Pinot Red or Dead?

Books by J. C. Eaton

The Sophie Kimball Mysteries
BOOKED 4 MURDER
DITCHED 4 MURDER
STAGED 4 MURDER
BOTCHED 4 MURDER

And available from Lyrical Press

The Wine Trail Mysteries
A RIESLING TO DIE
CHARDONNAYED TO REST
PINOT RED OR DEAD?

Pinot Red or Dead?

J.C. Eaton

LYRICAL PRESS
Kensington Publishing Corp.
www.kensingtonbooks.com

LYRICAL UNDERGROUND BOOKS are published by

Kensington Publishing Corp.
119 West 40th Street
New York, NY 10018

All Kensington titles, imprints, and distributed lines are available at special quantity discounts for bulk purchases for sales promotion, premiums, fund-raising, educational, or institutional use.

Special book excerpts or customized printings can also be created to fit specific needs. For details, write or phone the office of the Kensington Sales Manager: Kensington Publishing Corp., 119 West 40th Street, New York, NY 10018. Attn. Sales Department. Phone: 1-800-221-2647.

Lyrical Press and Lyrical Press logo Reg. U.S. Pat. & TM Off.

First Electronic Edition: March 2019
ISBN-13: 978-1-5161-0800-8   (ebook)
ISBN-10: 1-5161-0800-0   (ebook)

First Print Edition: March 2019
ISBN-13: 978-1-5161-0803-9
ISBN-10: 1-5161-0803-5

Printed in the United States of America

In memory of our dear friend, Harry Weymer, whose humor, sage wisdom, and bold energy will never be forgotten. We lift this glass of Pinot for you!

ACKNOWLEDGMENTS

When Beth Cornell, Larry Finkelstein, Gale Leach, Ellen Lynes, Susan Morrow, Suzanne Scher, and Susan Schwartz in Australia said they'd have our backs, we never expected them to hold on for the duration of our series. Boy, do we owe you!

We keep pinching ourselves because it's almost too good to believe we've got such incredible people helping us every step of the way. Tremendous thanks to our agent, Dawn Dowdle from Blue Ridge Literary Agency, and our editor, Tara Gavin, at Kensington. You're the best of the best!

Kudos to our production editors at Kensington and to their amazing art department. We're thrilled to be part of this team.

Chapter 1

Two Witches Winery, Penn Yan, New York

It was a little past eleven in the morning, Tuesday to be precise, and I couldn't believe what I heard when I walked into the Two Witches Winery tasting room. At first, I thought it was a joke, but when I saw our manager, Cammy, and her crew hanging festive tea lights around the huge fireplace, I realized they were serious about the holiday music that filled the entire room.

"Hey, guys!" I called out. "It's mid-November. We haven't even gotten to Thanksgiving yet."

Cammy placed a coiled handful of lights on one of the tasting room tables and stepped toward me. "It may be November, Norrie, but the annual 'Deck the Halls around the Lake' begins next weekend. We've got to get this place looking like the North Pole by week's end. This year we're adding some battery-operated lights in case the power goes out, and we bought some of those cottony things that look like snow. Can you believe it? The food-eating and gift-giving holidays are upon us."

"Yeesh. I almost forgot. Didn't we just take down the Halloween decorations?" I tossed my ski jacket over one of the chairs near the front counter and took a closer look at the room. "With that tight editing deadline I had for my screenplay and a new draft due in two weeks, I've kind of been in my own world."

"No kidding." Sam rubbed the bit of reddish stubble on his chin. "You've become the phantom of the bistro. Worse than some of my college profs who breeze in and out barking orders at their teaching assistants."

"What? I don't do that, do I?"

"He's giving you a hard time," Cammy said. She tightened the green ribbon around her loosely held bun, allowing more than a few strands of deep brown hair to spill about her face. "All we've seen of you is a blur. You rush in, head straight to the bistro for your lunch, and rush out."

"That bad, huh?"

"Oh yeah," everyone chimed in.

The tasting room crew, along with Theo and Don from neighboring Grey Egret Winery, was my second family here on Seneca Lake. My first one, consisting of my parents, the former owners of the winery, retired and couldn't move to Myrtle Beach, South Carolina, fast enough. They deeded the business to my sister, Francine, and me. She and her entomologist husband, Jason, were ecstatic, but I couldn't bear the thought of living in Penn Yan and managing a winery. Not when I had a degree in screenwriting and a decent contract with a Canadian film company to produce my romances.

In addition, I'd recently acquired my late aunt Tessie's apartment near Little Italy in Manhattan and had no plans to give that up. Crazy, I wasn't. So, I became the silent winery partner. Silent until Jason got a grant from Cornell's New York State Agricultural Experiment Station to study some elusive bug in Costa Rica.

Francine used her power as the "older by one year" sister to convince me to sublet my apartment and manage the winery. "You'll have lots of free time to write your screenplays. The place all but runs itself."

Yeah, sure. She should've gone into the used car business. The place might have run itself, but murders don't solve themselves. Yep, murders. No sooner did I arrive in June when their miserable next-door neighbor was found dead in our Riesling vineyard. Then three months later, a dead body cropped up across the road at Terrace Wineries, and I wound up tracking down the killer. It was no wonder I wanted to breeze in and out of the place.

"I'll try not to be such a stranger around here. I take it we're all set for 'Deck the Halls around the Lake.' How many people are we expecting?"

Before Cammy could answer, Lizzie looked up from her computer screen at the cash register and adjusted her glasses. "The wine trail has sold one hundred seventy-five tickets for next weekend and two hundred for the weekend before Christmas. Online sales for both weekend events are booming. Did you read the letter from Henry Speltmore? He sent multiple copies to all of the wineries."

I gulped. Another thing I must've ignored. "You mean the president of the Seneca Lake Wine Association?"

"How many Henry Speltmores do you know?" Cammy asked.

"Very funny, and no, I didn't get a chance to read it. What did it say?"

Sam waved his hands in the air and laughed. "I'll save you some time. It said, 'Blah, blah, wineries…blah, blah tourism…blah blah first impressions…Want me to go on?"

"Nah, I think I've got it. Besides, I got the lowdown from Stephanie Ipswich from Gable Hill Winery last week. According to her, Henry didn't want any of the wineries to skimp on the desserts they make for the customers. Seems there was a problem with someone's chocolate bread pudding a few years ago, and it still comes back to haunt us."

Glenda, who was busy tying green, gold, and red ribbons around the wine racks, stopped for a moment. I really must have blown past the tasting room these past few weeks because I didn't realize her hair was now a deep red with pink highlights.

"The problem was," she said, "whoever made those bread puddings forgot the chocolate. To make matters worse, they overbaked the things and some people actually broke their teeth biting into it."

"Ew, that better not happen to us. What are we making?"

"Pinot Noir truffles," Cammy answered. "And don't worry. We won't forget the Pinot Noir. This event is the major money maker for the wine association, and we don't want to be the ones to blow it. If they wind up short on their advertising budget, we'll never hear the end of it."

Without the Seneca Lake Wine Association, each individual winery would be on its own when it came to marketing and advertising, but with the thirty or so member wineries working together, it virtually assured the Finger Lakes Wine Region would be on the tourism map. Nope, no lousy bread pudding for us.

I immediately walked toward Lizzie. "Um, you said three hundred seventy-five tickets so far. Do we have a cap on the number of people?"

"Four hundred total," she said. "And not one person more. We already have the favors and goody bags, so that's not a problem. We're giving attendees little ornaments that feature two witches flying around a Christmas tree."

"What did we give them last year?" I asked.

Lizzie patted down her tightly coiffed grey hair and smiled. "Two witches flying around a snowman."

I rolled my eyes, hoping no one would notice, but Sam did. "Hey, at least it's better than that winery near Watkins Glen. They give out a small framed ornament in the shape of a wine bottle each year and it's got a photo of their owner inside it."

"Yeesh. I wouldn't even want us to give out photos of our goat and, believe me, Alvin really is quite popular, even though he spits."

"He only spits at you, Norrie," he said, followed by a chorus of "yeah."

"Very funny."

Just then, our ancient relic of a wall phone rang, and Lizzie turned her head from the counter to pick it up. "It's for you, Norrie. It's Theo Buchman. He said he tried the house and when there was no answer, he figured you were here."

"Thanks."

She handed me the phone and I walked behind her, leaving her enough room to man the cash register/computer monitor. Cammy, Sam, and Glenda went back to their decorating, and I took the call.

"Hey, Theo, what's up?"

"I take it you didn't catch the morning news, or you would've called."

"What? What happened? Who died?"

"No one died, but, get this, a tractor trailer truck was hijacked on the east side of the lake south of Waterloo. And not just any old tractor trailer truck. It happens to belong to Lake-to-Lake Wine Distributors."

"What? That's our wine distributor!"

"Norrie, Lake-to-Lake is the distributor for most of the wineries on Seneca Lake and certainly all of them in our little Winery of the West group. The truck was on its way over to our side when it happened. Imagine if they'd started with us. According to the news, the hijackers made off with forty cases of wine from four different wineries. Not a small-time theft, that's for sure. At least no one was injured, but this is a first."

"Yikes. I've never heard of anything like that. Did the news have any other details?"

"Yeah. They'll pass along more information as soon as they get it. Guess I'll be watching the six o'clock news tonight. You know, with the change in their compensation schedule, it makes me wonder if maybe we should be thinking about contracting with more than one distributor."

"Huh?"

"Their compensation rates for our wines has changed. It's lower. Not drastic but enough to make a difference. They blamed it on a shift in the market prices, but who knows? Anyway, they only distribute wines to New York and Pennsylvania. We're missing out in states like Ohio, Michigan, and Indiana. And those markets are growing. We wouldn't be the first wineries to use multiple distributors. Hey, it's just a thought. I'll catch you later, okay?"

"Sure thing. Thanks for letting me know."

"You won't believe this," I said out loud and then proceeded to tell everyone about Theo's call.

"They took off with forty cases of wine?" Glenda's question sounded more like a statement.

"That's what the news said. I don't know anything else."

Cammy, whose aunts owned Rosinetti's bar in Geneva, and whose family had been in that business forever, shook her head. "They'll be unloading it on the black market for sure. No legit business is about to buy wine that doesn't come directly from the winery or their distributor."

"Or maybe someone's going to have one hell of a frat party," Sam said. "After all, the holidays are coming."

"Seriously?" Lizzie asked. "Since when do fraternities hijack trucks of wine?"

Sam let out an extended groan. "I was only joking. Lighten up. At least it wasn't ours." Then he paused. "That sounded kind of callous, didn't it? Sorry. What I meant was—"

Cammy tossed some ribbons at him and pointed to the T-shirt bins. "Never mind. We get it. Let's hurry up and get this done before the next onslaught of customers arrives. They've been coming in spurts all morning, with that big crowd leaving a few minutes before Norrie walked in."

Sam gathered the holiday ribbons to his chest and headed to the bins, where Glenda was already fastening some bits of fake greenery. Lizzie turned her attention to the computer monitor, leaving Cammy and me to talk privately.

"Shh," I said. "I don't need Glenda to hear this or she'll want to hold one of her aura cleansing rituals, but you don't think this is an omen, do you? I mean, who on earth hijacks a delivery truck full of wine? The bottles are breakable."

"No one ever said thieves are intelligent. For all anyone knows, it could've been a gang initiation out of Rochester or Syracuse. Happens, you know."

I wasn't convinced. "Forty cases is a lot of wine. Not the kind of thing that fits easily into someone's car."

"No, but I wager those cases would fit very nicely into someone's van. Especially one of those oversized ones. Chances are the driver got a decent description and the state troopers are working on it right now."

"State troopers? Not the county sheriff's department?"

Cammy tightened the ribbon on her bun. "Oh, I'm sure they'll be involved, but it happened on a state road, so that's a clarion call for the New York State Troopers."

"Well, I hope they answer the call pretty soon. Last thing we need is a wine-stealing ring working their way around the lake right before the holidays."

"Better than a killer. We've had our fair share of those."

I shuddered and told Cammy I'd keep her posted if I heard anything—not that I expected to. After all, Two Witches wasn't one of the wineries whose cases were stolen, even if we had the same distributor as the victims from the east side of the lake.

Then something occurred to me, and I felt like a total imbecile. I had no idea who the representative for our distributor was, let alone the owner of the company. Francine probably told me when I first arrived, but most likely I glossed over it, figuring it was something the winemaker, Franz Johannas, dealt with, along with bottle labeling and packaging for shipments to restaurants and retail outlets. Crap. So much for a nice sandwich at the bistro.

"Um, I hate to walk in here and run, but I really need to grab something to eat and see Franz at the winery lab. I promise, next time I come in, I'll spend more time."

I swore I heard chortling noises coming from all of them as I grabbed my ski jacket and made a beeline to the bistro.

Fred, our sandwich and salad chef, who looked more like a long-haired high school kid than a graduate from culinary school, gave me a wide smile the minute he saw me. "Hey, Norrie, how's it going?"

"Faster than I'd like. Any chance you can make me a ham and cheese sandwich in a hurry? Whatever you have on hand is fine."

"Sure thing. Everything okay?"

"A delivery truck from our distributor was hijacked this morning, and thieves made off with quite a few cases. I found out a few minutes ago, and I need to see Franz in the winery lab. They're the ones who load our cases onto the trucks."

"Good grief! That's terrible. How much of our wine did they steal?"

"Oh, not our wine. It happened on the east side of the lake. They never made it to the west side for our cases. *If* we were even on our distributor's schedule today. I wanted to talk with Franz to find out what he knows about the company we use." *Or who our rep is.*

"I see. Hang on. I'll get your lunch."

A few minutes later I pulled up the zipper of my ski jacket and walked outside. We might not have snow yet, but as far as I was concerned, it was cold enough to rival the North Pole.

Chapter 2

The stunning array of autumn foliage disappeared overnight. Instead of a breathtaking view of reds, golds, and greens, I saw barren trees jutting up between the pines. Yep, it was November all right. Unlike Manhattan, where I had to rely on storefront windows to distinguish the seasons, in the Finger Lakes everything was left to nature. I rubbed my hands together and took long strides from the tasting room parking lot to the winery building, where Franz Johannas and his crew worked. Charlie, the winery Plott Hound, must've seen me. All of sudden, he was at my heels.

"You can wait outside," I said to the dog when I got to the door, "because Franz will have a conniption if I let you inside. Heck, I don't even think he wants *me* to go inside. They're really fussy about contamination."

The dog stared at me with his enormous brown eyes until something got his attention and he raced back up the hill toward our house. I rapped on the winery door a few times and Alan, the assistant winemaker, opened it. I swore, except for his height, he looked more and more like his boss each time I saw him—red hair and horned-rimmed glasses.

"Hi, Alan! How's it going?"

"Everything's good from our end. Come on in. We're almost done bottling the barrel-aged Pinot Noir. Boy, what a process it's been to age the wine. Of course, Franz likes to do a few things old school and that's one of them. It took all of us in the winery, plus a few of John's vineyard guys, to tip the barrel up so it could be charred for a minute. A regular pyrotechnic event if you ask me. The end-product was worth it, though. Not to say our stainless steel with oak-charred chips doesn't do the trick for most of our vintage. We still get the nuances in the flavors without all the drama."

"So, we wind up with two different Pinot Noirs?"

"Uh-huh. The really expensive ones with our specialty label are designated for upscale restaurants in New York and Pennsylvania. Some are under exclusive contract. The rest are sold to retail outlets and modest restaurants and chains."

Just then Franz appeared from the lab and gave me a nod. "That was quick. You didn't have to drive down from the house. It could've waited."

"What?" I wondered why he thought I drove. "What could've waited?"

Franz gave me a funny look. "I thought you were here because of the message I left you a few minutes ago."

"No. I'm coming from the tasting room. What message?"

Franz moaned dramatically. "I got a disturbing phone call from Gustav Geisler, the winemaker at the Red Salamander across the lake. Their shipment of Pinot Noir was stolen this morning outside of Waterloo. A truck hijacking. How utterly barbaric. And the Red Salamander wasn't the only winery whose wines were taken. Three others had cases stolen too. All red wines, according to him, but mostly Pinot Noir. Hooligans. That's what it was—hooligans."

"Guess those state troopers didn't waste any time tallying up the losses. That's why I came over here. Theo Buchman called me with the information. It was on the news, but I missed it. Franz, do you know who owns the wine distribution company we use and who our rep is?"

"The same owner since the late eighties—Arnold Mowen. The joke around here is he's the only man who can squeeze a nickel and get six cents. Undoubtedly, you've heard he lowered the rates he's paying us for our wines."

"Um, yeah. Theo said something about that. Market fluctuation, I think."

Franz let out a dry cough and patted his neck. "Not market fluctuation. Greed. Anyway, you asked about our rep. It's Miller Holtz. He's been with the company for a few years. Strikes me as a real hustler but, then again, I suppose that's the nature of the position. Alan's met him, too."

I turned to Alan and waited for his response.

He had just put his glasses back on, having wiped the lenses clean on his lab coat. "The guy's high energy and a real talker, but I'm not sure if that qualifies him as a wheeler-dealer. He's also a bit cavalier about things."

"Cavalier? I'm not sure I follow."

"I guess I'm referring to his attitude in general about wines. As far as he's concerned, we might as well be selling grape juice to the local school cafeterias. Don't get me wrong, he knows his wines. What he doesn't get is what a tremendously detailed and difficult process it is to create stellar varieties. It's all money as far as he and his boss are concerned."

"Hmm, do you think he would have an idea as to who might've hijacked their truck? Maybe he stiffed someone and they got even. Only they took everyone else along for the ride. Or should I say, *the loss.*"

Franz gave a sharp stomp on the floor with his foot. "If he does, those troopers will grill it out of him."

"Listen, I need his contact information. I want to get in touch with him to see what precautions his company plans to take so something like this doesn't happen again. We've had enough excitement at Two Witches since I arrived. Last thing I need is for our wine to go missing. Say, speaking of missing, where's Herbert?"

"Mandatory meeting with his advisor at Cornell," Franz replied. "All of the interns have them. Something about job placements, from what he told us."

"Oh. I hope he doesn't plan on taking a position elsewhere."

Alan shook his head. "Herbert has no intention of leaving us. He was tickled pink when he was offered a full-time position upon graduation."

"We're the lucky ones to have him. He's the first intern I've seen who was interested in producing great wines, not a great ego," Franz said. "Hold on a moment and I'll get you Miller Holtz's information."

He walked into the small room that housed the winemaker desks and file cabinets. I hoped he'd be quick before Alan launched into some long-winded explanation about wine making. I was wrong.

"So, as I was saying before Franz walked in, during the aging process, we use medium toast chips in our stainless steel barrels. We soak them in fabric sacks and allow their woody aroma and vanilla tones to permeate the wine."

Hurry up, Franz, before I go brain dead. "Um, that's very interesting."

"Notwithstanding, the desired effect is much better achieved with our French oak barrels. We've got two of those. When your father and the former winemaker started out, they were undecided about using American oak or French. I'm glad they chose French. American oak tends to produce wine that's so bold as to be considered overpowering. Of course, that's only my opinion."

"Um, uh, well…Oh, here comes Franz." I charged over to our short, stocky winemaker and took a business card from his hand.

"Miller left us a few of these," he said. "It's got all the information you need."

"Thanks. I'll give him a call tomorrow. I imagine he's besieged right now by the east side wineries. At least the businesses are insured, but still…"

"I know," Franz said. "It's disturbing."

I was about to say goodbye and head for the door, when I thought of something. "When are they planning on picking up our cases for distribution?"

"According to the calendar, it's scheduled for next week. That's why we're going nonstop on bottling the reds. Listen, this was most likely a one-time thing. I seriously doubt the thieves will try again. Besides, I'm certain our distribution company will ratchet up its safety precautions. Plus, the state troopers will also be on the lookout. If you ask me, those hooligans plan on selling it on the black market to pay for their drug habits."

"Don't you find it odd that the only cases they took were red wines?"

"Maybe those were easier to reach. It was a theft, remember? Not a lot of time to peruse wine cases."

"I suppose. Anyway, I'll call Miller Holtz. If I learn anything more this week, I'll let you know. Thanks, Franz. You too, Alan. Have a good afternoon."

I closed the door behind me and started up the hill. In retrospect, I should've taken off my jacket in the winery building because I was freezing by the time I got to the house. Even Charlie must've been cold outside because he was snuggled up in his bed in the corner of the kitchen when I walked in.

"You've only got one more week of freedom, dog, because after 'Deck the Halls around the Lake,' deer season starts. Well, it officially started with bows, so maybe I should've clarified."

The dog got up and ambled over to his food dish. I automatically poured out some kibble. "What I mean is, when hunting season starts, I have to lock the fence to your doggie area, so you won't be able to run through the woods."

With the zillion reminders and instructions Francine had left for me, deer season was ingrained in my head. True, we didn't allow hunters on our property, and our woods were marked clearly with no trespassing signs, but that didn't stop crazed enthusiasts in the past. I wasn't about to take any chances. Besides, half the time Charlie was sleeping in his bed or mine.

"So," I asked. "What do you think about that truck hijacking?"

The dog let out a burp and went back to his bed. I moved Miller Holtz's business card around in my hand for a few seconds and made myself a cup of tea. Frankly, if it wasn't for our Keurig and the microwave, I would've moved out months ago. Favors or no favors.

I wanted to get back to my real job of screenwriting with a draft that was far from completion, but instead I called Stephanie Ipswich from Gable Hill Winery. I knew she'd be stuck in the house with her twin boys.

She answered on the second ring. "Norrie! I was going to call you later. Did you hear about the truck hijacking and wine thefts this morning? Check your winery email. Henry Speltmore from the wine association sent all of us a nebulous, and I might add, ridiculous letter about it. All he said was that the authorities were looking into the matter and that it would be prudent for winery owners to review their business insurance policies. Now there's a vote of confidence if I ever heard one."

"I guess there's not much he can really say. I know Lake-to-Lake Wine Distributors is the big company around here and everyone's used them for years, but maybe things have changed."

"You mean in addition to them lowering our wine compensation rates? My husband was irate when he got that letter from the company. He and the owner got into it over the phone and, from the language that came out of my husband's mouth, I was only too glad they weren't face-to-face."

I took a breath, but it was more of a wheeze into the phone. "Whoa. That's the third time today I've heard about this rate lowering thing. Francine and Jason must've known but didn't say anything to me. Anyway, getting back to the truck hijacking…Could it have been an inside job? I mean, other than the winery workers who loaded the cases, who else would know what was on that truck? It wasn't happenstance that it got hijacked. It had to be planned. Geez, I wish we knew more."

Stephanie let out a little hum before she spoke. "As soon as the news comes on at five, I'm going to watch it. Our pickup for twenty cases of reds is a week from today. Maybe the state police will have the thieves in custody by then. I'd hate to think this could happen again. Especially with our wines. Bad enough we're losing money on the deal."

"Stephanie, is Lake-to-Lake the only distributor in this area?"

"It's the only one that goes into Buffalo and New York City. It's an either-or with the other smaller distributors. Why? Don't tell me you're thinking of switching. Besides, Two Witches has a signed contract with them. We all do."

"No, it's not that, but, well, okay, it's two things: maybe we should be thinking about having multiple distributors for a broader outreach into other states. If our wines are spread out and something happens to one company, the other will continue selling and delivering our stuff."

"Hmm, that's interesting. What's the other thing?"

"Aside from my thinking it could be a disgruntled employee or more than one, maybe another company wants to put Lake-to-Lake Wine Distributors out of business. What better way than to go after their goods?"

"You may be on to something, but again, isn't that what the state police will investigate? They don't just man the roads. They're involved in all sorts of criminal investigations. Uh-oh. Don't tell me you're thinking of getting involved with this. It's not like tracking down a little clue like we did two months ago at your Federweisser event. This could be an organized crime thing, for all we know."

"Don't worry. I wasn't planning on sticking my nose into this one—unless it lands on my front porch."

"Yeesh."

I told Stephanie I'd see her at the next Winery of the West meeting, which was scheduled a week from Thursday. We chatted briefly about "Deck the Halls around the Lake" and how wiped out we were all going to be afterward.

When I first arrived in June and discovered her neighbor dead in my Riesling vineyard, I had actually believed Stephanie might be a killer. Since then, we'd become good winery friends. She was the closest to my age, approaching-thirty-but-not-there-yet. So far, Stephanie hadn't tried to fix me up with anyone, unlike Catherine Trobert who did so every time she mentioned her son.

The news about the hijacking spread faster on the rumor mill and social media than in the newspapers and on television. It seemed as if everyone speculated about the incident, whether they were in the wine industry or not. Only one piece of information remained constant—the state police were working diligently to see where the wine had been fenced. Unfortunately, there were no leads by the week's end. What we had instead was four inches of snow, which began to fall Friday morning and ended late in the day.

"You think this is going to scare away festival goers?" I called out to Cammy as I opened the door to my office, adjacent to the tasting room. It was a little past ten, and I had broken my own rule of not leaving the house until I put in a decent amount of time on my latest screenplay. I had a good excuse. I was finally able to reach Miller Holtz from Lake-to-Lake Wine Distribution and he agreed to meet with me at ten-thirty.

"If this was Washington, D.C., it might," she said, "but not upstate New York. Stop worrying. This is nothing."

She was right. Even the schools would remain open. They only closed if it was a blizzard or an ice storm.

"Our winery looks amazing. If our decorations don't put customers into the holiday spirit, nothing will. I'm meeting with our new wine distributor any minute now, so if someone comes in looking for me, point to the office."

"You got it."

I booted up the office computer and, thanks to Lizzie's help a few days ago, pulled up the spreadsheets detailing our wine inventory and distribution records for the past two years. Lizzie was a retired accountant who did the taxes for Two Witches. She also managed other money matters when she wasn't working the cash register. When I met with her, she showed me the agreed-upon prices for each bottle of wine, per variety. The blends were notably cheaper, while the single varietals were pricier.

It was up to the distributor to establish the retail cost, thus jockeying up the price tag. Not surprisingly, an eighteen-dollar bottle of Merlot might go for as much as ninety-five dollars in a fancy restaurant once everyone got their cut.

Leaning back, I glanced at the light dusting of snow in our parking lot. At this rate, it would simply coat the ground. I was so engrossed in my thoughts, I didn't hear Miller Holtz come in until he announced himself and I all but jumped.

"Sorry. I thought you heard me walk in. One of your workers said I could come right in. I'm Miller Holtz and you must be Norrie Ellington."

I stood and reached across the desk to shake his hand. He was tall, at least six feet, and looked to be in his mid-forties. Well-built, short brown hair, with absolutely no hints of grey, and a decent smile. Not bad looking, but not what I'd call a heartthrob. *Good. I've had enough of those.* He was wearing a Lands' End navy-blue stadium jacket and grey slacks.

"Make yourself comfortable," I said. "Can I get you a cup of coffee?"

His smile got wider. "Thanks, but no. If I wasn't working and driving on these roads, I'd go for your wine. As far as coffee is concerned, I've already had more than two cups of java this morning."

He unzipped his coat and put it over the chair. Nice blue shirt that matched the ensemble.

"I'll give you a raincheck on the wine. Um, I really appreciate you driving over here today, especially in the snow. As I said when I spoke with you a few days ago, I'm managing the winery for my sister and brother-in-law this year. After that incident with your company's hijacked truck, I want to be assured that additional precautions are in place so something like that doesn't happen again."

"You and me, both. That incident took us all for a loop. I've been in the wine distribution business for nineteen years, and it was a first for me. Who'd imagine a van running the truck off the road and then threatening the driver with a gun? On TV maybe, but not on a small state road. Anyway, to answer your question, the company is no longer sending out single drivers. Not until the thieves are apprehended. We need to know if it was a one-shot deal or part of an ongoing operation."

"An additional driver isn't going to stop armed thieves," I said. *And it was a van, after all.*

"True, but he or she may be able to call for help inconspicuously. Lake-to-Lake Wine Distributors is also considering self-defense training for drivers."

"Guess it's a start. Tell me, who suffers the loss when something like that happens? The winery whose wines were stolen or the distributor?"

"Good question. Unlike mistakes that can happen at the wineries while the grapes are fermenting, this kind of loss depends on the contractual terms between the winery and the distributor. Bear in mind, wine distributors aren't transport companies, so the laws differ. Usually, the loss is split and the insurance companies duke it out. And, by loss, I mean, the actual loss, no mark-ups. Would you like me to review your contractual terms?"

"Uh, that's okay. I can pull up the information and call you if I have any questions. I guess I just wanted some reassurance our wines will be safe."

"No one can give you that kind of reassurance, but I can tell you this much, our company takes its business seriously. Your losses are our losses."

"Uh, yeah. About what you said a minute ago. Fermenting mistakes? I take it that means the winery is in deep you-know-what."

"Hey, you didn't hear this from me, but my boss tends to look at that type of thing differently."

"What do you mean?"

"If a winery loses a substantial amount of its product, but not all of it, then they can jack up the prices to compensate. Nothing like creating one's own supply and demand, according to him. Of course, we're talking varietal, not blends."

"Um, yeah. Right. By the way, the news said something about the stolen wines all being red wines. Was that because the truck carrying the wine only picked up cases of red wines? Or maybe the red wine cases were more easily accessible for the thieves?"

Miller paused for a moment and tapped his teeth. "I'm not sure about accessibility. The state police are delving into that. But I can tell you all four wineries involved in the incident loaded white and red varieties onto the truck."

"Where do you think that stolen wine went?" I asked.

"My guess, and it's only a guess, is black market distribution. Seedier outlets in the big cities. I do know the police are trying to track down the product. Unless someone alters the labels on the bottles, it shouldn't be too hard. The year is on the label and we've only now started to move the products along."

"What a nightmare."

"It may seem that way, but it's a small enough loss. It'll be absorbed."

"Like the lower compensation rates for selling our wine to your company for distribution? I only found out about that this week."

If Miller Holtz was a dog, his haunches would be up. "Compensation rates depend upon the market. We're not out to gouge our customers. Your success is our success."

Put it on a T-shirt and call it a day. "I imagine that didn't sit well with too many of your customers."

Miller gave a quick nod. "I'll admit, some of our long-standing customers were, well, shall we say, a tad upset, but they're business people. They understand how prices are set. Right now, the safe transport and sale of your wines is all that matters."

"I can't argue with that. Er...maybe this is none of my business, but do you make a profit on the lower compensation rates?"

"Huh? NO! Absolutely not. I get paid on commission. Number of cases sold to our outlets—restaurants, bars, etc. The case rate does vary according to the wine, but the amount that wineries are paid by the distributor has no bearing on my salary. I'm the salesperson/wine representative, not the distributor. Think of me as the conduit between the winery and the consumer."

"But it would result in more profit for your boss, wouldn't it?"

"I can't argue with you on that. Hey, speaking of my boss, I know for a fact he'll be attending your event this weekend. Our office secretary told me she ordered two tickets for him, but chances are he'll come alone."

"Huh?"

"Okay, this may sound strange, but Arnold always buys an extra ticket in case a business opportunity presents itself."

"That doesn't sound as if it's going to be much fun for him. It's the party atmosphere everyone enjoys."

"Arnold Mowen's not attending this event for the atmosphere. It's all business as far as he's concerned. He likes these events because the huge crowds allow him to sample the wines inconspicuously. Later, when he makes his purchasing decisions, he's one step ahead. Oh, and lest I forget, the man never shies away from gourmet food."

"What does he look like?"

"Sixties. Rotund. Bald dome with white frizz around the edges. Double chin. Used to have a moustache but got rid of it a few years back. If I were you, and you do spot him, please don't tell him we had this conversation."

"I doubt I'll see him. Unless his ticket lists Two Witches as his starting point, he'll be swept up into the crowd. Attendees are assigned starting point wineries where they pick up their complimentary grapevine wreath and our recipe cookbook. If we didn't do that, the crowds would be unmanageable and, worse yet, we'd have lots of downtime in between tastings."

"Interesting."

"Yeah, the Seneca Lake Wine Association really organizes their events quite well. Anyway, thanks for driving over here. I know you must have a busy schedule."

"Never too busy to meet with one of our customers. We'll be in touch. Nice meeting you."

"Likewise."

Miller put on his coat and pulled the zipper up in one quick motion before leaving the office. I wasn't quite sure what to make of him. He didn't seem like a hustler and I never expected him to be so candid about his boss. What did strike me was how defensive he got when I asked about his commissions, although I probably did cross a line.

I stood and glanced out the window. It was a "teaser" snowfall, warning us that winter was a lot closer than we thought. Heavy snowfalls. Icy roads. Winds. White-outs. Power outages. As if we didn't have enough to worry about running a winery. Then there was Miller's cavalier attitude about the wineries absorbing their losses from that hijacking. Wasn't he concerned that they would incur a loss, too? If I had to wager a guess, I'd say it was an inside job, but maybe Miller knew that all along.

Chapter 3

I promised Cammy I'd help with "Deck the Halls around the Lake" the next morning. Saturdays were notorious for drawing large crowds, and this one was almost a sell-out.

For all of us at the winery, it was going to be a busy day. The vineyard guys would do their winter pruning. The winemakers had a full schedule as well. Alan told me they were going to begin the final bottling of the barrel-aged Pinot Noir. They planned to start at seven. Yeesh. I planned to be viewing the inside of my eyelids at that ungodly hour. After all, Cammy didn't need me until ten, when the first stampede arrived.

I got the rundown of delicacies that our neighboring wineries were serving. Honestly, if I didn't have to help out, I would've made it a point to trot off to the different wineries and sample the stuff myself. Theo and Don from the Grey Egret were serving pork and chestnut in puff pastry with cranberry sauce. I told Theo to save three or four of them for me. In return, I'd let them taste our Pinot Noir truffles.

Stephanie Ipswich said she had a marvelous recipe for lemon shortbread cake. Rosalee Marbleton was sticking to one of her favorites—sun dried tomatoes and olives in phyllo baskets. I also got word there'd be artichoke and prawn canapes as well as beef tenderloin on black bread.

The time on my laptop read 11:22 p.m. and I could barely keep my eyes open. *A Soft Breeze at Dawn* would have to wait until I was done with this round of "Deck the Halls around the Lake." Charlie was already spread across the bottom of my bed when I made it upstairs and pulled back the covers to get in. That was the last coherent thing I remembered doing before the sharp ring of the bedside phone disrupted my brain cells.

The room was pitch black and, except for a fuzzy digital clock a few feet away, I couldn't see anything. My hand reached across the nightstand and I picked up the call. I couldn't even recall how many times it rang but the caller sure did.

"Norrie, thank God you answered. I was going to hang up on the sixth ring."

The voice sounded familiar, but nothing was registering. "Um, uh, what's up?" *And who are you?*

"I'm at the winery. On my cell phone. This isn't good. Franz is—"

"Oh my God! Dead? Franz is dead?"

Suddenly, it was as if I got jolted by a Taser. I was up, I was thinking, and I was panicked. The voice on the cell phone was Herbert's, and he wouldn't be calling me at seven in the morning to pontificate on the nuances of fermentation.

"Whoa. What? Dead? No, no, he's fine. Well, not fine. I think he's having a breakdown. Alan isn't doing so well, either. It's the Pinot Noir… the barrel…it's been—oh, heck, Norrie, you need to get down here. And it's freezing. Wear an extra sweater or something."

The call ended before I could say another word. I grabbed the first sweatshirt I could find in my chest of drawers. After a record-time shower, I tossed on jeans and my ski jacket. There was plenty of water in Charlie's bowl, so I poured out some kibble, snatched my keys from the counter, and raced to my car. Herbert was right. It was cold—cold enough for my car to turn over slowly. Forget about the heater—I'd be down the driveway and at the winery before it came on.

It was a good hour away from sunrise, but there was ample outdoor lighting at the back of the winery building, where some of our stainless steel and oak barrels were kept. As I approached the concrete slab that housed the barrels, I heard Franz spewing out the same word over and over again—*catastrophe*. Herbert motioned for me to come closer, but there was no sign of Alan.

I walked past two of the stainless steel barrels and stood directly in front of Franz, who was holding a wineglass in his hand. In the shadowy light, he looked like one of those silhouettes on the cover of a crime magazine.

"What happened?" I asked. "What's going on?"

"It's a disaster. A catastrophe." He kept shaking his head, swirling the red liquid around in his wineglass. "Smell this." He thrust the glass at me. "The Pinot Noir's been tampered with. The oak-aged Pinot Noir. Ruined. Utterly destroyed."

Herbert, thankfully, positioned himself closer to one of the outdoor building lights so I could see him. He rubbed his hands together and cleared his throat. "Alan's in the lab now, testing a sample. It shouldn't take him very long."

"How did this—I mean, when did this—oh hell! Does this mean all the cases of wine already bottled are destroyed too?"

And no, Miller, this cannot be "absorbed."

Franz inhaled and exhaled at least three times before he spoke. "We're fanatic about testing the wine. Everything we bottled was fine. Once we start the process, the barrels are under tight supervision. We finished yesterday at a little past four. After that, we cleaned the bottling machine and closed up. Whoever sabotaged our wine must've gotten to the barrel after we left for the day."

I looked at the other barrels on the concrete slab and felt momentarily numb. "Um, did you check the other outdoor barrels?"

"We did," Herbert said. "They're fine. No sign of tampering. Only the one oak barrel with the remaining Pinot Noir was tainted."

"I thought we set up security cameras and an alarm system."

Franz, who finally managed to breathe normally, pointed to the edge of the roof. "We do. The alarm system was functioning perfectly when we arrived at six thirty. But look closely at the security camera on the roof's overhang. Either yesterday's wind dislodged it, or someone knew exactly what they were doing. They could have easily hugged the building without being caught on camera, using a pole or something to knock it out of kilter. This was no accident. This was sabotage."

"I don't think the choice of barrels was any accident, either," Herbert said. "The oak-aged Pinot Noir carries a much heftier price tag than the others."

"A heftier price tag for a superb vintage," Franz added, "much of it lost."

"Um, I don't suppose you know how many gallons of wine that was, do you? Or how that translates into bottles? I mean, some of our oak-aged wine was already bottled so those are okay, right?"

I was desperate to get the answer I wanted. And terrified I wouldn't.

"It's relatively easy to calculate," Herbert said. "Our oak barrel was standard size—two hundred twenty-five liters or approximately fifty-nine gallons. With the standard seven hundred fifty ml bottles, that equals three hundred bottles or twenty-five cases. I'll pull up the bottling information, do a little subtraction, and let you know the damage. I was planning on getting that information to Franz when we were done here."

"As I said earlier," Franz added, "the wines we've already bottled are all right."

Unless they're doomed for the black market, like those on the east side of the lake.

"We might as well go inside," he said. "My hands are getting numb, and there's nothing more to do out here. We'll need to dispose of the tainted wine and thoroughly prepare the barrel for future use."

The three of us walked inside the winery building, past the lab and barrel room, to the small office that the winemakers shared. I caught a glimpse of Alan's back as we moved along the corridor. He was hunched over a table that reminded me of my eleventh-grade chemistry class.

"Alan shouldn't be too much longer," Franz said. "He'll be able to discern what the vandals used to destroy our wine."

I plunked myself at Alan's desk, since he was still in the lab. Herbert walked over to their coffeemaker and asked if I wanted a cup.

"Make it a gallon. It's not even eight and this is going to be one long hell of a day." From the small window across the room, I could see hints of daylight on the horizon. Black had turned to murky grey, and the sky matched my mood. "So, both of you agree this was sabotage and not something that inadvertently happened to our wine while it was, well, you know, aging and all that."

"Trust me. It was sabotage," Franz said. "Wine doesn't simply spoil on its own."

No sooner did he utter those words when Alan walked into the room and gave me a nod. He looked as if he had just buried his childhood dog. "Calcium carbonate. Someone knew what they were doing, all right. Not an amateur. They poured enough of the stuff in the barrel to ensure the wine would be undrinkable."

"Poured it how?"

"Easily, I'm afraid. All they had to do was pull the plug on the bung hole and pour in the chemical."

"That knob on the top?"

"Yeah, it has an official name. Along with chimes, hoops, and staves. I'll save that for another time."

I bit my lower lip and stared at the Keurig. No amount of coffee was going to set this day right. "So...sabotage. That's a crime—no different than if someone broke into our tasting room and made off with our goods."

Franz alternated between rubbing his hands and his chin. For a moment, I was afraid he'd develop a tic. "A crime, yes. And a catastrophe."

"And a call to the sheriff's department. That'll be another catastrophe if they send Deputy Hickman. He and I aren't always on the best of terms," I said.

That was a diplomatic way of me saying the deputy thought I was a meddlesome busybody who got in the way of his murder investigations. In fairness, he was partially right. I did do a bit of sleuthing on my own, but even he had to admit I wound up identifying the killers in two recent murders.

I dug in the pocket of my jeans for my cell phone and suddenly stopped. "Uh, I need to make another call. I have a hunch about something, but I sure hope I'm wrong."

Herbert handed me a hot cup of coffee with a splash of cream. "I'm going to log into my computer and see exactly how many cases of the oak-aged Pinot Noir we bottled. Easier than traipsing over to the barn to start counting."

I watched as he pulled up the screen. For a split second, I felt like one of those contestants on *The Price is Right. Let it be a big number. Let it be a big number.* While Herbert perused his screen, I took a quick sip of coffee, put the mug down on Alan's desk, and dialed Theo and Don's number. Meanwhile, Franz and Alan exchanged painful glances at each other and at Herbert's computer.

Don answered my call on the second ring. "I've heard of early starts for 'Deck the Halls around the Lake,' but this is ridiculous. What's up?"

"Our Pinot Noir's been tampered with. Someone put—hold on a second." I shouted to the winemakers, "What was that chemical? Calcium something?"

"Carbonate!" they all answered at once.

"Did you hear that? Someone put calcium carbonate in the oak barrel we used for aging our Pinot Noir. We bottled some of it earlier in the week and it was fine, but sometime yesterday someone put that stuff in the barrel and now the rest of our wine is useless. The stainless steel barrels are fine. The winemakers checked. Those things are enormous. Too hard to tamper with, I suppose, but the oak barrels are smaller and, oh my gosh, I really called to tell you and Theo to check your barrels. You have wine aging in oak barrels outside, don't you? My God, I'm rambling on."

"Take a breath, Norrie, and try to calm down. You said only one barrel was tampered with?"

"Uh-huh. The Pinot Noir. The oak-aged Pinot Noir, not the stuff with those flavored chips. Herbert's going to figure out exactly how much wine was left in the barrel. Oh, geez, I'll have to call the insurance company, won't I? I know we're covered for all sorts of farming accidents and product loss due to natural disasters, but this is an out-and-out crime. Oh, yikes. I've got to call the sheriff. I just wanted to make sure you and Theo check your barrels."

"We'll get right on it. Listen, call the sheriff and alert him. One of us will stop over as soon as we can, okay?"

"Okay. I really hope nothing's wrong with your wine."

"Yeah, me too."

The next call I placed was to the Yates County Sheriff's Department. Since it didn't classify as an emergency that required flashing lights and an ear-piercing siren, I used their general number and had to wait for what seemed like eons before someone answered my call. For a moment, I thought I had reached a recording.

"You've reached the non-emergency number for the Yates County Sheriff's Department. If this is an emergency, hang up and dial 9-1-1. Phones are answered daily from seven to six, including weekends. How may I assist you?"

A person! A real person. "Yes. Hello. This is Norrie Ellington from Two Witches Winery on Two Witches Hill in Penn Yan. I'm calling to report a crime. Not an emergency. I mean, there's no dead body or anything like the last two times, but someone tampered with one of our wine barrels and destroyed gallons of expensive wine."

"Are you the owner of the winery?"

"Yes. Along with my sister, but she's in Costa Rica looking for a rare insect. Can you please send a deputy over here?"

There was a long pause at the other end and I wondered if maybe I shouldn't've mentioned the bug trekking in Costa Rica. Finally, the voice at the other end answered.

"I've placed a call to Deputy Hickman. He's in the vicinity and will be at your winery as soon as he becomes available. Don't touch anything or otherwise compromise the scene of the vandalism. Is there anything else I can assist you with?"

"Um, er…no. That's fine. Thanks."

"Have a nice day."

Have a nice day? Have a nice day? How can I possibly have a nice day?

I walked over to Herbert's desk where everyone was standing. "The sheriff's deputy will be here as soon as he can."

"At least we'll be able to provide him with accurate information." Franz's voice was robotic and void of emotion. "We bottled fifteen cases yesterday so that means ninety liters, or ten potential cases, were destroyed."

"Deputy Hickman's going to ask for the monetary value."

"Right here on the computer!" Herbert shouted. "Lake-to-Lake Wine Distributors pays us seventeen dollars a bottle—two hundred four dollars a case. At ten cases—"

"Yeah, even I can do the math. It's a two-thousand-dollar loss, roughly speaking. Geez. I'd better have Lizzie pull up our insurance policy. For all I know, we could have a five-thousand-dollar deductible. No sense reporting something we can't recoup."

"Maybe that's what the thieves or vandals were counting on," Alan said, "winery losses that fall under the radar."

I picked up my mug and took a large gulp of the now lukewarm coffee. "But why? None of this makes any sense. It's not like that hijacking the other day. That wine could be resold."

Alan stepped away from Herbert's computer screen, looked out the window, and then turned his head toward me. "Like I said before, someone knew exactly what they were doing. This wasn't some idiotic frat-boy prank. They'd pour sugar or salt into the barrel. No, someone wanted us to think we overused the calcium carbonate. But that's something amateur winemakers do. Not trained professionals. What concerns me is their motive."

"You know what Deputy Hickman's going to ask, don't you? 'Do we have any disgruntled employees?'"

The room got suddenly quiet, and the only sound I heard was the faint buzzing of the desktop computers.

Chapter 4

"Is that someone pulling up the driveway?" I asked. "I hear a car. It's got to be the sheriff's vehicle."

Alan walked to the window again. "Nope. It's a Honda Civic."

"That's Theo's car. I'll let him in."

The corridor seemed longer than I remembered, maybe because I was in a hurry to get to the door.

"Must be the west side wineries' lucky day," Theo said when I opened the door and ushered him inside. Instead of following me back to the office, he remained standing in place. "Looks like your barrels weren't the only ones meddled with. They hit us, too."

"Oh no. That's awful. Bad enough they got us."

Theo looked as if someone had punched him in the gut. "Right now, Don's meeting with our winemakers to assess the damages. I take it you already called the sheriff's department."

"Yes. Deputy Hickman will get here as soon as he can. So, did they do the same thing at the Grey Egret? Calcium carbonate?"

"They did *something*. Our winemaker's testing a sample right now. Same deal as you, though. None of our steel barrels were disturbed, but the one French oak barrel we have has been tampered with."

"Pinot Noir?"

He nodded. "Unlike you, we hadn't started bottling that barrel. It's going to be a total loss for us. Crap! That's three hundred bottles! I can only hope our other varieties will make up for it."

Okay. Two wineries in one day. We can nix the disgruntled employee thing. I mean, how many miserable employees can there be who have a penchant for wine tampering?

"I'm so sorry, Theo. This is a nightmare. And on the first day of 'Deck the Halls around the Lake,' too."

Theo furrowed his brow. "I don't think the timing was a coincidence. Whoever did this most likely thought we'd be so preoccupied with the lake festival we wouldn't be checking our wines for bottling. I guess they didn't realize our winemakers have their own schedules—and working weekends goes with the territory. Listen, I'd better get back to Don. Do me a favor and send Grizzly Gary our way as soon as he's done getting your info."

"Sure thing. And we'd better stop calling him that. I'm afraid I'm going to slip one of these days and say it out loud in front of him."

Theo laughed. "He's probably heard worse."

I closed the door behind him and stood there for a moment before I walked back to the office.

"They hit the Grey Egret, too," I announced as soon as I got back to the room. "Theo was only here for a second. Worse for them. They hadn't even started to bottle their Pinot Noir."

"Oh no. That's too bad. Coincidence or not?" Herbert asked. "About it being Pinot Noir. Then again, I think it had more to do with the size and accessibility of the oak barrels than the actual contents, but I could be wrong. You think any other wineries were targeted?"

Just then there was a loud pounding on our winery door. I almost jumped out of my skin. "Must be Deputy Hickman. Geez, I didn't even hear the car drive up. I'll let him in."

Five minutes later, Franz, Alan, Herbert, and I were on the receiving end of Deputy Gary Hickman's personal version of a root canal. Talk about digging around.

"No, I don't know anyone who had it in for our winery," all of us said in our own way. That was followed by the men insisting it couldn't have been a love interest seeking to get even for a miserable breakup and me claiming I didn't have any jealous exes. What I did have were the occasional dates with hunky attorney Bradley Jamison—when he wasn't mired under working for his boss, Marvin Souza, in Geneva.

Deputy Hickman arranged for a forensics crew to dust for fingerprints, but he wasn't optimistic about the results.

"Even a moron would be wearing gloves in this weather," he said.

I told him about the situation at the Grey Egret and he agreed to stop over there as it was only a few yards down the driveway. That was after he lectured me about protocol and how Theo and Don should've called the non-emergency number to report the incident. All in all, it was a miserable morning.

Franz sent the other winemakers home for the day and said he'd stay while the forensics crew scoured the place for evidence. I prayed they would arrive in an unmarked car. Somehow, the thought of their van, parked in plain sight of the tasting room, wasn't exactly my idea of holiday ambience.

I drove home, scarfed down some toast, and changed into a red and green holiday-themed winery sweatshirt for the "Deck the Halls" event. The sweatshirt featured two witches (duh!) stirring a cauldron. The caption read, "Whip up your own holiday magic this season!" *Just don't do it in our oak barrels.*

I agreed to man the welcome table at the entrance of the tasting room. I'd present the attendees with their grapevine wreath and the small cookbook with the recipes for today's canapes—unless we weren't their starting point. In that case, they'd flash their tickets and go to another table for their little souvenir. From there, the customers would receive a complimentary wineglass and would be directed to the food and wine tasting tables.

At least one thing was in my favor—despite the early morning wake-up disaster, I got to the tasting room in plenty of time. Our parking lot had only begun to fill up.

"Good morning, Norrie!" Lizzie said from her spot at the cash register. "You look as if you could use a strong cup of coffee. Late night on your screenplay?"

"No. More like early morning with Franz and his crew. Have you seen Cammy?"

"She's in the kitchen getting a batch of Pinot Noir truffles ready."

"I'd better not disturb her. Looks like she has my welcome table set up near the first tasting room table. I don't suppose I've got time to grab that coffee, huh?"

"You won't need to. Fred's bringing a few carafes over here for us. We've got him well-trained for these events."

Fifteen minutes later, I was in full winery-event party mode: big smile on my face, enough caffeine to prevent me from falling asleep standing up, and a boisterous crowd of festival goers showing me their tickets with Two Witches listed as their starting point.

After the first hour, I hardly noticed my head spinning. I was on auto-pilot, repeating the same greeting over and over. Mercifully, most of the attendees had checked in by noon. At that point, the pace slowed down substantially. I couldn't say the same for everyone else. The tasting room tables were filled to capacity, and the food line snaked around the room. Our part-time college workers, along with the regular crew, were so busy none of us had time to chat.

At a little past one, Fred came around with bite-size sandwiches and a few pitchers of grape juice. We followed the golden rule during tastings—no alcohol for employees—not until we closed for the day. The last thing any winery needed was a reputation for employees drinking wine on the job, even if only a smidgeon.

I looked for a rotund, double-chinned man but saw no sign of Arnold Mowen. That wasn't to say he wasn't here, only that I hadn't seen him. I did see a few people I recognized from town, including Gladys Pipp from the Yates County Public Safety Building. She had the day off and, along with a friend, purchased tickets for "Deck the Halls around the Lake." Both were wearing headbands with big reindeer ears. Nothing like getting into the holiday spirit.

A zillion conversations buzzed around me, but when I heard the words "flashing red and blue lights," I froze. My eyes darted all over to see who was talking and I swear, my pulse started beating overtime. The forensic investigators should've been long gone by now. They should have been gone hours ago. And they shouldn't have used their flashers. Who the hell was talking? Who said the words "flashing lights?"

I stepped back from my table and took a few steps to the right, and then to the left. Whoever mentioned the lights had a shrill voice and a giggle. The giggle was coming from a group of twenty-something women. All of them wore black sequined T-shirts with appliques of wineglasses and/or bottles.

I moved closer and tried to isolate the speaker. Impossible. Finally, I motioned to the entire group. "Excuse me. Sorry to bother you but one of you mentioned seeing red and blue vehicle flashers. Were they on our property?" *Please tell me no.*

A tall blonde with one thin streak of bright red in her hair shook her head. "Nope. Big scene at the other winery. Which was one was it, Corina?"

Another blonde, heavy-set and no streaks in her hair answered. "Billsburrow, I think. It was the one off the main road and up the hill."

"What happened? Do you know what happened?"

"It couldn't've been that bad," the tall blonde said, "because there was no fire truck and no ambulance."

Unless they didn't need them because they were waiting for the coroner.

"Was the sheriff's vehicle at the winery or the house? Do you remember?" I tried to keep my voice at a normal pitch, but it wasn't working.

The blonde answered. "Neither. It was by their barn. All I could see were flashing lights and some of those big steel tanks."

"Okay, thanks. You're probably right. It could've been anything. Sorry to interrupt. Enjoy the event."

The women had already turned away from me and were on their way over to the food line. With no one at my table, I pulled out my cell phone and called Billsburrow Winery. Francine had insisted I add all the neighboring wineries' phone numbers to my contacts list, and I was glad she had. Someone answered on the third ring.

"Hi!" I said. "This is Norrie Ellington from Two Witches Winery. Is Madeline Martinez available?"

Madeline, the owner of Billsburrow Winery, along with her husband, was the head of our Wineries of the West group, formally known as Women of the Wineries but recently changed so Theo and Don could join us.

"Hold on," the voice at the other end said. "I'll get her."

I wasn't quite sure what I was going to say, but it didn't matter. Madeline spoke before I had the chance to say hello.

"Norrie! My God! The most awful thing happened. Oh dear, I shouldn't have phrased it that way because no one's hurt and no one's dead. But it's still awful. Someone drained the Pinot Noir from our oak barrel. They must've connected a hose and turned the spigot because the barrel wasn't set on its side for tastings. We didn't find out about it until a little while ago. A few of the festival goers decided to walk around on their own and thought they saw blood in the snow."

"Oh no. Was all the wine drained?"

"All two hundred twenty-five liters, I'm afraid. My husband called the sheriff and they sent someone over. My God, Norrie, who'd want to do something like that?"

"I could be wrong, but maybe the same person who sabotaged our Pinot Noir and the Grey Egret's."

"What?"

"Our winemaker woke me at the crack of dawn to tell me the wine had been tainted. He and his assistants arrived at the winery early so they could finish bottling. They tested the wine, and it had an overdose of calcium carbonate. I'm not sure if overdose is the right word, but you know what I mean. A similar thing happened at the Grey Egret. Their winemaker's still testing the product, so I'm not sure if the same substance was used to destroy the wine."

"My God! At first, I thought maybe someone had an issue with us. For the life of me, I can't imagine who. Our winery hasn't received any complaints from the wine association or the local business bureau."

"Is the sheriff's deputy still there? I called you because I overheard people talking about an emergency vehicle at your winery. Naturally I was concerned."

"Oh, Norrie, how sweet of you. Especially with all the 'Deck the Halls' hubbub going on. This place is a madhouse. People in, people out, and the same holiday music playing nonstop. I swear if I hear 'Frosty the Snowman' one more time, I'm likely to explode."

"Don't feel bad. 'Rudolph the Red-Nosed Reindeer' is on a loop at our place."

"Deputy Hickman left about forty minutes ago. Said he'd be back to speak with us after we closed for the day. Just what we all need. These events are always demanding, but this tops the cake. I'm really stressed about our loss. First thing Monday, we'll have to let Miller Holtz know they can't expect any oak-aged Pinot Noir from us. Not that it was that much, but it was the most expensive variety we had."

"Um, speaking of Miller Holtz, have you seen his boss at the event? Arnold Mowen?"

"No, I haven't. Trust me, he'll be hard to miss."

"Really? There are lots of balding, overweight, middle-aged men at these events."

"Not one with a voluptuous platinum blonde on his arm wearing enough gold to sink a ship."

"He has a trophy wife? I didn't think he was married. And I didn't think he was bringing anyone. At least not according to Miller Holtz."

"No wife. A trophy girlfriend, and it's not him she's attached to, it's his bank account. Maybe you'll spot him tomorrow. Frankly, I hope I don't run into the old buzzard. I'm still reeling about our lower compensation rates. Market prices my patootie! He's probably pocketing that extra money for her next piece of jewelry."

"How do you know all of this?"

"About a year ago, I met her at a fancy wine tasting benefit in Ithaca. Lavettia something-or-other. The competing rocks on her fingers nearly blinded me. All she could talk about was how Arnold promised to buy her a LeVian chocolate diamond bracelet for Valentine's Day. And to think, I'm happy if my husband stops at Walgreens and brings me a box of milk chocolates. Goodness, I can't believe I'm spouting off about all of this when I really should be concerned about our wines. I still can't imagine who'd want to hurt our business."

"Did Deputy Hickman ask you about disgruntled employees? Because that was his take when he met with us. Frankly, I don't think these damages were caused by a nutcase on our payroll. I hate to say it, but it doesn't take a real genius to figure out that only one wine has become a target for vandalism and theft. That hijacking the other day? They only stole red wines."

"*That* I can understand. The reds always yield a higher price. Even on the black market. But our wine wasn't stolen. It was eliminated. I'd like to talk more, but I've got to get back to our tasting room. Keep me posted if you hear anything else."

"I will."

I didn't hear another thing that day. Other than the morning fiasco, "Deck the Halls around the Lake" continued without incident at Two Witches Winery. By five thirty, after the event closed and we locked our doors, I told everyone about what had happened earlier in the day. I mentioned our place, the Grey Egret, and Billsburrow Winery. Roger, our resident French and Indian War expert, was certain it was some sort of conspiracy. Had it not been for Cammy insisting we all "get a move on or we'll be here until nine," we might've been forced to listen to another one of Roger's long-winded anecdotes about that war.

To further muddy the waters, Glenda insisted we all partake in a ritual aura cleansing that involved burning sage sticks, which she just so happened to have on hand, and lavender oil.

"The only cleansing I'm going to do is in my shower, in the privacy of my apartment," Sam said. "I've had enough hoo-hah for the day. And to think, we get to do the same thing all over again tomorrow."

"Ditto that," someone else said and the matter was dropped.

"Hey, before you leave for the day, did anyone happen to notice a stout, elderly man with a chrome dome?" I asked.

"You've got to be kidding me," Cammy said. "All I noticed were hands reaching out for wine or truffles. Why? Were you expecting someone?"

"Yeah, Arnold Mowen, the owner of Lake-to-Lake Wine Distributors was alleged to have purchased a ticket."

"Well, my dear," Lizzie said. "In the words of Scarlett O'Hara, 'After all, tomorrow is another day!'"

Whoa. No quotes from her favorite sleuth, Nancy Drew. Lizzie must be really tired.

Sam smiled. "Whatever tickles your fancy. I will be on the lookout for knockout redheads, but if it's a shiny bald head you're after, well…I hope you find it."

Chapter 5

Sam's words couldn't have been more prophetic.

I did get to see Arnold Mowen's chrome dome—but not the way I envisioned it. The sun reflected off his head as he lay face down in the hardened snow midway between our winery and the Grey Egret's. His body rested in a small ditch a few yards from the driveway. I wondered how long he'd been there. We found his car, a new model silver Audi A4 all-road that must've set him back at least forty-five thousand, parked at the edge of the Grey Egret's tasting room building. It teetered on the edge of a smaller ditch that bordered the adjacent property. The vehicle, obscured from sight by a row of mature pine trees, must've been there all night.

It was dark when "Deck the Halls around the Lake" ended on Saturday. It was no wonder no one noticed it. Or him, for that matter. If it hadn't been for Charlie, who was making the most of his last free days before deer season and the inevitable forced confinement in his dog run, I doubted anyone would've noticed the chrome dome until the spring thaw.

I woke up with the sunrise: six forty-two to be precise. The glow of the digital clock in my room was hard to miss. It was the sound of hunters sighting in their rifles that woke me. I should've been used to it, having grown up here, but that was years ago. I was more accustomed to cars backfiring, sirens blaring, cats yowling, the general rumble of trucks and streetcars, and the occasional scream.

Here, it was the pop-pop sound of a rifle that followed the hunter successfully bore-sighting it from twenty-five to a hundred yards. How did I know this? I dated hunters in high school. Opening day of deer season had the highest absence rate in the Penn Yan School District. At one point, they considered making it a mandatory teacher conference day, but the teachers objected. Most of them were hunters, too.

Every gunshot meant someone was about to measure yardage or adjust the rifle's scope. Even though hunters were not allowed in our woods, someone might ignore the 'No Trespassing' signs. It didn't matter. Sunrise or gunshots, I was awake and ready for another day of "Deck the Halls around the Lake." If I was lucky, maybe the forensics crew found a viable fingerprint during the investigation yesterday.

With a hot cup of coffee in my hand and a day-old croissant from the bistro, I planned on doing a bit of writing before I donned my happy holiday sweatshirt and left for another day in the tasting room. It was a good plan and one that should've worked. But it didn't. Charlie tromped through his doggie door and dumped a chewed-up piece of something at my feet.

"Not another dead thing, Charlie. At least it's a small one. A flattened mouse or vole maybe." Ugh. I reached for a paper towel to dispose of the small animal and caught sight of something else—a credit card. Huh? I gingerly reached for the dog's prize when I realized it wasn't the remains of an animal. It was a brown leather wallet—complete with Charlie's teeth marks. The credit card must've fallen out when Charlie started gnawing.

"Some poor customer's probably frantic." I said. "Let's see what the credit card says."

I turned it over and gasped. "This is a black card, Charlie! A black credit card from Citibank. They only issue these things to people who have so much money they don't need credit cards. Then again, who wouldn't want concierge services?" I was so fixated on the card itself, it took me a second or two to register the name embossed on the front—Arnold M. Mowen. Five years until the card expired, but Arnold didn't have that luck.

"Geez, dog, where did you find this? The parking lot?"

I fumbled trying to pull his contact information from the wallet. His work number was on my computer, but it was Sunday. Even Scrooge took that day off. I found his driver's license, Medicare card, and two other credit cards in the wallet, along with his list of medications—everything except his personal contact information—I guess most people don't carry around their own cell phone numbers.

My thumb rubbed against another card, a pink business card with small gold flowers around the edges. It read Lavettia Lawrence, Essential Oils for The Essential Life. Her phone number and email were on the card as well. I wasted no time placing the call, even if it meant waking her.

After four rings, she answered. She sounded groggy, and I knew I'd woken her. "Arnie, is that you?" Then a "Shh," but I didn't think it was meant for the caller. "I got worried when you didn't answer last night."

"Um, Miss Lawrence? Lavettia? This is Norrie Ellington from Two Witches Winery in Penn Yan. I'm calling because I found a wallet that belongs to Arnold Mowen and your business card was in it. The wallet has his license, credit cards—"

"OH MY GOD! Where is he? He'd never leave his wallet anywhere!"

"I don't know where he is. The wallet was found on our property." *Exactly where, I have no clue. Nonetheless, it was found here.*

"You have to start looking. Searching. Scouring. My poor Arnie could be lying in a ditch somewhere, for all we know. And he'll freeze to death with that all that snow underneath him."

"Okay, okay. Try to calm down. The wallet was found at our winery. Most likely he dropped it and didn't notice. Were you with him yesterday at our event?"

"No. He wanted me to go, but I needed to attend a company symposium on medicinal purposes for essential oils. I'm an area representative for The Essential Life Company out of San Francisco. It's a mecca for new-age living."

San Francisco. And all this time I thought they were famous for the Golden Gate Bridge and Chinatown.

As she was talking, I could swear I heard a man's voice in the background. Something about a Corvette. Then again, it was probably the TV or her radio. "Um, I feel as if I'm interrupting you."

"Interrupting? How can you interrupt me? You woke me."

Hrrumph. Good cover.

She continued, "With frightening news, too. You simply have to find my Arnie."

"I will. I mean, I'll try. I'll take a walk around the grounds, *because God knows, I have nothing better to do,* and call you back. You said you couldn't reach him. Have you tried his other contacts?"

"What other contacts? And what about his car? Where's his car?"

"I've no idea. What kind of a car is it?"

"An Audi. It's silver. An all-road vehicle. Brand new."

"That should be pretty easy to spot if it's in our parking lot. Okay, I'll start looking and I'll call you."

"Yes, yes. Call me."

She hung up before I could say another word. So much for early morning screenwriting. I put on the warmest socks I could find, then the usual jeans and a grubby sweatshirt, followed by a fleece-lined jacket. Charlie must've thought we were going out for playtime or at the very least a good romp around the grounds. He was bouncing up and down at my heels until I opened the front door to begin my search.

We started at the tasting room building. No Audi in sight. No cars whatsoever. From there I meandered down the road. Maybe he parked his car by the winery building, where our lab was. Maybe he'd gotten word about the sabotaged wines and wanted to check it out for himself. But who would've called him? I hadn't planned on speaking with Miller Holtz until Monday. Twenty-four hours from now.

Nothing at the winery building. Charlie and I moved farther down our driveway/road where our property ended, and the Grey Egret's began. That was when Charlie decided to roll on his back off the side of the drive, where a small, deep ditch widened before ending at the state road and the edge of the Grey Egret's parking lot. I watched the dog lift his legs in the air and dig his fur into the hardened snow At least the ground was frozen, and he wouldn't be filthy from mud or worse.

Lavettia's words popped into my head. *My poor Arnie could be lying in a ditch.* Why a ditch? Why couldn't he be two sheets to the wind under a porch or passed out behind the wheel of his car in a parking lot somewhere? Maybe it was just a figure of speech. I kept walking, eager to spot that car. Charlie got tired of rolling around and darted ahead of me. Talk about ditches. He took off to my left and, for a moment, he was out of sight. I scanned both sides of the road and didn't see any vehicles, especially not a shiny new Audi.

What I did see was Charlie tugging on something as he backed out of the ditch. I made a mental note to tell our vineyard manager to remove the debris and garbage from that spot. Unsightly trash didn't mesh well with winery ambience.

I took a few steps closer to see what had gotten Charlie's attention. The sun's reflection on Arnold Mowen's shiny scalp was impossible to miss. So was the small dime-size hole in the back of his neck. Dark red with a thin line of dried blood. I knew it was Arnold Mowen, because who else could it be? The guy was missing. Plain and simple. Plus, I was holding his wallet, presumably removed by the dog during an earlier encounter with his body.

He was lying face down. His arms were bent at the elbows, and his legs were splayed slightly apart. His black pants were only slightly dirty as was the long dark winter coat he was wearing. Oddly enough, the man was wearing shiny black dress shoes—not exactly the most appropriate attire for a winery event.

My feet were like two concrete blocks, and I stood fixed at the side of the driveway, trying to ascertain if the body was on our property or the Grey Egret's. As it turned out, we shared the prize.

"Leave it alone! Leave *him* alone!" I yelled to the dog. Somehow, I managed to free myself from the temporary paralysis that anchored my legs to the ground. I inhaled the frosty morning air and ran toward Theo and Don's house as if I was being chased by the zombie apocalypse and not our nosey Plott Hound.

"Dead body! Dead man! Dead Arnold!" I yelled. I almost took a header when I raced up their porch. The early morning frost had turned the wood into a veritable skating rink, and I all but skidded into their front door. I don't remember if I rang the bell, pounded on the door, or did both.

Within seconds, Theo opened it. He was in desperate need of a shave and a comb. I wasn't one to talk, considering I hadn't used a hairbrush either. Or makeup.

Not that it mattered. The words exploded out of mouth and the entire lake probably heard me. "We've got a dead man in our ditch and it's our wine distributor."

"*Our* ditch?" I heard Don call out from the back of the house.

Then Theo. "*Our* distributor? Arnold Mowen?"

"Yes. I believe so. Face down. Did I mention there is a bullet wound on the back of his neck? I saw the blood. It's a bullet wound, all right. It was either that or an arrow. You know, like a bow and arrow. Only, if it was an arrow and the killer pulled it out, the hole would be bigger, wouldn't it?"

Suddenly, I was the local forensics expert. The words kept babbling out of my mouth, making less and less sense as I talked.

Don came down the hallway and ushered me into their kitchen. "Stay here. Theo and I will go check it out. Where'd you say the body was?"

This time I pointed. It was as if I'd used up my vocabulary and was rendered mute. Nerves, I supposed. Not surprising. It was, after all, my third dead body in less than six months. Seasoned law officers didn't come across that many bodies.

"Help yourself to some coffee and there are some plain vanilla cookies if Charlie wants a treat," he said. "You look as if you could use a cup."

What I could use was a one-way ticket back to my apartment in Manhattan. I hadn't seen even one dead body there, and Manhattan has over a million and a half residents. Penn Yan has five thousand. Go figure.

I took Don's advice and made myself some coffee. I also nibbled on their cookies, along with Charlie, who had made himself at home under the chair where Isolde, their long-haired cat, was sleeping. It seemed like they'd been gone forever; but, according to the clock on their stove, it had only been fifteen minutes.

"It's Arnold Mowen, all right," Theo announced when they opened the door. "We found his car, too. It was at the edge of our lot, past the pine trees. What do you suppose happened to him? And don't you two start laughing. Other than the obvious, I mean. The bullet to the back of his neck. Blood and blackish soot. Couldn't be a hunting accident. No one's that stupid to sight in a rifle so close to our properties."

"Unless they wanted it to look that way." I wiped some cookie crumbs from my lip. "I don't suppose you called the sheriff while you were outside, did you?"

The guys grunted and looked at each other.

"Who wants the honors?" Theo asked.

"Don't make me call!" I shrieked. "Not after the Pinot Noir incident. I don't want to be in Deputy Hickman's line of fire. He takes one look at me and it translates to a heavier and heavier caseload for him. No wonder the guy despises me."

Don patted my shoulder. "He doesn't despise you, Norrie. What irks him is your, well, meddling, for lack of a better word."

"I'll have you know the word is sleuthing, and someone needs to do it."

Theo tapped his phone and dialed the number. "While the two of you play semantics, I might as well call the sheriff's department."

Don and I sat quietly as we listened to Theo's end of the conversation. "That's right. A dead body. At the midway point in the driveway between the Grey Egret and Two Witches Winery." Pause. "No, I have no idea how long it's, I mean *he's* been there, but I think it had to be overnight." Pause. "Well, because the body was stiff. Really stiff. They don't get that way in a few hours, do they?"

"Ew," I whispered to Don. "You touched the body?"

"Sort of. If you count the tip of my boot on his leg. It was like kicking a steel beam. By the way, how did you know his body was in the ditch?"

"I didn't." I handed him the wallet, complete with bite marks. "Charlie plopped this on the kitchen floor this morning and a credit card fell out with Arnold's name on it. A *black* card, I might add. I went through the wallet to get a phone number and found a business card for Lavettia Lawrence. That's his gold digger girlfriend, according to Madeline Martinez."

Theo and Don exchanged glances.

"Anyway, I called Lavettia and told her about the wallet. She was positive something awful happened to Arnold because she couldn't reach him last night. Guess she was right, huh? Oh, no! Lavettia! I probably should call her, shouldn't I?"

Chapter 6

"I don't know if that's such a good idea," Don said. "Better wait for the sheriff's deputy to contact Arnold's nearest and dearest. What kind of business card?"

"Essential oils. Why?"

"Curious, that's all."

He handed the wallet back to me, and I thumbed through it again. There were business cards in it I hadn't noticed. "Quick!" I said. "Turn on your printer. We should make a copy of everything that's in this wallet before I have to turn it over to Deputy Hickman."

Don chortled. "And you wonder why the man thinks you meddle."

"Come on. We don't have much time."

Theo held out his hand. "Give them to me. I'll line them up on the printer and get a copy. They should all fit on a single sheet of paper. If Grizzly Gary gets to the door before I'm done, stall."

I walked over to their large picture window. "You don't have to worry. I don't see any flashers and I don't—oh hell! Hurry up! He's on Route 14 and about to turn on to our road."

The photocopies were done in no time. Arnold's business cards, driver's license, and medical insurance cards were back in place. I pocketed the wallet and waited for the inevitable knock on the door. Theo and Don motioned for Deputy Hickman to step inside, and the four of us stood in their foyer—uncomfortable as ever.

Deputy Hickman clasped his hands together, gave his head a shake, and looked directly at me. "If I had my way, Miss Ellington, I'd have the entire Seneca Lake area from Route 54 in Dresden all the way up to Two Witches Hill designated to another county!"

"It's not like I'm trying to find dead bodies."

He shuddered and shook off a light dusting of snow. "No, but you seem to have a penchant for attracting them. Now, suppose you tell me about your latest find. I take it you were the one who found the deceased?"

I nodded.

"Good. Tell me the circumstances and show me where the body is located."

I began with Charlie and the wallet, continued with my call to Lavettia, and ended by having Theo and Don describe the crime scene. Deputy Hickman used the same small pad and pencil I'd seen him use before for note taking.

When he was done, he leaned against the doorjamb. "The coroner should be here momentarily, along with a forensics crew. Will one of you please walk me to the body? I don't require an entire parade."

"I'll do it," Theo said. "Give me a second to grab my jacket."

"Um, Deputy Hickman," I said, "if you want my opinion about the gunshot wound to the back of Arnold's neck, I think—"

Two hands flashed in front of my face. "I most certainly do not want, need, or require your opinion. Gun season for deer hunting begins on Tuesday. Every overzealous hunter from here to Canada has been sighting in his or her gun. Most likely this was a hunting accident, but, until we get a thorough report from our trained investigators and our coroner, I refuse to speculate any further. And you, Miss Ellington, should do the same. Cease and desist from speculating and theorizing."

With that, the deputy and Theo left the house. Don and I went back to the kitchen. Instead of sitting down, we looked out the window that faced the driveway.

"This is a disaster. How long do you think they're going to be there with the body?" I asked.

Don shook his head. "Who knows? With a gunshot wound, they'll be looking at the trajectory and all that neat stuff."

"Aargh. That could take, like, forever." I looked at the clock on their stove. "It's eight fifty-three now. My tasting room crew's going to be arriving in less than twenty minutes, if not sooner. Much too late to call them. At least the vineyard guys are off today, and the winemakers won't come in until much later. Franz wanted to get that tainted barrel cleaned, provided the forensics guys are done with it. I really should go home and change."

"Yeah, I've got to get washed and changed, too. Because our tasting room building is so close to the main road, party goers for 'Deck the Halls around the Lake' aren't as apt to notice the active crime scene when they first arrive. It's only when they start up the hill for your place that—"

"Don't say it. I know. They'll wonder who got knocked off this time. At least it's cold out and they won't be traipsing around. I'll catch up with you and Theo later. Oh, geez, I almost forgot. We didn't tell the deputy about Arnold's car in your parking lot."

"Don't worry. He'll get to that soon enough. Besides, the car wasn't killed, Arnold was."

"Yeesh."

"Want me to drive you up the hill? It's a long walk."

"Nah. You've got to get going. Besides, it'll give me a chance to have a word or two with Deputy Hickman. Not my fault I have to pass right by there on my way home."

Don laughed. "Grab a few cookies for the trek."

"I'll need them to lure Charlie out of here. He's fast asleep under your chair."

It took me all of two seconds to slip back into the fleece-lined jacket I had draped over my chair and head out the door. With the cookies as bait, Charlie was at my heels once again. Deputy Hickman was right about the other county vehicles. There were more flashing lights in our driveway than strobes at a '70s disco.

Geez. It's not like you're chasing a speeder. This one's a slam-dunk.

As I got closer to the spot where Arnold Mowen took his last breath, I could see a heavy-set man wearing a dark vest that read "Yates County Coroner." Next to him were two other deputies—probably the forensics team. Deputy Hickman was standing cattycorner from them, a good two or three yards away. His arms were crossed, and he barely moved.

Someone had already cordoned off the area with that familiar yellow crime scene tape. No way were the tourists going to think we roped it off to shelter part of our vineyard. A knot formed in my stomach just thinking about it.

"Excuse me." I approached the deputies. "Do you know how long this is going to take? Um, not to sound callous, but we've got a winery event starting at ten."

The coroner, who had bent over to examine Arnold's neck wound, looked up. "Could be another half hour or more before we remove the body."

"A half hour? Can't you move it any quicker? How long does it take? I've seen mattresses moved in less time, and they were heavy mattresses, too."

"Miss Ellington," Deputy Hickman's voice bellowed. "If you don't leave the crime scene immediately, I'll have you arrested for interfering with an investigation."

"Fine. I'll be on my way."

I turned away, but not before overhearing the coroner say something to Deputy Hickman about antacids. No surprise there. That job would give me indigestion too.

I thundered up the rest of the hill, threw off the clothes I had grabbed earlier, and put on a cheerful holiday tunic. Nothing like basking in the joys of the season with a corpse to welcome our visitors.

"You stay here," I said to Charlie. I added kibble to his bowl and made sure his doggie door was sealed shut. Last thing I needed was for him to return to the scene of the crime. Then I was off to the tasting room, anticipating a round of questions from the staff. I wasn't wrong.

Glenda rushed over to me the minute I set foot in the place. "I had an awful premonition that another restless soul would be haunting the winery," she said.

I groaned. "If anything's getting haunted, it'll be the ditch between us and the Grey Egret."

"Norrie! What the hell happened?" Cammy shouted as she opened the kitchen door and spied me. "Was someone shot? There are two sheriff's cars off the side of our driveway, not to mention the coroner's van. You can't miss it."

"Sorry, guys," I said. "It was too late to call you."

Roger, Lizzie, and Sam walked over to where I was standing. They were joined by the part-time college students who were also working the event.

"Can someone get Fred over here?" I asked. "He's at the bistro, and I really don't want to repeat this."

"YO! FRED!" Sam yelled across the large room. "You gotta get over here. Like now!"

I rolled my eyeballs and took a breath. Fred came running as if the place was on fire. "What? Is this about all the sheriff's cars in our driveway?"

"I'll make this as short and succinct as possible." I tried to sound professional and matter-of-fact. "Our wine distributor from Lake-to-Lake Wine Distributors was found dead in the ditch by the side of our driveway, midway between us and the Grey Egret."

"Dead like heart attack or dead like bludgeoned to death?" Sam asked.

I swallowed. "Dead like bullet wound to the back of his neck."

A chorus of "oohs" followed.

I went on to tell them how I found the body, from Charlie gifting me with a partially chewed wallet to Deputy Hickman threatening to arrest me for interfering with an investigation.

"How long are they going to be there?" Cammy asked. "Did they tell you?"

"Nope. No clue."

"They usually load up the body and get it on a gurney right away," Roger said. "It's those forensics guys who take their time with everything. Want me to have a look-see?"

"No," I said. "There's nothing any of us can do about it, and we've got to get ready for today's event."

Lizzie furrowed her brow and pursed her lips. "As the account keeper for this winery, I've had my share of dealings with Mr. Mowen. Most of them quite unpleasant. I wouldn't be at all surprised if his death was ruled a homicide. The man didn't get along with anyone. When I went to make a deposit at Seneca Lake Communities Bank last week, I found out he had moved his business accounts to First Liberty Federal. The teller told me he had a falling out with 'one of the bigwigs' at her bank."

Glenda caught her breath and held it. "I'm sensing his death was the result of a personal vendetta."

I shook my head. "Deputy Hickman thinks it might've been a hunting accident."

"The season doesn't start for two more days!" Sam blurted out. "Is he nuts or what?"

"None of us will know anything until they complete their investigation. Heck, we don't even know what kind of a bullet it was."

Roger took a step closer to me. "You said you saw the body, right? And the wound? What was the diameter?"

"I didn't exactly take out a ruler, guys! Aargh. Less than a half inch. The size of a dime."

"Could be a .22 caliber. A shotgun would use a plug and a 30-30 would leave a larger hole. Now, if this was the French and Indian War, we'd be talking the flintlock musket, but you probably know it by its nickname, the Brown Bess."

Oh, God help us! Roger's about to launch into one of his lectures about that war.

"We don't have time right now," I said. "Customers are going to be walking in that door. Later! We can talk about vendettas, bullet wounds, the French and Indian War, and Arnold Mowen much later. After we close for the day."

No one argued or added another word. One by one, everyone went over to their tasting tables, or in Fred and Lizzie's case, the bistro and cash register respectively. I took my spot at the welcome table and prayed our customers would be more interested in Pinot Noir truffles than who was in that ditch. Turned out I was wrong.

Someone working for Channel 13 WHAM in Rochester must've had nothing better to do than listen to the sheriff's scanners from Yates County. The TV channel wasted no time sending a bright yellow and black news van to us. It was déjà vu all over again. This time with a light snowfall.

"We saw the coroner's van removing a body from the side of your driveway," the first customer said, as I handed her a grapevine wreath. "Car accident in your driveway? I think the light snow is much more dangerous than inches of the stuff. It's so slippery, and there's nothing anyone can do."

Before I could answer the svelte, twenty-something with the Brazilian blow-out, she snatched her wreath with one hand and grabbed the small cookbook with the other. "Oh, do I smell truffles?"

She was gone in a nanosecond. Unfortunately, the topic of conversation wasn't. The questions kept hitting me like my own personal barrage of bullets.

"What happened in your ditch?"

"Why are there a zillion sheriff's deputies parked down the driveway?"

"Did someone plant a bomb on your property?"

I decided to go with the most innocuous response. "Gun sighting mishap. Hunting season starts the day after tomorrow."

An hour after we opened, the traffic at the welcome table remained steady. I had developed a certain rhythm as I greeted people. I was even beginning to feel comfortable with my own lie about a possible hunting accident, but that ended abruptly when the gold charms from Lavettia Lawrence's chain bracelet brushed against my wrist. She latched on to every bone that connected my hand to my arm and wouldn't let go. In fact, I could feel her long nails pinching my flesh.

"You, you…monster! You knew he was dead and you didn't tell me. I had to find out from my…my… never mind. I found out. It was all over the news. On TV, on the radio. The dead body in your ditch *must* be my Arnold. The moment I heard what happened, I got in my car and drove right over here." Then she paused for a second and loosened her grip slightly. "Oh. You *are* Norrie Ellington, aren't you? The cashier pointed in this direction, but there's another table behind yours and there's a woman at that one, too."

I used my left hand to extricate her fingers from my wrist. "Yes, I'm Norrie and I thought the sheriff's department would be contacting you. The sheriff's department has Arnold's wallet. I gave it to Deputy Hickman. Honestly, I expected him to call you."

"Well, he didn't. No one did. So, tell me, did you see the body? Was it my Arnold?"

"Um, it was a bald man with some hair below the crown of his head. And nicely dressed."

"Florsheim Hamilton Wingtip Oxfords? Shiny black?"

"Well, some kind of shiny black dress shoe."

She pressed her hand to her chest. "What about the car? Did you find a silver Audi?"

"There was one parked in the Grey Egret's lot. I think it was there all night."

Lavettia rubbed the edges of her eyes and stood still. I wasn't sure what to say or do.

Finally, she spoke. "I warned him something like this might happen. But did he listen? No. Or he'd still be alive. I kept telling him, 'Arnie, you can't keep squeezing money out of people. One of these days someone's going to make you pay.'"

Then, without warning, Lavettia flung her faux rabbit coat across the nearest chair, grabbed the side of the welcome table, and threw herself across it. Her sobs could be heard across the room.

Behind her someone said, "My God! I don't get that upset when I lose an event ticket!"

Chapter 7

Fred happened to be making the rounds with coffee for us at that very moment, and helped me move Lavettia from the tasting room to our kitchen. The part-time worker assisting Lizzie at the cash register immediately took over for me at the welcome table.

I handed Lavettia a cup of coffee and a handful of napkins. She sank down in the closest chair at our long rectangular table.

"You going to be okay?" Fred mouthed to me as Lavettia wiped her eyes.

"Yeah," I mouthed back. "You can go back to work."

He gave a quick nod and got out of there in a flash. It didn't surprise me. I'd never met a man who could stand being around a crying woman. Heck, I couldn't stand it either, and I *was* a woman.

"Miss Lawrence, um, Lavettia, please calm down."

It was pointless to tell her the body in the ditch might not have been her boyfriend, We both knew it was. The wallet, the car, the clothing, the bald head...Duh. No wonder Lavettia was beside herself. As for me, the last thing this winery needed was a reputation as a dumping ground for bodies, or worse yet, a killing ground. True, Arnold's rock-solid corpse was equidistant from us and the Grey Egret, but that was a small consolation.

Lavettia took a sip of her coffee and, as she put the cup down with a trembling hand, she said, "Channel 13 WHAM announced it was a gunshot wound to the victim's head. My God! How can someone mistake a well-dressed, portly man for a deer? No, it was personal all right. It had to be. Now all I have to figure out is which SOB killed him."

"If I'm not mistaken, isn't that what the sheriff's department is supposed to do?"

"Oh, please. They couldn't locate a lost cow if it opened up a milk stand on Route 14!"

With the histrionics behind her, I figured now was as good a time as any to get Lavettia to open up about Arnold.

"I don't suppose you'd know if he had any close relatives. Or any, for that matter. They always seem to crop up when there's a mention of a will."

"A will? Who mentioned his will?"

"Um, er, uh…I was talking in general. Not specific."

"It doesn't matter. Arnold's an only child. Parents passed on years ago. No wife. No children. He was all about work. Everything for that business."

"Speaking of which, do you have any idea who inherits his business? Lake-to-Lake Wine Distributors is a big-name company."

Lavettia rolled the gold charms around on her bracelet and answered me without looking up. "Me. I inherit the business. He left it all to me."

I opened my mouth, but nothing came out. Thankfully, Lavettia didn't seem to notice. I rubbed my hands together and took the seat next to her at the table. "Lavettia, this isn't good. If you stand to inherit his business, you could be the prime suspect in his murder."

Murder. I'd said the word out loud. Me. I was the one who said it. Not the sheriff's deputy. Not the forensics crew. Not the coroner. Not Channel 13. Me. I had opened my mouth and there was no going back. I did the only thing possible—I dug myself a deeper hole.

"You probably should hire an attorney. Just in case. And don't say a word to Deputy Hickman when he questions you unless you have an attorney present. Then again, that might look as if you're guilty. Okay. Have someone you trust at your side when he questions you. And whatever you do, don't tell him about the business."

"The business. Oh heavens. The business. I don't know the first thing about it. But Arnold's sales rep does--Miller Holtz. Oh, and then there's the secretary, Clayton LeVine. Should I be calling them?"

"If I were you, I wouldn't be doing anything just yet, until you hear from the sheriff's department. Your business card was in Arnold's wallet. Naturally, they're going to contact you. Right now, they're probably trying to track down next of kin and when that doesn't pan out, I guarantee they'll send one of their deputies to Arnold's office and another to your house. Right now, all anyone knows is that a dead body with an apparent gunshot wound was found on Two Witches Hill in Penn Yan. That's not really unusual during hunting season." *Oh, who am I kidding? Last time someone got shot around here during hunting season was when one of the Munson brothers mistook his twin for a deer and grazed him in the butt.*

"What about the news? It'll be all over the TV, not to mention social media."
I brushed an annoying strand of hair from my forehead. "No worries.
The news media won't be able to release the name until they get clearance
from the sheriff."

"How do you know so much about these things?"

This isn't my first rodeo. "Uh, I happen to read a lot."

Lavettia reached for a napkin from the small stack we had on the table
and dabbed her eyes. "This will all land on me, you know. His funeral.
His eulogy. His final wishes. There's no one else."

"What about his lawyer? I'm sure his lawyer will be able to handle the
business end of things."

"You're right. First thing tomorrow morning, I'll call Marvin Souza's
office and insist he see me."

"Marvin Souza in Geneva? *That* Marvin Souza?"

"How many Marvin Souzas are there? You know him?"

"I know another lawyer in that office. Bradley Jamison."

"Bradley, you said? Sounds like an old coot. Well, if they saddle me
with him, I'll simply have to deal with it."

My cheeks warmed. Lavettia would be in for one hell of a surprise if
indeed she "got saddled" with Bradley.

Just then, Lizzie stuck her head in the doorway and called out, "Norrie,
Godfrey Klein's on the phone for you. Isn't that the entomologist from
Cornell who keeps you informed about your sister and brother-in-law? His
department must have deep pockets for him to be on that satellite phone
all the way from New York to Costa Rica. Said he tried your cell but it
went to voice mail. I told him I'd get you."

*Oh no. As if this day couldn't get any worse. Godfrey's probably calling
to tell me my sister and brother-in-law contracted some awful insect-borne
illness in Costa Rica.* "Tell him I'll be right there, Lizzie!"

Lavettia was still dabbing her eyes and twirling around the charms
on her bracelet. I swore I could hear her humming. For a split second, I
pictured Dr. Manette, from *A Tale of Two Cities,* hunched over a table in
the Bastille as he made shoes. *His* mental lapse I could understand, but
heaven help us all if Lavettia went off the deep end.

"I've got to take this call," I said to her. "There are trays of truffles on
the counter in here. Help yourself."

I rushed out the door and into the tasting room, where the phone was
located. Wedging myself behind Lizzie at the cash register, I picked up
the receiver. "Godfrey! Hi! Is everything all right?"

"You tell me. I turned on the news this morning and caught the tail end of a report about a body being found in the ditch by the side of your driveway. Who? What happened?"

"Long story but it was our wine distributor. And the body was actually equidistant from our property and the Grey Egret's."

Somehow, I wanted to absolve Two Witches from the entire burden of shouldering yet another corpse on our property.

"My God! That's horrible. Do you know what happened?"

"The sheriff's deputy thinks it was a hunting accident. Someone who goofed while sighting in a rifle. I think it was deliberate. Um, listen, there's no way my sister and brother-in-law can find out about this, is there?"

"They won't find out from me when we make our satellite calls, if that's what you mean. At some point, however, they'll be airlifted out of the rainforest for an R & R along the coast. Even the best researchers need a break from time to time. Of course, I wouldn't worry about it if I were you."

"Why? Francine will get hysterical and insist Jason abandon his research project and come home. I'd feel miserable about that."

"Well then, I've got stunningly good news for you."

Wonderful. I could use stunningly good. "What?"

"They've located the Culex corniger in a remote area. Normally, this is an urban mosquito species found in the Greater Puntarenas area on the west coast."

"And this is a good thing...because?"

"It will open up a whole new field study area for us."

"Oh, I see. Anyway, not a word about the dead body, okay?"

"You said you thought it was deliberate. Mind if I ask why?"

"Because, out of the blue, our wine distributor, whose name hasn't been released to the public yet, lowered the compensation rates on all of the wines in our area. In other words, he was paying us less than he did in prior years. That's a major business loss for the small wineries. But someone was making a profit on the retail sales, and that someone was him. Everyone was ticked. Everyone!"

"And you think one of the winery owners killed him?"

"*Someone* did. Of course, it could be personal, too. His girlfriend's sitting in our tasting room kitchen at this very moment. She drove here because she thought I might have some answers about his death. Which, by the way, hasn't officially been deemed a murder, yet."

"Oh, brother. Look, if there's anything I can do, let me know. And be careful. That hill of yours is becoming a regular magnet for every kook and nutcase on the lake."

"I will. And thanks, Godfrey. For everything."

I hung up the receiver and raced back into the kitchen. Lavettia was still rolling the gold charms around on her bracelet.

"I really should get going. Is Arnie's car still where you said it was or did the sheriff's department have it towed?"

My gosh. With all the chaos going on, I hadn't thought about the car. I wasn't even sure if Deputy Hickman knew about it. "Um, I think so. It was parked by the far edge of the Grey Egret's lot."

"Good. I need to get something out of it. Don't worry. I have a key."

"Uh, er, gee, I'm not so sure that's a great idea."

"Why? It isn't as if someone ran him over with it. Besides, my extra makeup bag and overnight jewelry are in there. Under the front passenger seat. You know, in case Arnie and I were out somewhere, and he decided to get romantic and book us a room along the lake. He did that sometimes. A nice, romantic…"

And then the tears again. And the sobs. People handled grief differently and they went through all sorts of stages, but watching Lavettia Lawrence was like having a front seat at Wimbledon.

With this morning's light snowfall, I was positive Lavettia's footprints would be found next to the car. That stuff didn't melt. It became crusty and imprints lasted a long, long time. It was a really bad idea for her to retrieve some lipstick and more bracelets or whatever she had stashed in her overnight "just-in-case" bag. Worse yet, when Deputy Hickman got around to dealing with Arnold's car, he'd badger Theo, Don, and me about why there were footprints going straight to the passenger door.

Lavettia pushed her chair back and stood. "I'm sorry if I went off on you when I first got here. It was the shock, you know. I'm fine now. Really, I am. And I'll call Marvin Souza first thing in the morning. He'll know what to do, I'm sure."

"Yeah, me, too."

She reached for the black and white faux fur jacket that she had tossed on her chair and buttoned it up. I followed her past the tasting room to the main doors, hoping she'd take my advice and stay away from Arnold's car.

She didn't.

Hours later, when "Deck the Halls around the Lake" ended and four or five stragglers headed out the door, Deputy Hickman walked in. I was standing next to Lizzie, looking at the total sales for the day. It was only when my eyes left the screen that I noticed him standing only inches from me.

"Good afternoon, Miss Ellington. I'm coming from the Grey Egret, where I had a word with the owners. The key to a new Audi A-4 all-road was found in the victim's pocket. And surprise, surprise—his car was parked at the far end of the Grey Egret's lot. Our protocol called for the vehicle to be towed to a forensics lab in Syracuse. The lab is closed on Sunday, so we made arrangements for that process to take place tomorrow morning."

"Um, is there a problem?"

His face was expressionless. "One of our deputies drove over there this afternoon to tag the car. When he arrived, he noticed a fresh set of footprints by the passenger door. I don't suppose you'd know anything about that, would you?"

"I, uh…"

"The owners of the Grey Egret were equally surprised."

The last thing I wanted to do was rat out Lavettia Lawrence. I figured if anyone might have an idea of who Arnold's killer was, it would be Lavettia. I stepped away from the counter and looked straight at Deputy Hickman. "Today was a major winery event. Lots of cars were parked in their lot. That Audi was brand new and pricey. Maybe someone wanted to have a closer look."

"Maybe."

"The news commentators are saying the cause of death was a bullet wound. Would you happen to know—"

"No, I would not. I should receive the coroner's report sometime tomorrow—along with a positive identification of the body."

"I thought it was pretty obvious. I mean, the driver's license photo, and all the other papers and stuff in his wallet."

"In this county, we turn to blood type, dental records, DNA, surgical implants, and/or fingerprints to make a positive identification, not 'stuff from someone's wallet.' The only stuff I want to see is a piece of paper with a county seal on it."

I smiled and gave him a shrug. "What if the coroner determines it wasn't a hunting accident?"

"Then, Miss Ellington, I'm afraid the wineries on Two Witches Hill will be seeing a lot more of me."

Chapter 8

Glenda, who'd been standing a few feet away, presumably cleaning up the tasting room tables, rushed over to me the second Deputy Hickman exited the building.

She adjusted the flowing green and gold caftan that draped over her winery T-shirt and whispered, "It's your aura, Norrie. It needs to be cleansed. The negative forces circling around it will only attract all sorts of unwanted energy."

"The only thing I want cleaned is this tasting room. I'm fine. Honest."

Glenda shook her head. "You can cleanse your own aura with a few simple steps. All you need is a candle and a quiet place. You light the candle, stand in front of it, and visualize positive spiritual essences flowing into you. Then you step away from the candle and use your hand to grab the negative energies and throw them into the flame."

Terrific. One sudden move and I'll set the whole place on fire. "Glenda, I really don't have the time to—"

"Once the negative energy is in the flame, draw an X in the air with your hand."

"Fine. Fine. I'll keep that in mind."

With an armload of dirty glasses on a rack, Sam turned to us. "What did Grizzly Gary want? Any updates?"

By now, Cammy and Roger were only a few feet from where I was standing.

"Not really. They're towing Arnold Mowen's car tomorrow. Anyway, it's been a long day for all of us. If I hear anything, I'll let you know."

A half hour later, we all exited the building and went our separate ways. Shouts of "See ya tomorrow" came from everyone except Sam. He reminded us he had classes the first part of the week and wouldn't be in until Wednesday afternoon. I trudged up the hill and immediately opened the door to let Charlie out.

The light snow had stopped hours ago, but a cold wind made it really uncomfortable for anyone to be outside for more than a few minutes. I wondered how Theo and Don fared at their establishment today, but I was too hungry and exhausted to call them. Instead, I nuked a frozen mac and cheese dinner and poured ranch dressing over a chunk of iceberg lettuce. I also refilled the dog's bowl.

As I sat at the table, spooning the gooey pasta into my mouth, I thought about Lavettia. She had to be the most bullheaded woman I'd ever met. Why on earth would she risk getting in trouble with the sheriff's department by opening Arnold's car? No one needed makeup that badly. Then again, she was probably smart enough to wear gloves to avoid leaving fingerprints. After all, she was his girlfriend. She was always in that car. I was pretty sure those forensics guys could determine which prints were recent and which were dated. I didn't think it was the brightest move, on her part, to retrieve her things.

The lettuce crunched between my teeth and, coupled with the ranch dressing, filled my mouth with a watery mix. It also made an odd popping sound in my left ear. An annoying, repetitive sound that, for some reason, reminded me of a gunshot. In that instant, I froze. What if it wasn't jewelry or makeup she was after? What if it was a gun? And not just any gun. *The* gun that was used to put a bullet in the back of Arnold Mowen's neck.

Sure, she had an alibi. If what she said about being at that essential oils symposium was true. But if it wasn't…it would've been easy for her to ditch the gun in the car after she fired it. Of course, that would mean she had an accomplice who drove her home. Unless…Oh My God!

I dropped a full spoonful of the mac and cheese on my plate and called Theo and Don.

"Do those winery buses still make the rounds up and down the lake?"

Theo chuckled. "Hello to you, too, Norrie. Always glad to answer the question of the day."

"Sorry. This is important. So, are those buses running?"

"Yeah, the wine shuttles still make the rounds—but only during the fall or for special events like the one we just had."

"So, they would've been running on Saturday?"

"Uh-huh. Why?"

"Because Lavettia Lawrence went from victim to possible murderess."

"Uh, suppose you slow down and tell me what's going on. By the way, your favorite deputy dropped in to see us about Arnold's car. Seems someone might've had themselves more than a look-see."

"I know. I know. It was Lavettia. I think she might've been the one who killed him. Theo, the woman has a really good motive. One of the oldest in the book—greed. She could have killed him when there was a lull in the driveway traffic. Besides, no one would notice if she got on a winery bus. Heck, half those people are so intoxicated they wouldn't notice a thing and the other half would be too busy texting on their cell phones."

"Norrie, before you go all hog-wild with one of your theories, take a breath and fill in the missing pieces for me, okay? And remember, this isn't one of your screenplays. You can't make it up as you go along."

"I'm not making this up—Lavettia's about to inherit Arnold Mowen's wine distribution business."

There was silence at the other end, and then I heard Theo shout, "Don, you've got to hear this." Then he was back on the line with me. "Norrie, can I put you on speakerphone?"

"If we get disconnected, call me back."

Thankfully, we didn't. It took me a good two or three minutes to give Theo and Don the complete rundown, beginning with Lavettia making her grand entrance into our winery and concluding with me insisting that she *not* go to the car to fetch her jewelry and makeup. In between, I mentioned the will, Marvin Souza, and the possibility that maybe Lavettia planned to fetch the gun she used to kill her boyfriend.

"So you see, that's why I wanted to know about the Finger Lakes Wine Trail Buses. The flyers with their schedules are everywhere, even online. The buses stop at each winery, making the rounds before they drop people off in in Geneva, Seneca Falls, and Auburn. She could've used that bus to get home."

"Geez," Don said. "This is almost making sense. *Almost.* That scares me. Whatever you do, don't go spouting off about this to Deputy Hickman."

"My God!" I gasped. "That's like the last thing I'd do."

"Good. Because right now you have no evidence whatsoever to indicate she might've been involved in the guy's death. Heck. The sheriff's lab hasn't even completed the autopsy or determined what kind of bullet was used. When they do, they're not about to share it with us. I'm afraid the public is going to have to wait. And you should, too."

"Aargh. I suppose you're right. I mean, this wasn't like the last time when a friend of ours was the suspect and we needed to get her off the hook. No one here is a person of interest, even if the situation isn't pretty for our wineries."

"Speaking of situations, Theo and I are more concerned about the wine sabotage at this point. Not to sound callous about Arnold's unfortunate demise."

"Yeah, about that. Did Madeline Martinez invite you to an emergency Winery Owners of the West meeting at her house to discuss it?"

Before Don could answer, Theo broke in. "Yep. Day after tomorrow at two. Works for me. Nothing like fueling the fires with more rumors at the WOW meeting."

"Madeline's really freaked about what happened to her wine. She told me her husband wasn't about to sit idly back while some lunatic wreaks havoc on all of us. Said her husband planned to meet with the wine association board to address this."

Theo groaned and snorted. "And what are they going to do? Print out signs that say, 'No tampering with our wine'?"

"I really don't know what they *can* do. Seems more a matter for the sheriff's department. Now that they've got a homicide on their hands, our wine loss will be taking a backseat."

"Don't be so loose with the 'H' word, or the 'M' word for that matter. Even though we think Arnold's death was intentional, the sheriff's deputy is operating under the assumption it was a hunting accident."

"Poof to that! Unless the hunter was Mr. Magoo. Look, I sat through an incredibly boring documentary about how gunshot wounds are evaluated."

"Yikes!" Don said. "Why on earth did you do that?"

"Long story. I was dating a guy who majored in criminal justice. Anyway, the only thing I remember from watching that show was that there are four categories of bullet wounds. They're broken down by range of fire—or how far away the gun was from the victim."

"And?"

"The closer you get to the victim with the gun, the more gunk from the gun lands on the victim."

"Boy, if that isn't a scientific explanation, I don't know what is."

Theo cut in again. "Norrie may have a point. When I saw the body, I noticed black powdery marks around the wound. I mentioned it to you both that day. If she's right about proximity, then whoever shot Arnold didn't do it from twenty-five feet."

"See? It was up close and maybe personal, which brings me back to Lavettia. The woman stands to inherit a lucrative business."

Theo continued with his groans. "True enough, but keep in mind, Arnold was fast developing a long list of angry winery owners. Any one of them could've pulled the trigger. Let's all sleep on this tonight. We can talk more when we get together on Tuesday. I'm sure those women won't hesitate to add their two cents."

We left it at that, and I went back to my now-cold mac and cheese. I wasn't sure what was worse, eating it cold or re-nuking it until it resembled plastic. I opted for plastic and poured myself a glass of juice to wash it down.

That night, I tossed and turned. My mind conjured up all sorts of scenarios involving Arnold's death and our wine sabotage. I'd exhaust one idea and flip to another. When I finally managed to fall asleep, I dreamed that a dead body was found floating in one of our stainless steel tanks. When the face surfaced, it was Lavettia's. I tried to turn away from her cloudy, blueish eyes, but I couldn't. I woke up hearing Glenda's voice in my head, shouting, "You didn't cleanse your aura!"

* * * *

Mondays were notoriously slow in November compared to other weekdays. I told Cammy not to expect me in the winery until the weekend, but that she should call me if they were slammed I desperately needed the time to get my screenplay to the script analyst and make my deadline.

Surprisingly, it was a quiet day—no frantic phone calls from the winery, and no news about Arnold's death. I didn't expect to hear anything on the morning news, but I was certain the news anchors would release the name of the victim during the noon segment. I was wrong. At a few minutes after four, the phone rang.

It was Miller Holtz, of all people. "Good afternoon, Miss Ellington, heck of a thing. Heck of a thing. I'm reaching out to all the wineries in my territory. Heck of a thing. Poor Clayton's been inundated all morning with phone calls: 'Is the business still operational?' 'What's the status of our wine?' 'Who's taking over?' Poor guy was about to have a breakdown. No one should be put in that position. Even if Clayton LeVine is, or should I say *was*, Arnold's secretary. Heck of a thing."

"So, you know," I said, "about your boss. Did one of the county deputies stop by the office? Is that what happened? How did everyone else know it was Arnold's body in the ditch? A positive identification hasn't been made public yet. Look, I wanted to call you myself, but I was advised not to. Sheriff department protocol and all that."

"Don't worry about it. The sheriff's department sent a deputy to the office. I was on the road checking in with some of the wineries at the lower end of the lake when Clayton called me. They've got enough evidence, official or not, to be certain it was Arnold."

Stuff in the wallet works for me. "That still doesn't explain how everyone else knew. The other wineries, I mean."

"Really? Well, for starters, Arnold's ditsy girlfriend posted a large 'Rest in Peace' banner on the guy's Facebook page and went on a Twitter storm. If that wasn't enough, she called everyone in his phonebook and hers! One thing led to another, and boom!"

"Yeesh. Not a great way to break the news."

"I'll say. Now we're up to our ying-yang in damage control. Every winery is going nuts wondering whether we'll continue picking up and distributing their wines."

"You *will,* won't you?"

"Of course, we will. Arnold may be out of the picture, but Lake-to-Lake Wine Distributors isn't. He left a very solid business plan and even named his successor. I should know, because it happens to be me. I stand to inherit the business."

"You, uh, you….you…" For the life of me, all I could sputter out was the word "you."

"Are you okay, Miss Ellington?"

"Um, fine. Yeah. I was surprised, that's all."

"Arnold didn't have any family, and he worked his butt off for the business. When I last spoke with him, which wasn't all that long ago, he told me he'd be leaving the company to me in his will. Not his house or personal effects. Who knows about those? The girlfriend will most likely get her claws into them. Frankly, it's not my concern. The business is. As soon as we get things straightened out, a new sales rep will be hired to replace me. I'll need to take the helm, so to speak."

First Lavettia, then Miller. They were like vultures circling around fresh meat. "What happens in the meantime?"

"Business as usual. Payroll's been set up. Bills are on autopay. Listen, I've got at least three more calls to make. I'll be in touch."

"Uh, before you hang up, any news on that wine hijacking?"

"Zip. But like I told the Martinez family, the demand for Pinot Noir is going to increase. We'll sell it for more and come out ahead. As for the wineries, they have their own accountants and know how to handle business losses."

Terrific. We just traded Ebenezer Scrooge for the Grinch. "I don't mean to keep you, but when will you know for sure? About inheriting the business?"

"Sometime this week, I'd wager. Guess it's time I put Marvin Souza's number on speed dial, huh?"

Not if Lavettia has a thing to say about it. "Okay, then. Thanks for getting in touch."

Holy Cow! Who else did Arnold Mowen deed his business to? And why wasn't Miller Holtz the least bit concerned about who killed his boss? As if I didn't know.

Chapter 9

"We've got hot chocolate, coffee, and tea," Madeline Martinez said. "Help yourselves. I made a few batches of snickerdoodles, too. Got a hankering for them last night."

As planned, the WOW crew was gathered in her living room on Tuesday. Two o'clock, to be precise—Rosalee Marbleton from Terrace Wineries, Stephanie Ipswich from Gable Hill Wineries, Catherine Trobert from Lake View Winery, and of course, Theo and me.

Unlike the other ladies who complained about the rifle noise in the morning, the pop-pop sounds didn't wake me. Maybe I'd gotten used to them with so many hunters sighting in their rifles over the weekend.

"Guess it's official now, huh?" Stephanie said. "Why on earth did the five o'clock news have to be so graphic yesterday? My kids were in the room. First graders don't need to know about carotid arteries being severed by a bullet. And I didn't need to hear them asking over and over again, 'What's a corroded eatery?'"

"Did you tell them it was a bad bakery?" Theo laughed.

Catherine snapped the cookie she was holding in half, bit into the smaller chunk, and swallowed it. "Is that what they said on the news? I hadn't heard."

I jumped in before Stephanie could respond. "Did they mention whether the gun was fired from a long or short distance?"

She shook her head. "No, but they showed a sketch of the human head, zeroing in on the carotid artery."

"Too much information, if you ask me," Catherine said. "A simple name, and perhaps a nice photo of Arnold Mowen when he was alive, would've been more than enough."

Stephanie nodded. "I agree. At least the speculation is done. The county made a positive identification from the guy's dental records. Apparently, he had implants and lots of them."

Theo and I looked at each other, and then I spoke. "We knew it was him the minute we found the wallet and the driver's license. Hunting accident, my you-know-what."

Rosalee stood and poured herself some tea. "They might have to conduct this investigation like the deli counter at Wegmans: Get in line and take a number. Let's be honest, the man all but had a target on his back. That's what happens when you get too greedy. And talk about greedy, that Miller Holtz isn't too far behind. Imagine what it'll be like with him as the CEO. I wouldn't be surprised if he finds a way to pay us even less for our wines."

"Unless he's behind bars for murder," Theo said. "Talk about motive. That guy was chomping at the bit to tell all of the wineries he was going to inherit the business."

I shifted in my seat, debating whether to open my mouth, but I figured 'what the heck'. "He wasn't the only one. Lavettia Lawrence, the platinum blond with the dangling gold jewelry, told me *she* was about to inherit the business."

Madeline slapped herself on the cheek, making an audible noise. "You *don't* say. Really?"

"Really." I began to feel as if I'd left a business meeting and somehow returned to my seventh-grade lunch table. Worse yet, it was my fault for telling tales out of school. My mother would've been appalled. "Maybe we should forget about Arnold and actually discuss the real reason we're here—the wine thefts and sabotage."

A few groans followed.

"This isn't coincidence, you know," Theo said. "I think these are calculated acts, deliberately designed to boost the market price on the Pinot Noir. True, those oak barrels were easier to tamper with than stainless steel, but how do you explain the wine truck hijacking? Only the red wines? And only the Pinot Noir?"

He turned to me. "Don got that tiny little detail from Clayton LeVine—before all hell broke loose."

"So, now what do we do?" Stephanie asked. "Sit back and wait for the next winery to be hit? We can't afford round the clock surveillance and all of you know that these crooks, or whatever you call them, know how to render our alarm systems useless. Face it, they're always one step ahead of the good guys."

Suddenly, that gave me an idea. Not the best idea, mind you, but an idea. "Suppose we go old school and double-cross them?"

Theo looked ashen, but the ladies seemed intent on hearing what I had to say.

"Listen, if it's Pinot Noir they're after, let's fool them. All of us have oak barrels we're not using for one reason or another. Fill them with water and make sure there's a visible number chart. We all use barrel number charts that list the wine and year. So what if someone tampers with our water? It's not like we plan on bottling it. Besides, this is only for another few weeks. Everyone should be done bottling the reds by then."

Theo rubbed his chin and paused. "So, if I understand you correctly, the real number chart would be under lock and key while the fake one would be in plain sight near a barrel. Like hanging on a building wall or something."

"You got it."

"That's not a bad idea, Norrie," Stephanie said. "I'll run it by my husband."

Catherine gave a quick nod. "Same here."

"I don't have to run anything by anyone," Rosalee said. "I'll just do it. It can't hurt."

I reached for a cookie and held it for a moment. "Hold on, there's more. The fake number chart should be written on transparency paper with a marker, and then put on a white clipboard. That way, when those scoundrels check it out, their fingerprints will be on it. Staples and OfficeMax both sell white clipboards. Francine's obsessed with them."

"If it's water in the barrel, how will we know it's been tampered with?" Catherine asked.

"Have your winemaker pull up a sample each day and test it in the lab for calcium carbonate. They should be able to do that. If it shows up, we notify the sheriff's department and have them check the transparency paper for prints."

"Goodness, Norrie," she said. "How do you come up with this stuff?"

"I don't. But Nancy Drew does. One of my employees is a real aficionado and she insisted I become familiar with *The Official Nancy Drew Handbook*."

"Really? It's still in print?"

"In print, on Kindle, on Nook..."

Theo shrugged. "It can't hurt. Well, one 'Deck the Halls around the Lake' down, and one to go. I can't believe the wine association even considered running a third weekend."

"It's the biggest money maker for them," I said. "Besides, it isn't until after Thanksgiving. It's always the second weekend in December."

Madeline stood and poured herself another cup of coffee. "Tell me about it. No sooner am I finished with one holiday, the next one begins. At least I won't have to cook a giant turkey for the winery event. Or figure out what to do with the leftovers, for that matter. So, are we all agreed on Norrie's plan?"

A chorus of "yes" followed, and the meeting concluded in record time. Theo and I had driven over together in my car and we all but raced out the door.

"I'm glad you'll be joining Don and me for Thanksgiving this year. He's already browsing through cookbooks to find new and different side dishes."

"I really wish you'd let me bring something."

"And what? Spoil his fun? If you insist, you could pick up a pie at Wegmans. Anything except rhubarb."

"Done! I hate rhubarb too, and I can always taste it no matter how many strawberries they bake into it."

"What did you just say?"

"That I hate rhubarb?"

"No, something about tasting it."

"I said I can always pick out the rhubarb, why?"

"Because the most unsettling thought popped into my head. What if the people who tampered with our wine didn't want us to notice? Maybe they didn't realize the winemakers keep testing it before it's ready to be bottled."

"Meaning?"

"Maybe some unscrupulous individuals wanted to ruin our wines for the customers and give all of us a bad reputation. Maybe it was about that all along."

"Then how do you explain what happened to Madeline? Or the hijacking?"

"I can't. Not right now, anyway. That's not the worst of what's going on. He might not show it, but Don's pretty rattled about having someone killed on our property. I seriously don't think he's going to get a good night's sleep until it's resolved."

"I understand. Remember? Sometimes I still think about Elsbeth Waters."

"Face it, the killer had to be someone who wanted Arnold out of the picture. Narrows it down to two suspects in my book—Lavettia and Miller. Both of them had a strong motive to get him out of the way."

"When that ballistics report is complete, and Deputy Hickman realizes it was no accident, he'll turn his attention to those two for sure. Trouble is, how long do we have to wait?"

It was a question neither of us could answer. I dropped Theo off at his winery and drove home to focus on my real job—screenwriting. I received an email from Renee, the movie producer, telling me the company would begin filming *A Swim under the Waterfall* in late spring, possibly summer. The location was somewhere near Niagara Falls, but she wasn't too specific. It didn't matter. After that screenplay left my hands, it belonged to her and the director. She wanted to know if I'd meet my next deadline. Apparently contemporary romance was still in.

As soon as I settled in with my laptop at the kitchen table, my cell phone rang: Bradley Jamison. That name could get my pulse rate up—even if I was standing perfectly still. I hadn't spoken with him since Sunday, the day Arnold's body was discovered, and the news stations broadcasted the event. He'd called to make sure I was all right and we agreed to get together for dinner soon. I supposed this call meant that time had come.

"Hey, Norrie! Hope I'm not interrupting anything. Believe it or not, this is the first break I've had all day. You won't believe what's going on around here."

"Let me guess—you met Lavettia Lawrence."

"You could say that. She came in demanding to see Arnold Mowen's will. She insisted Lake-to-Lake Wine Distributors was willed to her. Among other things."

"Did you read her the will?"

"Look, I'm really not supposed to talk about this. I called to see if you were available on Friday for dinner at Port of Call."

"That depends. Will you be able to talk about it then?"

"Very funny. This much I can tell you, and it's a doozy. Marvin and I have never had a situation like it."

"What?"

"Arnold Mowen had a Memorandum of Understanding with our law firm to ensure that his will was not read until twenty-nine days after his death."

"Huh? That's a first."

"Oh. It gets better. Believe me. The MoU stipulated that our office was to contact certain individuals to inform them of his demise, and request that they memorialize him in some way prior to the reading of the will. He even listed the options."

"Options?"

"Want the long list or the short list? The long list is *really* long. I'll give you the short version—a memorial bench at the Museum of Modern Art in New York City, a memorial brick walkway at the Boston Aquarium, and my personal favorite, the placement of a life-size statue of him at the capitol building in Albany."

"Isn't there a statue of someone there already? Someone on a horse? We visited the place when I was a kid."

"Yeah. Some general, but I can't remember who. Anyway, how about I pick you up at seven-thirty and we can talk about it then. If I'm still sane."

"Good luck with that. I've already met Lavettia."

"Lavettia wasn't the only one demanding to hear what was in that will. Look, I can't stay on the line. See you Friday. I've missed you."

With that, the call ended. I was positive Miller Holtz was the other bottom feeder anxious to learn what Arnold had bequeathed him. Honestly, hearing the words, "I've missed you," was all I could think about. At least for ten minutes. Eventually, the rainbow-rosy-romance portion of my brain gave way to the cognitive side and I realized something—whoever was on Arnold's memorialization list might have had a motive for murdering him. A statue at the capitol building? Really? What kind of a person demanded such a thing? And, even more puzzling, who on earth would have the means and the wherewithal to do it?

I groaned and went back to work on the screenplay, stopping a few times to stretch and to make sure Charlie was doing okay in his doggie run since hunting season officially started this morning. Now the poor Plott Hound was relegated to being under house arrest. He could go from inside to a fenced-in area but couldn't roam freely, the way he did the rest of the year.

Alvin's pen was located adjacent to the winery's tasting room building and our parking lot, so I knew he'd be safe. Still, our vineyard manager posted bright orange warning signs around the fence, so it would be visible from a distance. They read, "Caution—Farm Animals." I was half tempted to cross off the "s" and add the word "spits" instead, although it seemed like I was the only one afforded that treatment by the goat.

It was almost dark when I emerged from my writing to answer the landline. It felt like every muscle in my body was tight, and my stomach was grumbling because the last thing I'd eaten was a snickerdoodle.

"Hello, this is Norrie."

"Did you catch News at Five on Channel 13?" It was Stephanie—and she was talking a mile a minute.

"Um, no. I was working. What happened?"

"They made it official. Our wine distributor's death was ruled a homicide. The news anchor went on and on about why the sheriff's department made that determination. Honestly, I don't have a degree in forensics, but I could've put two and two together."

"What was it?"

"Common sense. Duh. They explained about the powdery marks on the victim's neck and went on to say that someone fired a twenty-two from a close distance—close enough that the shooter clearly knew he was aiming at an individual and not a clump of trees or something."

"That's what we've been saying all along."

"I know. I know. Now maybe they'll start investigating. Frankly, I'm getting un-nerved with all these dead bodies showing up. I keep having horrible nightmares that my boys are going to go out to play and wind up crawling over a corpse in our backyard."

"Yeesh."

"Anyway, thought you should know. I already spoke with Madeline and she watched the news. She also said she was going to call Rosalee and Catherine. I told her I'd ask you to let Theo and Don know."

"No problem. Thanks, Stephanie. I'll catch you later."

"Don's got the six o'clock news on now," Theo said when I called him seconds after hanging up with Stephanie. "Hold on a sec, will you?"

He asked Don if they'd reported it yet.

"So," I said when Theo got back to the phone, "what's the verdict?"

"They mentioned it as a teaser when the news first came on. According to Don, they said there was new information about the man found in our winery ditch. If we all hurry, we can catch it at the same time."

"On my way. Talk to you later."

Sure enough, Stephanie was right. They gave Arnold's name, occupation, and cause of death. The news anchor followed up by directing the audience to call Silent Witness if they had any information. Then they showed an aerial photo of Two Witches Hill, probably archived on Google Maps. To make matters worse, they zoomed in on the Grey Egret and then Two Witches. I've heard that even bad publicity is good publicity but in this case, I wasn't too sure.

Chapter 10

Unfortunately, I had to wait until Friday night to get the dirt from Bradley. *If* he'd say anything—client confidentiality and all that. Of course, Bradley wasn't the only means I had of securing information. Gladys Pipp, secretary at the Yates County Public Safety Building, would toss little tidbits of information my way on occasion, and I always thanked her by dropping off jars of Francine's jams and jellies.

Thanksgiving was only a week and a half away, so I figured Gladys might enjoy some currant jam. Besides, I needed to drive into Penn Yan anyway to pick up Charlie's bulk food from the Grain and Feed Farm Store. Our vineyard manager offered to send one of the guys, but they had enough to do with winter pruning. At least the early snowfalls had stopped, and we were back to normal Finger Lakes November weather—cold and dreary.

Gladys was at the front window when I walked in at noon the following day. She looked up from the computer monitor and adjusted her rhinestone eyeglasses. "Norrie, what brings you here? Is that jam I see?"

"Uh-huh. Thought you might enjoy it at Thanksgiving. I had to pick up dog food at the grain store and I knew I'd be right down the block from you."

Gladys laughed. "You don't fool me, but I can never turn down your sister's jams. So, does this have anything to do with that wine distributor's death? I'm wagering it does, since the guy was found on your hill. I'm not sure if I can tell you anything you don't already know from watching the news or reading the paper." Then she looked at me for a second. "Or on whatever device it is you millennials carry around with you. See, I'm up on things, too."

I chuckled. "It's a long story, but I'll speak fast."

"Relax. Your favorite deputy's not in the office."

"Whew. Here goes—and you cannot repeat this. Promise?"

Gladys moved her index finger across her lips and leaned closer to the window.

We were the only ones in the front office, but I still looked around before I spoke. "Arnold Mowen's attorney is Marvin Souza in Geneva. I found out that Arnold left specific instructions not to have his will read for twenty-nine days, during which time certain people were to be contacted."

I left out the part about the man's demand for memorialization because it was way too weird, and anyone could walk in at any time. "So," I continued, "I want to know if you know who Deputy Hickman is interviewing. Suspects? Persons of interest? Names on Arnold's contact list?"

"I don't know who he's interviewing," Gladys said, "but I do have his weekly schedule in front of me." Then she gave me a wink.

"Just tell me, other than Lavettia Lawrence, Clayton LeVine, and Miller Holtz, who else is he grilling?"

"You should quit your day job and come work for us. There's only one more entry, but I don't show a name. All it says is Penn Yan Airport—private plane."

"When?"

"This afternoon. Three fifty-one. Flight out of Buffalo. Not as exciting as when Congresswoman Nancy Pelosi's plane landed here a few years ago. We were the closest airport to Seneca Falls, where she was inducted into the National Women's Hall of Fame."

I tried not to roll my eyes. "Is there any other information about the plane? The recent one, not Nancy's."

"None that I see. Oh, wait, there is a small note. It reads 'per Marvin Souza.' Hmm, that's the name you mentioned. The attorney. Interesting, huh?"

"I'll say! Anyway, I'd better get a move on. If I don't see you, have a happy Thanksgiving!"

"You, too, dear. And I hope they catch whoever murdered your nice wine distributor."

Nice wasn't exactly the word I'd use for Arnold Mowen, but go figure. Gladys was bound to learn all about him soon enough. Meanwhile, I couldn't exactly go traipsing off to the small, private airport, especially if Deputy Hickman was there. There was only one thing I could do—tell Bradley I knew all about the private plane's passenger and see if he would fill in the blanks. Ugh. It was only Wednesday. A long wait.

At least Gladys didn't mention the winery owners. We all had motive, too, and some of us, like Theo, Don, and me, had means and opportunity. I tried not to think about it, but I knew eventually, it would cross Deputy Hickman's mind as he probed further and further into Arnold Mowen's murder.

I was particularly antsy the next two days as I anticipated my conversation with Bradley. It was business as usual at the winery. The tasting room crowds slowed until the next "Deck the Halls around the Lake." Cammy and the crew didn't need my help, and it was just as well. I had deadlines looming over me, and I wasn't about to miss them.

On Thursday I touched base with Franz, and he told me they had finished bottling the reds. Labeling would wait until winter. He also mentioned running into Leandre, Rosalee Marbleton's winemaker, who was losing his mind over the possibility of something happening to his wines.

Leandre discovered that two other wineries at the upper end of the lake had compromised Pinot Noir barrels as well. Those wineries were in the Seneca County jurisdiction. A different sheriff's department but the same distributor.

"Whoever is behind this wants to ruin us all!" he lamented to Franz.

I had to admit, Leandre probably wasn't too far off. In fact, his take bordered on that short-lived theory of Theo's the other day.

"By the way," Franz said, "Leandre liked that idea of yours. They've made the swap already, just in case. With treated water."

"Will they be able to tell if it's tampered with?"

"Absolutely."

"It's a start. Not that I want more trouble to find its way to Rosalee's, but maybe if someone does mess with that barrel, they'll be dumb enough to leave prints."

"We can only hope."

It felt as if Friday would never get here, but sure enough it did—with a spring-like break in the weather that had every hunter royally annoyed. Apparently, the hardened snow afforded them the opportunity to follow deer tracks. The ground was now a mushy, muddy mess strewn with leaves. Charlie reveled in it. He rolled, dug, and even snorted the stuff, leaving his messy paw prints all over the kitchen floor.

After running the mop over it for a third time, I gave up and turned my attention to picking out a decent outfit for my dinner with Bradley. Between Francine's closet and the small wardrobe I'd brought, I finally settled on a cream cowl-neck top over black leggings. My favorite mid-calf boots pulled the ensemble together. Now all I needed to do was gather the information Bradley had and compare it to what I already knew.

I'd only been to Port of Call a few times with Theo and Don, and it was always during the summer when we sat on the huge wrap-around deck. The interior, as I discovered that night, was equally impressive in an elegant, homey way. Cushioned captain's chairs in groups of four, six, and eight surrounded the round tables. A giant gas fireplace, not too different from the one we had at Two Witches, stood against the only wall that didn't have a picture window.

Bradley picked me up at a little past seven, hoping we'd avoid the usual dinner crowd that arrived after eight. We sat across from the fireplace, and had a gorgeous view of the lake and an even more stunning view of the lit-up airport runway. It was the perfect opportunity for me to get right to business.

"Wow," I said. "The airport's got the runway lights on. Must be they're expecting a corporate jet. They don't do that for little old Piper Cubs. You know, I found out Deputy Hickman was over there the other day. You wouldn't happen to know which VIP he was meeting, would you?"

"Boy, you don't miss a beat, do you? It's like sleuthing is in your blood or something. If you must know, he was meeting with one of our clients."

"Client or murder suspect?"

"Client for now. And no, I'm not at liberty to divulge a name. Come on, check out the winter menu. It's spectacular."

"Fine. I'm more interested in Arnold's will anyway. You got off the phone in such a hurry, I never did find out who else thought they were going to inherit the business. And before you answer, I'll spare you the breath. It was Miller Holtz, wasn't it?"

Bradley looked dumbfounded. "What? No. At least not as far as I know. But if he's on the list, that'll make three. Well, five actually, if you want to get technical."

"How do you figure that? And who?"

"More like what—A triumvirate of nuns from the Holy Sepulcher Convent in Lodi."

"Nuns? Did he distribute holy wine to them?"

"No. He was their former student. Went to school there until he was ten. Then who knows where. Anyway, dear little Arnold wrote them a letter before he left telling them that, when he grew up and had a business of his own, he would leave it to the convent in his will."

"You have *got* to be kidding me. That can't possibly hold up in court, can it?"

"Not in my book, but according to Sisters Mary Katherine, Gloria Mae, and Celeste, it does and it will. No pun intended."

"Holy cow! I'll have the rosemary chicken with new potatoes."

"So, why did you think it was Miller Holtz?" he asked.

"Because Miller made it a point to call the Seneca Lake wineries to tell them he was 'next in line.'"

"Not if Lavettia has anything to say about it."

"How do you think she'll stand up to those nuns?"

"Sister Celeste can be quite feisty, but her claws don't scratch like Lavettia's. All I can say is I'm going to have a good supply of Tums and aspirin when we read that damn will. And, by the way, that rosemary chicken sounds good. Think I'll order it, too."

"All of those people are tearing into Arnold's will like some families do with the Thanksgiving turkey. What about his funeral? Did anyone even hold a funeral? I haven't heard anything. Not that I expected to."

"It's only been five days, but Lavettia informed our office it would be a private burial with a public celebration of his life to be scheduled following the reading of the will."

I all but choked. "She wants to make sure she's inheriting the whole lock, stock, and barrel before she commits to celebrating anything. Yikes, if the business goes to those nuns, or, worse yet, to Miller Holtz, Lavettia won't be grieving over the grave, she'll be spitting on it."

"Yeah, I had the same thought."

The rest of the evening was the date Bradley probably intended it to be. We talked about ourselves and our interests. Like me, he grew up in the Finger Lakes, so winter skiing was on his to-do list. We agreed to go to Bristol Mountain when the season officially opened. No doubt the guy could get my pulse racing with a mere touch, so why, of all things, did Godfrey Klein keep popping into my head? It wasn't as if we needed to identify an insect in our food.

When I got home that night, I realized the juicy tidbit about the nuns more than made up for not getting the information I wanted about the mysterious plane passenger. Two seconds after tossing my bag on the couch, I got on my laptop and Googled the Holy Sepulcher Convent. The results nearly knocked me out of my chair. Whatever happened to vows of poverty?

The Holy Sepulcher had a thriving bakery business—cheesecakes and specialty tarts. They sold their goods in boutique restaurants in all five boroughs in New York City. But that wasn't what grabbed my attention. A small article appeared in *The Villager*, an online news source for locals in the city. Apparently, the Sisters were excellent bakers, but they were lousy investors. Their business was on the verge of going under unless they received a substantial boost in revenue.

What better way to avoid losing their business, I thought, than to inherit Arnold Mowen's business and the monies that went with it. Would those

God-loving women really commit murder? Especially if their claim to the will was written by an underage kid who probably wanted to avoid being held back?

The tangled web seemed to get bigger and bigger, but no one was any closer to solving it.

* * * *

"Nuns," I said to Theo and Don the next night when we got together for pizza at their place. "Nuns! Of all people!"

"It's like a soap opera leading up to the reading of the will," Theo said. "I'll laugh if more people claim to be Arnold's beneficiary. By the way, what did you make of that thread on the Seneca Lake news forum? The one entitled 'Pinot No-more?' Is that supposed to be a take on Pinot Noir? Very funny. Someone's digging into the wine sabotage, and I'm not all that sure it's a reporter."

"Of course it's not a reporter," Don said. "The forum is for every kook and nutcase on the lake to voice his or her opinion about something. If I want the real news, I'll read it on their website, or any other news agency's site."

Theo looked at me and then back at Don. "Nutcases or not, whoever wrote that opinion piece knew what's going on. They claim none of this is coincidence or the result of disgruntled individuals, thieves, or vandals. They believe it's a covert operation meant to drive up the price of next fall's Pinot Noir, since it won't be on the market until then. Let's be honest, the Pinot Noir we've bottled was outstanding. No, even more than that, it was spectacular for all of us on this side of the lake. All of the elements were in place—climate, soil, grapes, and winemaker skill."

"But there's still plenty more of that wine," I said. "Those rats didn't get everything."

Theo plopped his elbows on the table and leaned forward, his head barely resting on his hands. "Don't you see what's happening? Articles and opinions like this are going to crop up all over social media. When the buzz starts, there'll be no stopping it. Restaurants, hotels, fancy liquor stores…all of them will be jacking up the price on that wine. They'll create the illusion of a major shortage, even if it means they hold back some bottles for sale."

I opened my eyes as wide as I could. "You're kidding?"

"Wish I was. Everyone will make a profit except us. Dammit! We need to find out who's behind it. My first thought was Arnold, but we can rule that out."

"I'll tell you who it is," I said. "After listening to the two of you, it's pretty clear cut. It's got to be the person who put a bullet in Arnold's neck. Get Arnold out of the way, inherit his business, monkey with the supply and demand for a particular wine, and watch your profits multiply."

"Whoa, Norrie," Don said. "What business school did you graduate from?"

"Connect-the-dots University. Didn't Deputy Hickman say something about the body being twelve or thirteen hours cold, according to the coroner? That puts the time of death around Saturday afternoon. Since Arnold's body was face down in that deep ditch, with his head toward our driveway and not your parking lot, it would seem logical someone fired a shot at him from the clump of trees that borders your lot. Whoever it was, they picked a good spot. I couldn't even see a body. I figured there was road trash in the ditch."

"Got to admit," Theo said. "It adds up. Arnold was either on his way into the Grey Egret or on his way out when it happened. No one would've batted an eyelash if they heard a gunshot. It's almost hunting season. Too bad we don't have surveillance cameras for the tasting room building."

"What about Lavettia?" I asked. "She could have lied about that essential oils symposium. Maybe she told him she had a headache or was too tired to go inside. She could have stayed in the car the entire time, just waiting for an opportunity to blow his head off."

Don rubbed his chin and grimaced. "Someone should have heard the gunshot."

"Maybe, but remember, like I said before, it's hunting season," Theo replied. "Gunshots are going off all the time. And even if someone heard one, it would've been too dark to notice our guy taking a header into the ditch. The sun goes down about four thirty this time of year, and it's really overcast and dark even when it's daylight. The only lighting we have is around the building plus those low-level lights by the bushes. There would be enough light to make your way to your car, but not enough for anything else."

"Maybe our killer knew that all along," I said. "Think about it—a crowded event, slightly inebriated people, and an early nightfall."

"Are we talking murder, or one of your screenplays?" Don laughed.

"I try to steer clear of Gothic horror."

Chapter 11

"Lavettia Lawrence most definitely wasn't your murderess," Glenda exclaimed the second she saw me enter the tasting room. It had taken me a while, but I was getting used to her dramatic overtures. The last full meal I had eaten was pizza the night before, so I'd decided to pop into the bistro for a quick lunch before returning to my laptop.

"Huh? What do you mean?" I asked.

"Last night, my friend Zenora and I had our Chakras read by another friend of ours."

Of course. Why not? What else is there to do on a Saturday night in Penn Yan?

"Zenora?"

"Actually, her given name is Mabel Ann, but it really doesn't suit her, so she goes by Zenora."

"I see."

"Anyway, we were having our Chakras read when Zenora told me she ran into Lavettia at the essential oils symposium. Zenora also works for The Essential Life Company. The symposium was held at the La Tourelle Hotel in Ithaca and Lavettia was there the entire time. Zenora said she looked like hell."

"Why would she look like hell? It was before her boyfriend was found dead."

"According to Zenora, who's run into Lavettia at scads of these conferences, Lavettia was in a bland eye shadow rut with washed-out colors and a neutral face foundation that made her look as if she was ready to go to confession and not a symposium. Oh, and she said Lavettia's hair looked like someone took a wig and blew it up like an air mattress."

"Was Zenora sure it was Lavettia?"

"Of course, she was sure. The two of them spoke to each other. She thought Lavettia might've caught a cold, but other than that, everything was as normal as could be."

I stood perfectly still, trying to absorb what Glenda told me.

"Are you all right. Norrie?"

"Just ducky."

I waved hello to Cammy before I walked to the bistro for my lunch. The truth of the matter was, I wasn't all right. My theory about Lavettia blew up in my face, and there was nothing I could do about it. It was time to revisit the list of suspects, beginning with Miller Holtz.

Miller was so positive he was going to inherit the whole kit and caboodle, he wasted no time telling everyone. Heck, if he could've hired a helicopter to drop flyers across the Seneca Lake communities, he would have done so, which was why I was kind of reluctant to point the finger at him. Way too obvious. Then again, weirder things had been known to happen. And my phone call from Bradley the following day proved that point.

It was late in the afternoon and I had just come inside, following a brisk walk around the vineyards with Charlie at my heels. Poor dog had to be leashed. I couldn't trust that he wouldn't dart into the woods without notice. He could run toward deer and either get shot or land this family a major citation and fine.

When I got back to the house, the phone was ringing, and I picked up.

Bradley's voice was as chipper as ever. "Hey, Norrie, I had a terrific time Friday. I'm heading home to spend Thanksgiving with the family. I should be back to work on Monday. Let's do dinner when I get back, okay?"

"Sure. I had a great time, too."

"Listen, that was only part of the reason I called. You may want to sit down for this part. When Marvin went through Arnold Mowen's documents, he didn't realize our secretary had filed a separate letter related to the will. The letter was addressed to our firm."

"Uh-huh."

"Here's where it gets bizarre. Really bizarre. In addition to the MoU that Arnold had with our law firm regarding the reading of the will, this letter specified the place."

"The place? I thought wills were read in law offices."

"Under normal circumstances, yes. But like I said, this isn't normal. Arnold directed our firm to read his will at Two Witches Winery at midnight, twenty-nine days after his death."

"What???"

"Oh, you heard me. And there's more. Good news actually. He directed our firm to pay Two Witches Winery the sum of five thousand dollars for their trouble. And another two thousand dollars for the food and drink he requested."

"Two thousand dollars for food? Who does he think is coming? I mean, other than the vultures we already know about. Which reminds me, Lavettia didn't kill him. I'll tell you about that later."

"So, can you do it? There's more than enough money to pay your staff overtime, too."

"Yeah, we can do it. The question is why. Why Two Witches? Did the letter say?"

"In a cryptic sort of way, I think. The exact sentence reads, 'It's all in the name.'"

"Oh brother."

I looked at the wall calendar Francine had in the kitchen. Twenty-nine days past Arnold's death would fall on a Thursday night—two weeks after Thanksgiving and right before the next "Deck the Halls around the Lake." Not the best timing, but it was doable.

"Fine. Send out the invitations. Did Arnold specify what he had in mind for refreshments?"

"Not exactly, but he used the word 'extravagant' at least three times when he mentioned food and drink. Look, it doesn't matter if a handful of people attend or a brigade. Hire your entire staff and be sure to serve wine."

"Extravagant? What does he mean by extravagant?"

"I take it to mean anything other than reheated canapes from the frozen foods department at Costco. Look, don't overthink this, Norrie. It's not a wake. It's a colossal waste of money, if you ask me. Who's going to be hungry at midnight?"

"The entire room, I imagine. Only not for food."

Bradley chuckled. "That's what I adore about you—that sense of humor."

"Right now, I have more of a sense of foreboding. Keep in mind, one of those so-called mourners may be our killer."

"Then I'm sure you'll figure out who it is. Talk to you later. I've got to get going."

When I hung up the phone, I glanced at the clock on the microwave. Still plenty of time to give Cammy a heads-up about the reading of Arnold's will. I started to dial the tasting room and then hung up. This was something that needed to happen in person.

I tossed a fleece jacket over my sweatshirt and darted out the door. If nothing else, I was getting my exercise, unlike Charlie, who scratched his ear and plopped into his dog bed.

"Back in a flash, dog," I said. "I'm about to give new meaning to the word 'drama.'"

Lizzie looked up from the cash register when I walked into the tasting room. "Nice to see you. Any news yet on the murder? I figured since the body was found by the driveway, you and the guys from the Grey Egret would be the first to hear from the sheriff's office."

I shook my head. "Nope. The only thing I hear from Deputy Hickman are directives to mind my own business."

"Don't fret. Nancy Drew was told the same by many a person, but she was undaunted."

And fictional.

Cammy walked over on her way to the kitchen with a tray of used glasses. Only fifteen minutes until closing, so the tasting room was no longer bustling with customers. Only two women remained, and they were off to the side of the room looking at the holiday sweatshirts. Glenda was tidying up her table, and Sam was re-stocking the wine racks. It was Monday, so I knew Roger had the day off. Each season the tasting room schedule changed—amazing that I even remembered who was on and who was off.

"You're not going to believe this in a million years," I said to Cammy and Lizzie. Before they could say anything, I continued. "Get Glenda and Sam over here and I'll run over to the bistro to grab Fred. It's important."

"Is everything okay?" a panicked Glenda asked.

I was already a few yards away, but in good hearing distance.

"There are unstable energy fluctuations in the atmosphere today," she went on, "so it wouldn't surprise me if things were in flux."

I turned my head and gave her a quick look. "Don't worry about it. There'll be more instability in this room by the end of next week. I guarantee it." With that, I took off to find Fred, leaving Glenda with her mouth wide open.

"Please tell me you didn't find another body," Fred said. I frantically motioned for him to leave the bistro, where he was cleaning up, and follow me to the tasting room.

"Not yet. This should only take a minute or two, but it's important."

The two ladies who were perusing the sweatshirts finally decided on their purchases. They were standing in front of Lizzie when Fred and I returned to the tasting room. Cammy, Glenda, and Sam positioned themselves near the kitchen and were conversing under their collective breaths.

"As soon as these customers leave," I said to Cammy, "please lock the door and hurry back."

"My God, Norrie, you're giving us the heebie-jeebies."

Finally, when the doors were locked and the *Closed* sign placed on the outside of the building, I took a deep breath and groaned. I told them everything Bradley had told me, beginning with the twenty-nine-day wait time for the reading of Arnold's will and the final directive to hold the damn thing at our winery at midnight.

"Holy crapola!" Sam said. "Was that man a nutcase or what? Does he think his spirit's going to emerge from the grave and point out his killer?"

At the mention of the words "spirit" and "grave," Glenda held out her hands as if she was about to conduct an orchestra. "We could always hold a—"

"No!" I said firmly. "Not another séance. All we need to do is serve refreshments to the mourners, or whatever you call these people, and let Marvin Souza read the will. It will mean one hell of a long day for us, since you'll need to leave at closing time and get back here by eleven to set up. Fred and his wife might need more time. That is, if you agree to do it. And wait! There's more! Arnold's paying for this shindig so that will mean overtime pay. Time and a half before midnight and double time after midnight."

"What the hell. I'm in," Sam said.

"Me, too," Lizzie added. "With or without the overtime, I wouldn't want to miss such a…"

Sam chortled. "Sideshow?"

Lizzie pressed her lips together and narrowed her eyes. "I was going to say 'presentation.'"

"My wife and I won't let you down," Fred said. "We'll figure out something tasteful and tasty for the occasion."

Cammy's face resembled the Cheshire Cat, with a huge grin and wide eyes. "You think I'd miss something like this? Not on your life. Heck, I'm up later than that when someone doesn't show up to work at my aunts' bar in Geneva and I get stuck because 'It's family.' Count me in."

"What about Roger?" Lizzie asked. "Would you like me to call him?"

I thanked her but told her I'd take care of it. "I'm also going to ask Theo and Don from next door to attend. I have a funny feeling it's going to be a challenging night."

Glenda, who had been fairly quiet, rubbed her forehead and closed her eyes for a moment. "I think what we all are feeling is Arnold's restless spirit. I sense he cannot and will not move on until the person responsible for his death is apprehended."

"Well, I don't know about Arnold, but I'm movin' on," Sam said. "I've got a hot date with a girl in my computer systems class, and I don't want to keep her waiting. I've got two racks of glasses to put in the washer and I'm out the door."

I looked around at the tasting room and realized the crew still had some clean-up left. "I'll load the dishwasher," I said. "You guys need to finish up and get going. Listen, thanks for agreeing to do this. It really goes way over what's expected."

"Everything at Two Witches goes way over what's expected," Cammy laughed. "That's why we love it so much."

When I got back to the house, there was a message for me on the answering machine. The caller ID said Catherine Trobert and after hearing the first two words of her message, I knew I was in trouble.

"Steven's coming for the holidays! Isn't that splendid news? Now you can get together, finally. Oh dear, I didn't mean Thanksgiving. I meant Christmas. I'll chat later. Bye, Norrie."

As if I didn't have enough on my plate. The last thing I wanted to do was get together with her son, who was a few years older than me and who had ignored me all through high school. Why she wanted to fix me up with him was anyone's guess. I was sure Steven wasn't lacking in the dating department. He was a practicing attorney in Maine, and when Catherine showed me a recent photo of him on Facebook, he was still the same good-looking, self-assured guy I remembered from Penn Yan Academy.

I shuddered and deleted the message. Then I realized there were two messages on the phone. The other caller ID read "Yates County Public Safety." Crap! It had to be Deputy Hickman, unless, of course, Gladys Pipp had uncovered some choice gossip that couldn't wait until morning. I tapped the phone and held my breath.

"Miss Ellington, this is Deputy Hickman. I wanted to let you know our forensics department was unable to secure viable prints from your wine barrel. The perpetrators must have been wearing gloves."

Duh. You think?

The message continued, "We will continue to pursue this case via our normal investigative means. Should you have any questions, please contact our office. Thank you."

I figured Theo and Don had received a similar message because they would've called me otherwise. I wasn't really expecting the sheriff's department to strike it lucky with prints. Still, I was bummed. Not the best mood to be in when writing a romance screenplay. What the heck. If I had to suffer through wine sabotage and another dead body cropping up, my characters could deal with their own problems.

Chapter 12

The weather turned cold again, and the forecast called for three to five inches of snow for Thanksgiving. Like most of the wineries on the trail, the tasting room closed early on the Wednesday before Thanksgiving, but a skeleton crew remained to sell bottles of wine for last minute shoppers. That crew was Cammy and me.

"My aunt Luisa decided a giant turkey wasn't going to be enough, so she made lasagna and manicotti. I'll just spoon it over the cornbread and gravy dressing," Cammy said. "By the way, Marc and Enzo send their regards. They got in yesterday. Come to think of it, that's probably why my aunt's been on a cooking rampage."

Cammy's two cousins, who were now officially college juniors, had helped me out with a sticky situation regarding a land developer. Without them, I might've said or done something I regretted.

"Tell them I said hi and if they've got some free time, please stop by Two Witches."

"I'll send them on my day off," she replied and gave me a wink. "I take it Theo and Don are doing the cooking tomorrow?"

"You shouldn't even ask. I picked up two pies and homemade whipped cream at Wegmans. That's as close to cooking as I get."

I figured we'd be lucky if two or three customers stopped by to purchase wine, especially since a light snow had started to fall. Surprisingly, people kept trickling in, and every one of them left with at least two bottles.

"Excuse me," a twenty-something man with a buzz cut and freckles asked. "Can you tell me what wines go well with turkey? I'm kind of new at this, and I promised my girlfriend I'd get the wines for Thanksgiving dinner at her parents' house."

"Absolutely. The two favorites are Riesling and Chardonnay. We have three different varieties of Riesling—dry, semi-dry, and semi-sweet. Dry means there's no residual sugar left after the fermentation process, while semi-dry and semi-sweet have increased levels of sugar."

"Okay. I'm going to play it safe and buy one bottle of semi-dry Riesling and one bottle of Chardonnay."

I smiled. "Sounds like a good plan to me. I'm sure the family will enjoy them."

When the man left, Cammy whispered, "You're holding out. You know more about this stuff than you let on."

"Not really. I just get stuck listening to Alan and Herbert all the time."

We were in the final twenty-minute stretch when a woman with short curly hair in shades of brown and honey approached me at the cash register. She was wearing a black mid-calf winter coat and had one of those tan, black, and red tartan scarfs around her neck. Cammy had already closed everything down, so we could make a quick exit at precisely five-thirty.

The woman started to say something when her phone buzzed, and she stepped to the side. "Sorry, I really need to take this."

I could hear her end of the conversation, even though I tried to be discreet.

"I know, I know. Why do you think I'm making the rounds? I'll be home as soon as I can."

"Sorry about that," she said to me. "My husband insists that I buy up as much Pinot Noir as possible. You do sell it by the case, don't you?"

For a second, I was stunned. "That would be over three hundred dollars. Are you sure?"

"Oh, I'm sure all right. Make it two cases. Red wines keep for years, unlike whites. Everyone in these parts knows what's going on. The prices for next year's vintage will skyrocket and none of us will be able to afford it. Pinot Noir is a staple for our Sunday dinners, not to mention Christmas and Easter."

"Is this because of the wine hijacking a couple of weeks ago?"

"That, and the fact there's a conspiracy in the works to limit the number of bottles on the market."

Cammy, who was standing a few feet away from me, moved in closer as the woman went on.

"I know this for a fact. The woman who sits next to me in church has a son who happens to work in the industry. Let's just say, he gave her the heads-up. If anyone would know, he would. Oh, do you have a way of getting those cartons into my SUV? I can move it to the front of the building."

"Um...uh...sure." I was so taken aback by what came out of the woman's mouth, I stood there like a blithering idiot.

"No problem," Cammy said. "I'll get the dolly and load the cartons. See you out front."

The woman handed me a credit card and, as I processed her purchase, I asked, "What part of the wine industry does this woman's son work in?"

"Wine distribution. To listen to her speak, you'd think her son was about to own one of those companies."

"You wouldn't happen to know his name, would you?"

"I only see the woman at church, but she refers to her son as Scottie. It could be a nickname though. Oh my goodness. It really is getting late, isn't it? I'd best be going. Thank you for all your help and have a happy turkey day!"

"What a terrific last-minute sale!" Cammy walked back through the doorway. "But maybe we shouldn't be that ecstatic. That woman used the word 'conspiracy,' didn't she? Even if there's really no major shortage of the Pinot Noir, a perceived shortage will be enough to drive prices up. You know as well as I do, we can't very well undercut the commercial businesses and restaurants that sell our wine."

"It's not our fault this is happening. I mean, sure, people are used to paying more for a bottle of wine in a restaurant than at our winery, but the distributor's the one who works that deal out. The individual establishments set their own prices."

"Arnold must've worked it out, all right, and look where it got him. Maybe the winery owners weren't the only ones gunning for him."

"Are you saying you think he was the mastermind behind all of this and that's what got him killed?"

"If the Florsheim shoe fits..."

"But the wine sabotage continued, long after he was found dead."

"Honey, didn't you ever hear of the word 'accomplice'?" Cammy asked.

I paused for a minute and bit my lower lip. "Looks like the trail of bread crumbs surrounding Arnold's death gets more and more complicated. First, his murderer...now, his accomplice...unless..."

"Yeah," Cammy said. "I thought about that, too."

"Is the door set to lock?" I asked.

"Uh-huh. I did it as soon as I came in from loading the wine into that woman's SUV."

"Good. I'll be quick. I need to write down the name on that credit card. Tracking down that woman's source of information might not be a bad idea."

"You're going to find out what church she belongs to and attend one of their services?"

"Good Grief! No. I intend to show the name to Lizzie. She's on the ecumenical council for the Tri-County area. She'll be able to come up with something, I'm sure."

"You never cease to amaze me, Norrie."

We locked up and wished each other a happy Thanksgiving. "Eat hearty and hit the sack early," Cammy told me. "Black Friday makes 'Deck the Halls around the Lake' look like a cake walk. You *are* coming to help, aren't you?"

"Seriously? You think we'll get that many people? The only thing we discount are our gift items and clothing."

"Trust me. They're not coming for our discounts, they're coming to reward themselves after doing battle at the big box stores."

* * * *

Thanksgiving dinner with Theo and Don looked like something out of a Norman Rockwell painting, beginning with the ginormous herb-seasoned turkey Don prepared, complete with chestnut dressing, fingerling potatoes, sweet potatoes, and a medley of vegetables, each in its own savory sauce. We paired it all with our semi-dry Riesling and their Chardonnay.

Charlie was invited to enjoy his own version as well—turkey juices poured over the kibble I brought. The guys felt bad that the dog had to be cooped up for hunting season, so they indulged him with gourmet food to compensate. Isolde was pampered, too—tiny morsels of turkey blended into her regular feline diet.

It was after five when we got to the Dutch apple pie and the French silk chocolate one. I told Theo and Don about the woman who bought two cases of Pinot Noir from us, and they said they'd had similar requests all week.

"Talk about panic mode," Theo said. "The odd thing is, right now it's giving us some income, but I think we're in for a dramatic shift pretty soon. Lower comp rates and less inventory."

I cut myself a small slice of the Dutch apple pie and spooned on some whipped cream. "Did either of you hear anything from Deputy Hickman?"

"No viable prints," Don said. "Or we would've called you."

"Same here. I figured as much. Listen, since we've crossed Lavettia off our list, we really should concentrate on Miller Holtz."

Don groaned. "What a cocky son-of-a-gun, huh?"

Theo looked up from his dessert plate. "That doesn't make him a killer. A jerk maybe, but not a killer."

"Miller's kind of a hard guy to miss," I said, "but given that huge crowd for 'Deck the Halls around the Lake,' he could've slipped into our tasting rooms unnoticed. In fact, he could've been the other person in Arnold Mowen's car. I was dead set on it being Lavettia, but maybe Arnold brought Miller along for the ride instead. Maybe Miller was the one who killed him. They never found the gun, but that doesn't mean he didn't take it with him. It was late in the day, so if he timed things right, no one would've noticed Arnold falling into that ditch. Too shadowy. Everything on the landscape blends together."

"And then what?" Theo asked. "Miller's going to stand around in the parking lot twiddling his thumbs?"

"Of course not. Same scenario as before, only with a different suspect. Miller would've taken one of the wine shuttles back to Geneva or wherever. I should have thought of this before. Those buses accept major credit cards and debit cards as well as cash. Most people don't carry around that much cash. If Miller hopped on that shuttle and paid for his ride with plastic, the bus company should have a record of it."

I caught myself in mid-thought and paused. "Oh no. That means I'll need to run this by Deputy Hickman. The bus company certainly isn't about to share its information with me."

"Got to admit," Don said, "it's a thought."

"First thing tomorrow, like it or not, I'll call him."

As things turned out, I didn't like it and neither did Deputy Hickman. I phoned the public safety building at a little past nine the following morning and asked to be connected to him.

"I hope you had a nice Thanksgiving," I said, trying to pave the way for a smooth conversation.

"I didn't. Combat duty would've been preferable to a full day with my relatives. Anyway, how can I assist you, Miss Ellington?"

I took a quick breath. "I may have a lead...well, actually, more like a hunch about Arnold Mowen's killer. It may be his wine rep, Miller Holtz. Miller could've driven over with Arnold to the 'Deck the Halls around the Lake' event and killed him. Then he could've hopped on one of those wine shuttle buses and gone back to Geneva or Seneca Falls. If you could get the bus company to check its credit card transactions for that day, you'd be able to see if Miller Holtz was on that bus."

"Let me see if I understand you correctly, Miss Ellington. Out of the clear blue sky, you've determined Miller Holtz to be a suspect. Or should I say *the* suspect?"

My mouth suddenly felt scratchy, which made my voice sound raspy. "Miller thinks he's about to inherit Arnold Mowen's wine distribution business. He said that to everyone on the wine trail. If that doesn't spell out motive, I don't know what does."

"Miss Ellington, people bequeath property and businesses all the time. They write wills. They write trusts. They write letters. If that were the case, our county would be swarming with homicides. Just because someone stands to inherit something does not automatically make them a murder suspect."

"Not everyone. No. But why take a chance on letting Miller Holtz slip through your fingers when you could easily place a call to the wine shuttle company and demand to see their credit card transactions?"

"Based on what evidence? Your hunch? Our department will need something stronger than that, I'm afraid."

"Okay. Okay. What about a pistol permit? You can check to see if Miller Holtz has a pistol permit. Unless the news stations got it wrong, Arnold was shot with a .22. That could be a rifle or a pistol. No way to tell from the bullet. Miller could've concealed his gun easily. Holsters... pockets... heck, he could've been wearing it around his ankle for all we know."

"Miss Ellington, we don't know."

"That's what I'm trying to tell you. *If* Miller Holtz owned a gun and *if* he was on that late day wine shuttle, it would be a no-brainer."

"It would be circumstantial and a bit far-fetched."

At this point, my voice had gone from raspy to whiny. "So, you're not going to do anything?"

"I didn't say that. Your call will be taken under advisement. Now, please go about your business and let the trained professionals go about theirs. Good day, Miss Ellington."

Click. The call ended before I could eke a syllable out of my mouth. That man had to be the most pig-headed, obtuse, obstinate sheriff in the history of the county. I grumbled for over twenty minutes before making myself a second cup of coffee and booting up my laptop.

My producer, Renee, had emailed me requesting a status report on the screenplay. I sent her back three words: "It's coming along." And it was, albeit slower than usual. I found myself sidetracked with thoughts of wine sabotage and murder instead of budding romance and deceit. At a little past eleven, I took a break and nuked some of the leftover turkey and dressing from yesterday. Don had made sure I'd have at least four meals before I had to fend for myself. I devoured the fixings as if I'd never eaten a holiday meal before. I'd promised Cammy I'd be in the tasting room to help with the late day Black Friday crowd, and I figured I'd be better off going on a full stomach. Unlike the retail stores, our crowds intensified after lunch.

"I put some leftover manicotti and lasagna in the freezer for you," she said when I walked in. "When you leave tonight, don't forget it. My aunt Luisa says hi and told me you are way too skinny."

"I knew I liked that woman!"

I had met Cammy's aunt not too long ago when Cammy and I were chasing a lead on another murder.

From what Cammy and the gang had told me, I'd expected a full crowd, but what I didn't expect was such a boisterous one. It was impossible to hold a conversation, let alone talk about wines. The Black Friday shoppers were getting an early start to the holiday season partying. The limousines were in full force and the weather was mild by November standards. Low forties and no snow.

At a little past four, Lizzie waved me over. "Norrie, you have a phone call from Godfrey Klein at the Experiment Station. Said he tried your house first."

Although Godfrey called to provide innocuous updates about Francine and Jason's progress tracking down that stupid bug, I always felt a certain amount of trepidation until I knew, for sure, that my sister and brother-in-law were all right. Visions of viper snakes and poison dart frogs came to mind, along with crocodiles and pumas.

"Hey, Norrie, I just got back from Lodi with another entomologist. We were called over there for the worst infestation of Boisea trivittata I've ever encountered. Not to be confused with the Boisea rubrolineata. The Boisea trivittata unleashes a horrible odor unlike the—"

"Stinkbugs? You're calling me about stinkbugs?"

"What? Oh no. That's not why I called, although you'll find it quite interesting. We were surprised ourselves. I mean, when people have insect infestations, they usually call an exterminator, not a scientist. But these nuns were adamant they were not about to have any pesticides used on their premises. They were hoping we'd be able to recommend a process for the removal of the Boisea trivittata without the use of chemicals. They said this was the first time anything like this had ever happened. Frankly, it's not that unusual. Did you know there are entire categories of what we refer to as overwintering pests?"

"Well, no. I hadn't given it much thought." *Or any thought.*

"Oh, yes. I believe that's exactly what happened to the Sisters of the Holy Sepulcher Convent. Most likely they had pumpkins out for their fall decorations and those pests fed on the pumpkins and found a way into a warm home."

"Did you say Holy Sepulcher Convent?"

"Yes. Are you familiar with it?"

"In a roundabout way. The Sisters who run the convent believe they're going to inherit Arnold Mowen's business. You know, Lake-to-Lake Wine Distributors. It's a long story."

"Hmm, that might explain something. While I was checking out the desks and armoires for Boisea larve, I came across a detailed set of plans for expansion. Major expansion. It called for new dormitories and a separate building for their bakery enterprise. I figured it was one of those architectural pie-in-the-sky kinds of things that lots of institutions have on file in the event a generous donor leaves them his or her estate."

"Oh my gosh. That's not pie-in-the-sky, that's prepping for the future. No one hires an architect unless they're certain there's going to be a building project. And building projects don't happen without the funding in place. I should know. It took the Penn Yan School District years to get bond approval, not to mention voter approval, to expand the high school. Of course, those nuns don't need a taxpayer vote, but they do need money and lots of it."

Suddenly the Holy Sepulcher raced to the top of my suspect list in Arnold Mowen's death. I know. I know. It was a dreadful and horrible thought—nuns committing murder and all that. Still, I'd seen enough true crime drama to know that if someone wanted something badly enough, they might be willing to sacrifice their moral fortitude for cold hard cash.

"Godfrey, do you remember where you found those blueprints? What drawer? What room?"

"All I remember was that it was an upstairs room and they all look alike. Crucifix over the bed, small nightstand with a bible, and the occasional painting of the Virgin Mary. Why? What are you getting at?"

"I could go straight to hell for saying this, but…what if those nuns collaborated to murder Arnold Mowen in order to inherit his business? That business isn't any small potatoes. The guy's worth a fortune, from what I understand."

"You might be putting two and two together and coming up with five. Maybe at one time the convent thought they had funding for expansion. I have no idea how far back those blueprints go."

"Chances are you're right, but still, you have to admit it's a possibility."

"What? Gun-toting Sisters poised and waiting at a winery event to shoot someone so they can inherit his fortune?"

"When you put it like that, and by the way, you sound just like my friend Theo, it does seem like a made-for-TV drama, but I'm not discounting anyone at this time. Not to be rude or anything, but was there a reason for your call?"

"I was so busy talking about infestations and nuns—I nearly forgot to tell you the real reason I called. Jason checked in on the satellite phone early this morning. I wanted to call sooner but I was tied up. Remember when I mentioned the Culex corniger and how they located it in a remote area?"

Vaguely...

"Anyway, they think they may have stumbled upon another species that's now inhabiting urban areas. Fantastic, isn't it?"

I'd like to inhabit an urban area. Manhattan, to be precise. In my own apartment. "Um, yeah. I guess."

"Say, Norrie, I know it's a ways off, but if you're not doing anything for Christmas, you're more than welcome to join our crew. There are seven or eight of us who get together each year at a different entomologist's house. We all bring a dish to pass and chip in for a prime rib roast. I promise—there won't be any insects."

"I, er..."

"You don't have to answer right away. I just thought—"

"That's awfully nice of you, Godfrey. I'm not sure if Theo and Don next door are expecting me, so let me get back to you, okay?"

"Sure thing. And listen, don't decorate with pumpkins adjacent to your house next fall. Remember that. The Boisea trivittata can be quite invasive. Those poor nuns. It's either kill the damn insects or convert them."

Unless those Sisters have bigger plans.

Chapter 13

The phone practically screamed in my ear the next morning and I fumbled to reach it. I was groggy, and my thought processes hadn't kicked in. I could see the murky, grey daylight outside my window, so I knew whoever called wasn't a late morning sleeper like me. I barely uttered the word "hello," when Lavettia Lawrence's voice ripped through me like a razor.

"I'd like to know what on earth is going on. I just got a certified letter informing me that Arnold's will is going to be read twenty-nine days past his death. What's that? A Friday? A Saturday? And at midnight, no less. Midnight at *your* winery. Whichever one of those idiotic lawyers wrote that letter, they had the audacity to tell me my presence was requested. Damn right it was requested. I'm about to inherit the business. I'll tell you what I told Marvin Souza on the voice mail I left him five minutes ago."

"Good morning, Lavettia."

I was still trying to focus and all I heard was a jumble of words including "midnight," "inherit" and "Marvin Souza."

Lavettia got louder and I had to move the receiver away from my ear. "Was the man insane? Who insists on the reading of a will at midnight? And at a winery, no less. If that business of his isn't left to me in its entirety, I'll have the will contested. I cannot, for the life of me, imagine who else he would've named as his beneficiary. He didn't have any family. He had me. And I better have what's coming."

I didn't dare mention Miller Holtz or the nuns, for fear Lavettia would really go off on a tear. It didn't matter. She was on a roll, and she wasn't about to stop.

"What if he was insane? Well, not insane, but cognitively diminished. Isn't that what they call it? Oh my God! I've seen this on *48 Hours.* The boss loses his faculties, but his assistant covers for him, all the while paving the way for the business to be handed over to him. That sneaky, sniveling lowlife Clayton LeVine. I'll bet he's behind all of this. Well, he's got another think coming. I won't let him get as much as one of his grubby little fingers on Arnold's money."

"You mean 'business.'"

"Business…money…it's all the same. Tell me, was this your idea? To have the will read at your winery?"

Finally, the real reason for the call. "What? Of course not. I have to pay my employees overtime and stay up late, not to mention provide refreshments."

I failed to mention the generous compensation Two Witches would be getting for the shindig.

"Then it's obvious," she said. "Arnold was losing his wits. Let me ask you something. Did Marvin Souza indicate how many people he expected for the reading?"

"Sort of a ball park figure. Anyone's guess."

"Tell me."

"Well, there's Marvin, naturally, and the other lawyer in the firm, Bradley Jamison…and of course, you."

"Three people do *not* constitute refreshments and employee overtime. Spit it out. What do you know?"

"This doesn't mean anything, really, but we're expecting between five and ten others. Winery contacts, that sort of thing."

I tried to sound matter-of-fact, but I was sure she could sense I wasn't being completely honest.

"So help me, if that mealy-mouthed Clayton LeVine gets so much as a penny out of the business, there'll be hell to pay."

"What makes you so convinced Clayton LeVine might be on the receiving end of the will?"

"Don't you know? Clayton's been holding something over Arnold for years. Probably some scandalous piece of gossip he plans to unleash posthumously if the business doesn't go to him."

"How do you know?"

"Arnold talked in his sleep."

Yep. That should hold up in the Supreme Court. "Lavettia, what do you know about Miller Holtz?"

"Only that he's in the right profession. At least, according to what Arnold said. Miller's an expert when it comes to wheeling and dealing. Got lots of accounts for Arnold. Why? Is there something I should know?"

Not right now. "No. Not really. Wine reps are more than salespeople. They get the winery names out there and promote us in the big cities."

It was way too early to be grilled by Lavettia, and I needed to end the call. I was about to tell her I'd see her next week when something gnawed at me. "Oh, by the way, how did your essential oils symposium go? A friend of a friend was there and said she saw you."

"Who?"

"Zenora. I don't know her last name."

The line got quiet for a moment and then Lavettia spoke. "Of course. Zenora. I did see her. I saw so many people, it's difficult to remember who I spoke to."

"My friend saw a Facebook post and said Zenora looked kind of wild and wooly at the event."

Again, a pause. "Well, that's Zenora for you. Anyway, I need to make a few more calls. Maybe even leave another message for Marvin Souza. Oh, and if that certified letter wasn't bad enough, do you know the Yates County Sheriff's Department sent someone to my residence to question me. Why, I'm practically the grieving widow."

"At least you have an alibi. And a witness."

"What witness? Who?"

"Zenora, the lady we were just talking about."

"Right. Zenora."

Lavettia sounded a tad agitated. Either she was so unnerved about that certified letter and it made her jittery, or she really hadn't attended that essential oils symposium—even if Glenda's friend said she saw her. Zenora could've been mistaken, or high on some essential herb. I'd met some of Glenda's friends before. All of them had one thing in common—they seemed to occupy an alternate universe.

Now, wide awake and famished, I washed up quickly and went downstairs for my coffee and whatever else I could dig up. At least Charlie could count on his kibble. I glanced at the wall calendar and counted the days until the midnight fiasco—thirteen, if I included the day of the event.

Deputy Hickman was no closer to finding Arnold's killer than I was to figuring out who had sabotaged our wine. What I really needed was an insider in the sheriff's department, but the closest I could get was Gladys Pipp. Still, she was better than no one. I made a mental note to call her on Monday and see if she was privy to any new information.

Miller Holtz moved to first place on my list of possible assassins, but Lavettia was back in the race as well. With nothing but a free morning on my hands, and a screenplay hanging over my head, I turned to the one place that could give me some answers—social media.

Delving into social media was like falling into a never-ending pit, but what choice did I have? If I could focus on Miller and Lavettia and not get sidetracked by cute kittens or craft projects I'd never make, I'd be okay.

I began by searching for Miller Holtz via LinkedIn. Because Miller was a businessperson, LinkedIn was a good place to start. Although I belonged, I didn't utilize the site often. My producer had suggested it as a means for networking and business contacts. She thought I should get my name out there. I had to admit, Norrie Ellington, screenwriter, did have a certain flair.

There were lots of Holtzes, but only one Miller. A slam-dunk. The guy listed himself as a wine distributor/manager and highlighted his experience and education. He graduated from Clarkson University in Potsdam, New York, with a degree in Global Supply Chain Management. I didn't know there was such a thing. He also listed his prior experience working for various businesses in upstate New York. While his age wasn't exactly spelled out, I did the math. Miller was in his forties, just as I thought.

His profile didn't offer anything that would scream *Killer*. I scrolled through his endorsements, a LinkedIn thing that job seekers need to impress would-be employers and recruiters. Miller's included community outreach, business management, and technology communications: three things that were completely nebulous. I scrolled further to his recommendations. I stopped to rub my eyes and look again.

There was a recommendation that dated back eight years. One of Miller's former professors from Clarkson had written, "Mr. Holtz has an innate understanding of how to maximize efficiencies, price, and ultimately, profit. The man is a veritable genius when it comes to manipulating the profit-loss margin."

Did that mean Miller was sabotaging the wines to ensure a greater profit on the restaurant market? Or was it merely one of those jacked-up recommendations meant to get the guy a job? I shrugged and moved to the next name on my list—Lavettia's.

LinkedIn wasn't exactly the neighborhood she'd play in, but still, I gave it a try and bam! There she was. I almost choked. Her photo reminded me of Ginger from those old *Gilligan's Island* reruns, only Lavettia's hair was as platinum as could be.

Under education, she listed The New York Etiquette School for Social Success. Under endorsements, there were at least thirty. They ranged from personal branding to masterful manners and communication. Were we talking about the same Lavettia Lawrence? Then again, her profile didn't mention a degree or even if she lasted past the first semester. Still, what this woman was vying for she most assuredly found with Arnold Mowen. Fine, so she majored in gold digging. That didn't necessarily make her a murderess.

I was about to call it a day and get back to the real work I had on hand when I decided to look up one more person—Clayton LeVine. It didn't surprise me when I didn't find him on LinkedIn, but when he didn't appear on Facebook either, I began to wonder. Heck, it's almost un-American not to be on Facebook.

I tried a few other social media sites and met the same fate—no Clayton LeVine. I tried Clay LeVine, C. LeVine, and even CLeVine. Still nothing. Then, for some unknown reason, I checked out Pinterest. Lo and behold, the guy had his own board devoted to disguises using wigs. To top it off, he had four hundred and eighty-three followers. At first I wasn't sure it was Clayton, even though the name said as much. One photo showed a man wearing some sort of wig meant to look like a green dragonfly head. The man stood in front of a door with a glass window with lettering that read, "Lake-to-Lake Wine Distributors." Figuring out who that man was wasn't rocket science.

The whole thing was downright weird, but, like Miller and Lavettia, it didn't make Clayton a killer. A whack-job maybe, but not a killer. When I finished my online sleuthing, I was no better off than when I started. Unless, of course, I needed a cool costume for Halloween next year—I could always call Clayton.

I did receive some good news that morning, news that was a long time coming. The sheriff's department finally removed the crime scene tape from the area where we found Arnold's body.

John, our vineyard manager, called to let me know. "I imagine there aren't any more clues they can uncover. Anyway, thought you'd be glad to know. They left a few minutes ago."

"Did you talk to them? Who? Who left? Was it Deputy Hickman?"

"No. It was their regular patrol making the rounds on Route 14. When they pulled into the driveway, I was nearby doing some pruning, so I walked over. The deputy who stepped out of the car said there was no further need for the crime scene tape. He yanked it off the poles, wadded it up, and took off."

"That's it? That's all he said?"

"Pretty much. Left me to deal with the wooden stakes. No big deal."

"Geez, I wish I knew what they found."

John laughed. "I think you already do—nothing. I don't think they've made a shred of headway on the case. From what I hear, they're still clinging to that hunting accident theory."

"That's crazy."

"What's that saying? Oh yeah. 'If you can't move forward, retreat or hold your position.'"

I thanked John for keeping me posted. I shot off a quick email to Theo. If he or Don glanced through their tasting room window, they'd see the yellow tape was gone, but once customers rolled in, it was impossible to catch a break.

I felt a little guilty for spending so much time sleuthing online, but I made myself a quick peanut butter and jelly sandwich before getting back to my screenplay.

It wasn't until late afternoon, after I shut down the computer and put on a warm jacket for a fast walk outside, that I realized something. If I was going to make any headway on my so-called investigation, I really needed to eliminate one of my suspects, but who? Lavettia was the logical choice because she had an alibi, but then again, did she?

I certainly wasn't going to eliminate Miller Holtz—he did everything but measure the corpse to see if the suit would fit. And what about the Convent of the Holy Sepulcher on the other side of the lake? They weren't any better than Miller, what with their architectural plans for expansion. Where else were they going to get their money? Certainly not from their little cheesecake business.

No matter how hard I tried, it was impossible to narrow down the list. Worse yet, as I traversed the back of our property with Charlie on his retractable leash, I added yet another person to the list—Clayton LeVine. Who else would know more about wine distribution than a guy who managed his boss's every interaction? It would be easy for Clayton to slip into that role.

The most horrific thought came to me—if Arnold Mowen's killer didn't inherit the business, would that killer then go after the beneficiary? Killing the beneficiary might not net any money, but anger ranked high as a motive.

Off in the distance, I heard the pop-pop of someone's rifle, and I instinctively pulled back on Charlie's leash. "I might have an idea about getting some answers."

The dog was busy pawing at the ground.

"Too bad it'll have to wait until tomorrow."

Chapter 14

When I spoke with her on Monday, Gladys Pipp was no help whatsoever with Arnold's murder. I don't know which one of us was more frustrated.

"I have to keep my voice down," she whispered. "People have been in and out of here all morning like it was Grand Central Station."

I laughed to myself. That was an expression my mother used all the time. She had gotten it from her mother. I doubted either one of them had ever stepped foot in the New York City train station.

"Any chance you can get your hands on that ballistics report?" I asked.

"Unless Deputy Hickman printed it out and left it lying around on his desk, like he usually does with stuff like that, I doubt it. I can't open his email."

"Has he given any indication they're getting close to making an arrest?"

"Honey, he hasn't given any indication they're getting close to making lunch. The man's as tight-lipped as they come."

"And no news on the wine sabotage either, I suppose…"

"Hmm, I may be able to help you out with that one."

I perked up immediately and begged her to tell me.

"They got some new information from the Seneca County Sheriff's Department about the van that was used in the truck hijacking."

"Why didn't they make it public?"

"Maybe they are keeping it hush-hush for the investigation. Up until now, all they had was a general description—white cargo van, possibly a Chevy. The license plate was deliberately covered with mud. But there was a dent on the rear passenger side bumper and a long scratch along the driver's side, almost as if someone keyed the van."

"Sounds pretty thorough to me. Of course, white cargo vans are as common around here as snow. And as for dents and scratches, they're pretty common, too. So, what's the new information?"

"A van matching that exact description was seen making deliveries to local restaurants in the Geneva, Penn Yan, Waterloo, and Seneca Falls areas. Sheriff's investigators in all three counties are looking into it as we speak. They're talking to the restaurant owners to see what items were delivered and from what sources. Restaurants usually use big chains like Sysco Foods, but they do contract with lots of local bakers. Not to mention farmers who supply anything from organic vegetables to goat cheese."

"Wow! That *is* a break. Whoever's making those deliveries might've loaned their van to the thieves or they *are* the thieves."

Gladys's voice sounded like a recording. "That's correct. The office is open until five and you can file your complaint any time before we close."

"Is Deputy Hickman right there?" I asked.

"Yes, that's the right address."

"Thanks, Gladys. I really appreciate it. Goodbye."

"Very well. Have a nice day."

As soon as I hung up the phone, it rang. I was in the kitchen and had used the landline because the connection was a zillion times clearer than my cell phone.

"Hello?"

"Norrie, it's me, Godfrey. You left a message for me, but it was on my office number and I didn't get it until this morning. Remind me to give you my personal cell phone number. What's up?"

"Are you planning to go back to Lodi this week about those stinkbugs at the convent?"

"As a matter of fact, we are. Tomorrow, in fact. Alex Bollinger and me. Same entomologist as before. We might be able to ameliorate that situation by infusing the area with pheromones to confuse the Boisea Trivittata. They may seek another location. Why?"

"I need to look at that architectural blueprint. You said you found it upstairs. It had to be in one of the Sister's rooms, but which one? Those blueprints always have the architect's firm or name on them. Godfrey, you've got to let me join you and your buddy tomorrow."

"Norrie, I don't think—"

"Listen, I won't do anything to mess up your pheromone plan. Honest. I won't so much as step on a single one of those disgusting stinkbugs. I promise. While you and Alex are setting your traps, or whatever it is you plan to do, I'll keep a low profile and try to find out which of those Sisters stashed the blueprints."

"So breaking and entering, essentially."

"Entering. I could pretend to be taking photos of the infestation for scientific research. In fact, I could take photos. I have a smartphone."

"It's not that...it's...well, this is government work we do. Government research. We can't compromise it."

"Godfrey, one of those nuns could be a killer. A bona fide killer who goes free because she has the perfect ruse. No one would ever suspect a nun. I could join you as an observer, couldn't I? Surely the Experiment Station allows observers."

I wasn't sure if Godfrey was groaning or humming. "Fine. Meet me at my office at eight tomorrow. I'll think of something to tell Alex."

"You're the best, Godfrey. The absolute best!"

Opportunities like this didn't come along every day, and I was positive Theo and Don would agree. Unfortunately, they didn't. I called them at a little past seven that night. I was absolutely brimming with enthusiasm.

"Are you insane?" Theo asked. "You actually plan on sneaking into the nuns' private bedrooms? It's a religious order. What if you get caught?"

"I'll whip out my phone and tell them I'm documenting the infestation."

"Geez."

"Look, Godfrey found those blueprints. You know as well as I do people don't have blueprints drawn up if they're not serious about building something. And those architects don't come cheap. I keep thinking something fishy is going on and I need to be sure."

"Oh brother. Here, talk to Don."

"You'd better be really careful, Norrie. This isn't like snooping around in a warehouse or something. And how are you going to go about it if those Sisters are milling about?"

"I doubt they'll be in their rooms during the day. It's not a dormitory. They'll probably be praying or something."

"If you're not careful, you'll be the one praying. Make sure your cell phone is charged, just in case."

"You make it sound as if I'm going into Dracula's Castle."

"Castle, convent, it's all the same."

When I got off the phone with Theo and Don, I revisited my earlier Google search on the Holy Sepulcher Convent. This time, I focused on images. I wanted to get a general sense of what I would face tomorrow. In my mind, I pictured a combination of The Cloisters in Manhattan and that enormous Romanesque structure in the 1966 classic, *The Trouble with*

Angels. What I saw instead reminded me more of an English countryside estate, only instead of a barn and horses, there was a chapel and another larger structure—a Tudor Revival with a steeply pitched roof, high chimneys, and dormer windows.

It looked as if a more modern addition had been added within the last decade, given the style and the fact that it bore no resemblance to the original building. Maybe it was the industrial kitchen the Sisters needed for their thriving bakery business. The last thing I noticed was a Morton garage with a side overhang. It was located between the chapel and the residence—and was large enough to accommodate two vehicles plus lawn mowers and a snowplow.

If I was lucky, the Sisters would be baking in the kitchen or praying in the chapel. Unlike *The Trouble with Angels,* the religious order no longer ran a boarding school. Arnold Mowen's class was probably one of the last ones to grace its hallways. Cheesecakes, tarts, and prayers replaced unruly kids and demanding parents.

With absolutely no plan of action for the following day, I decided to take a "look-see" approach—and hoped that Godfrey spent lots of time on the second floor, where the dormitories were located. Like the nuns, I did some praying of my own. Mainly that Alex Bollinger wasn't a stickler for following the rules.

I arrived at the Experiment Station promptly at eight, dressed in assorted layers of clothing in case it got warmer, colder, or wetter. The fact that it was in the mid-thirties didn't mean a thing. Weather in the Finger Lakes could change in a matter of minutes. Godfrey and a tall, thin man, in his early forties, met me at the front entrance. The guy had wavy brown hair and wore rimless eyeglasses with a slight tint.

"Norrie, this is Alex Bollinger." Then Godfrey turned to Alex. "This is Norrie Ellington from Two Witches Winery. As I mentioned, she's very interested in our project today since all the wineries are always concerned about overwintering pests."

Alex held out his hand and I shook it. "Nice to meet you. It's not often we get community members joining us on our off-site visits. Of course, you're Jason Keane's sister-in-law, so that might explain it. Lucky guy getting that grant, huh?"

I smiled, nodded, and held myself back from saying anything I'd regret.

The three of us piled into the Experiment Station's van, and Godfrey drove us to Lodi. He made a quick stop at the Dunkin' Donuts on Hamilton Street so we could grab coffee. The conversation consisted mostly of their pheromone plan to rid the convent of the stinkbugs, although I was privy to all kinds of information regarding winter pests, including some things I would have rather not heard, including the mess caused by cluster fly excretions. How anyone could revel in this knowledge was beyond me.

Lodi, a village that made my hometown look like a metropolis, was directly east of Penn Yan, on the opposite side of the lake. We took two county roads and made it there forty minutes later. The convent was situated on the lake and, had it not been winter with barren trees, it would have been obscured by foliage.

The sign in front of its long driveway read "Holy Sepulcher Convent." The words "and School" were painted over but still visible. Godfrey drove us directly to the Tudor Revival house. It looked exactly like the image I saw yesterday on the computer.

"Come on," he said. "I've got to let Sister Mary Katherine know we're here. She's the one in charge of operations. Sister Celeste runs the bakery and Sister Gloria Mae does the accounting and bills."

He used the brass doorknocker to let the Sisters know we had arrived. A young nun, who looked like she might be in her teens, answered the door and ushered us inside. She told us to wait for Sister Mary Katherine.

If I could describe the convent in one word, it would be imposing. Everything seemed to be struggling to breathe under the layers of dark curtains, dark furniture, and dark rugs. Even the circular staircase looked like it would be better placed in a Gothic horror movie. I half expected to hear a blood-curdling scream as a body was hurled from the top floor. Instead, Sister Mary Katherine arrived and greeted us.

I hated to admit it, but my mind was stuck in that stereotypical image of nuns, so when I found myself face to face with her, I was taken aback. For one thing, she was on the young side of middle age, probably in her late thirties, had a clear complexion and high cheekbones, and wasn't wearing a long black habit—or any habit, for that matter. She was wearing a plain white blouse and a non-descript beige skirt that came below her knees. Not ankles, knees. I noticed that she wore heavy beige stockings, and a gold cross around her neck. No veil, but a small beige covering that looked like a starched scarf. Her hair was dark brown and cut fairly short, just below her ears. She wore no makeup whatsoever. Without the drab attire and with a little blush and eyeliner, she could've passed for a coed.

Godfrey introduced me but didn't provide details. He explained to Sister Mary Katherine that he and Alex would begin the pest removal process using pheromones to lure the stinkbugs out of their recently discovered abodes. Alex would start in the chapel, as they found a large concentration of the insects there. Godfrey would begin upstairs in the dormitories, and he suggested that the Sisters do the preliminary work in the kitchen, since that infiltration was prominent. They would need to vacuum all visible bugs and take the vacuum cleaner outside. There, they would dump the insects into bags that they would seal carefully. Godfrey and Alex would take the bags for further research or obliteration. In addition, the baseboards and cabinets would have to be wiped down with Clorox. The nuns considered Clorox a cleanser and not a chemical, so Sister Mary Katherine had no objection.

"After we have vacuumed the visible insects, we'll introduce the pheromones," Godfrey explained. "More bugs will emerge from the cracks and holes. They should be vacuumed up immediately. We've brought two small, handheld machines for the upstairs and the chapel. I take it you have a decent upright or canister model for the kitchen."

"We have both," Sister Mary Katherine said. "Thank the Lord we completed our baking yesterday and sent the cheesecakes and tarts out for delivery. I anticipated we'd need at least a full day to take care of our situation. Oh dear. We have the garage to consider as well."

"I wouldn't concern myself too much about the garage," Godfrey told Sister Mary Katherine. "Right now, concentrate your efforts on your residence. How many Sisters will be assisting?"

"There are eight of us in all. We're a very small order and, unfortunately, dwindling. When we closed our school due to lack of enrollment, we feared something like this would happen. Most nuns study education as well as theology because they wish to teach. We cannot compete with the larger convents and monasteries like Bishop Grimes in Syracuse. Anyway, we genuinely appreciate your help. You said the kitchen contained the greatest number of those pests. What about the rest of the house?"

Godfrey and Alex exchanged glances and Alex spoke. "When we were here the other day, we noticed a number of ornamental plants. The insects feed on those as well as any fruits, like apples or berries, you may have lying around. It's always a good idea to remove the food source or at least make sure it's refrigerated so they can't get to it."

"And the plants?" Sister Mary Katherine asked.

"If you don't wish to discard them, scrutinize them carefully. Of course, the insects do lay eggs, although during the winter months they tend to remain in hibernation mode."

"Yes," Godfrey added, "The female of the species is known to lay four hundred eggs in her lifetime."

Sister Mary Katherine gasped and then put her hand over her mouth.

"Don't worry," Alex said. "Have your Sisters begin with vacuuming and the bleach treatment. We'll add the pheromones to the mix and your dilemma should resolve itself."

Suddenly, the only thought in my mind was houseplants. So help me, if I saw so much as one stinkbug on Francine's spider plant, out it would go. Bug and all!

"If you'll excuse me for a moment," Sister Mary Katherine said. "I'd better let Sister Gloria Mae know what's going on. She's working in our office, the small room on our left, past the devotional room."

I wasn't sure what all those rooms were, but it didn't matter. I needed to scope out the dormitories to see which of the rooms housed the blueprints. I knew Godfrey had arranged for us to be upstairs so I could have access to those rooms without Alex, or anyone else, breathing down our necks.

"Off to the chapel I go," Alex said. "I expect to be done within the next two hours."

Godfrey gave him a quick nod and turned to Sister Mary Katherine. "Guess Miss Ellington and I had best get started as well. I need to go back to our van to get the hand-vac. Our pheromone vials are in the van as well, in my briefcase. Shouldn't be more than a minute or two. Would it be all right if Miss Ellington heads upstairs or would you rather she wait right here?"

Sister Mary Katherine glanced at the long circular staircase before turning to me. "No sense waiting. You might as well go up there and see for yourself what we're up against. All of the rooms are identical, and all of the light switches are on your right."

"Thank you. It was a pleasure to meet you."

The steps creaked as I walked up the stairs. The worn carpeting no longer muffled the sound of footsteps. When I got to the landing, I stared at a long corridor with an open door at the end. A row of sinks was clearly visible, and I figured it had to be the community bathroom. I shuddered. One year of living like that in college was enough for me. I much preferred my ratty apartments with one or two roommates to communal living.

It was eerily quiet upstairs, and I felt as if I was about to commit a sin by opening someone's private drawers and closets. I told myself it was sleuthing, not snooping. Still, it was creepy, and I muttered "It's a murder investigation, not a scavenger hunt." Of course, Deputy Hickman might've had another word for it, but I tried not to think about that.

I had always thought the Shakers and the Amish lived simple lives, but their simplicity was nothing compared with the Sisters from the Holy

Sepulcher Convent. I was glad I dressed in layers. Clearly, the Sisters didn't believe in overspending when it came to heating the place.

I had gone through every conceivable corner in the first room when Godfrey finally made it upstairs.

"What took you so long?" I asked.

"I spotted a few boxelder beetles in the kitchen when I peeked inside. This place is a veritable winter hotel. It appears as if the Sisters didn't bother, or didn't have the resources, to have their windows caulked and sealed. Not to mention the doorplate areas."

"Yikes. I don't do that either."

Godfrey looked as if I said I left all of our windows and doors open at night. "Unless you plan on sharing your house with a host of unwelcome guests, you might want to consider it."

Consider it? I'm calling the vineyard manager right this minute and having him line up the first carpenter he finds!

Chapter 15

The hum of Godfrey's vacuum cleaner was a soothing sound as I worked my way through each of the rooms. With the exact same layout and amenities (one dresser, one nightstand, one small, non-walk-in closet), it was easy to poke around.

The mattresses were lightweight and twin-sized, so it didn't take any Herculean effort to lift them and see if any of the Sisters was hiding something. Three rooms down and the only thing that caught my attention was the bugs. Ew! They were everywhere. The worst clusters were in the corners of the closets and in some of the drawers. I hoped Godfrey had brought lots of vacuum cleaner bags or garbage bags if his vacuum was one of those bagless ones.

"Hey, Norrie, how's it going?" he asked when we bumped into each other in the corridor.

"Do you have any idea where you found those blueprints?"

Godfrey shook his head. "It wasn't one of the end rooms, but that's the best I can do."

"Okay. I'll plod on."

Plod on was definitely the expression for what I was doing. The entire process was mind-numbing, and I wasn't getting anywhere. Finally, when I left one of the rooms and walked toward the next one, I caught a whiff of something. It was faint, but discernable. It was a scent I recognized, even though I couldn't place it. It was someone's perfume. Until now, most of the rooms smelled like a mixture of mildewed wood and Ivory soap.

Working in the tasting room, I inhaled all sorts of aromas, or in some cases, odors. This was definitely an aroma. Maybe I'd smelled it on one of the customers. Normally, I wouldn't notice this kind of thing, but this was a convent, and I didn't think nuns were allowed to wear perfume.

I don't know why, but I looked to my left and my right before entering the room. Godfrey was across the hall, or at least I thought he was because I heard the vacuum. I walked into the room, expecting to get a good dose of the perfume, but like the lingering aroma in the hallway, it was diluted.

By now I had worked out a routine—check the nightstand first, check the dresser drawers, look at the closet, and finish with the mattress. Too bad Hilton and Marriott weren't hiring in our neck of the woods.

Other than the usual Bible and, in this case, a box of tissues, there was nothing of interest in the nightstand. The dresser held an assortment of white undergarments and stockings, as well as white blouses and two cardigan sweaters, both tan. The closet held a few beige skirts and a heavy winter coat. Two pairs of clunky black shoes were lined up on the closet floor.

Next, I moved to the mattress and I heard footsteps approaching. It was one of those Stephen King moments when the small hairs on the back of your neck stand up. I told myself to relax, that I was searching for stinkbugs and what? Boxelder bugs now? Before I could turn my head, I heard a woman's voice.

"There's a false bottom on the second drawer down. Unless you're really looking for more of those horrid stinkbugs."

Standing in the doorway was another Sister, about the same age as Sister Mary Katherine but much taller and thinner with reddish hair and bangs.

My face suddenly warmed and, for a moment, I didn't know how to respond.

She went on. "Don't worry. I've often wondered what Sister Celeste keeps in that drawer."

"I, uh, um…"

"Shh, your secret's safe with me. I'm Sister Gloria Mae, and you are?"

"Norrie. Norrie Ellington from Two Witches Winery in Penn Yan. I'm friends with one of the entomologists and he said I could join them today."

"Fair enough. Mind telling me why? Like I said, the last thing I'm about to do is go scuttling off to Sister Mary Katherine."

I had to phrase my words carefully, or I'd be making an accusation I'd regret. "One of the Sisters in this convent may have knowledge about our wine distributor's suspicious death."

"So, you're trying to find out what that knowledge is?"

At first, I was hesitant to tell her the truth, but something about her demeanor told me I had nothing to worry about.

"Uh-huh. In a roundabout sort of a way. I'm looking for blueprints. Architectural blueprints for your convent's expansion. One of the entomologists saw them when they were checking for insects."

"Shh. We've got to keep our voices down. I didn't know anyone else knew about it. It's not common knowledge. I know this doesn't bode well, what with Mr. Mowen's unfortunate demise, but our convent stands to inherit a tremendous amount of money from his will. He was your wine distributor, I presume."

I nodded.

"And our benefactor. The Holy Sepulcher Convent has been in dire financial straits. Without this major infusion of funds, we'd have been forced to shutter the place by next summer."

"I think I heard something like that."

"Now our prayers have been answered. Once the will is read and the arrangements are made, we'll be able to proceed with that expansion. Sister Mary Katherine explained the entire process to us."

I'll just bet she did.

"That kind of money would offer us new investment opportunities as well as a chance to lure some of our students back. We weren't very savvy with our prior investments, but we've learned from our mistakes."

"Um, you do realize that by standing to inherit Arnold Mowen's money and/or business, you become prime suspects in his murder?"

Sister Gloria Mae put a hand over her mouth and held it still.

I wasn't sure if she was about to gag or lose her lunch. "Are you all right?"

She shook her head and looked as if she was about to cry. "Murder suspects? We're having a hard time killing insects. We could never take a human life. No amount of money is worth losing one's soul. Are you sure about that?"

"I'm not making an accusation, just an observation. Usually, when someone stands to benefit from another person's questionable death, they become suspects."

"Oh dear. I don't think any of us considered how it would look. We were all so caught up with the possibility of restoring our convent to its original thriving place of worship and knowledge."

"Sister Gloria Mae, are you certain it's money that's going to be left to you or Arnold's business?"

"His business? The wine distribution business? That would be a disaster. We have our own problems running our little bakery operation. If he were to leave us his business, we'd undoubtedly sell it. We're nuns, not business entrepreneurs, even though we try to make a profit from our cheesecakes."

"What about the blueprints? Are they in Sister Mary Katherine's room? I really need to look at them."

"The only reading material you'll find in her room is the Bible. You'll be wasting your time. Come on, I'll show you where they are. Walk softly."

I hadn't done anything like this since summer camp on Keuka Lake when I was twelve and snuck off with Heidi Bunchmeyer to peek in the boys' cabin. Sister Gloria Mae turned and glanced down the empty corridor before continuing. Then she motioned for me to follow her down the corridor. Thankfully, I could still hear the hum of Godfrey's handheld vacuum. We took a few steps and she opened a door on the left. The room looked like the others—devoid of anything homey.

"This is my room. I don't mind if you sit on the bed. Or you can take the chair near the dresser."

"Um, I..."

"Sit wherever you're comfortable. Oh, and keep your voice low."

I opted for the chair by the dresser. Something about sitting on a nun's bed gave me the creeps. I know it was ridiculous, but still…it was unsettling.

Sister Gloria Mae closed the door to her room without making a sound. "The blueprints are in here. We should be all right for a few minutes. Sister Celeste is running the kitchen. She'll be bossing everyone around for hours with that cleanup."

With that, she opened her dresser drawer and pulled out a ream of dark blue sheets.

"The actual blueprints are on a flash drive. These were some earlier ones dating back to the nineteen eighties when the convent had its original expansion. They must've been the ones the entomologists came across when they were in this room."

"I, um, er..."

"Did you think I was going to show you these old blueprints and leave it like that? You don't have to answer. We're not hiding anything. Not about the expansion and certainly not about poor Mr. Mowen's death. The blueprints on the flash drive are recent. Within the past year. If you think they'll help you in any way to figure out who might have killed him, I'll email them to you. Fair enough?"

I was so dumbfounded I couldn't speak.

"Whatever you do," Sister Gloria Mae said, "please don't breathe a word of it to Sister Mary Katherine and especially Sister Celeste. It's not that they're hiding anything, but everything around here requires a major decision and it gets very tedious."

"Don't worry. I won't say a thing. But why do you have the blueprints?"

"Because I handle the business end of things and that includes the expansion project."

I reached into my small bag and pulled out a Two Witches Winery business card. "The winery email is listed and, give me a second, I'll write my personal email on the back of the card."

"So," Sister Gloria Mae said, "do you think we'll ever be rid of those nasty bugs? If it was up to me, I'd buy a can of Raid and call it a day, but you never heard me say that."

I was beginning to like her more and more. "Yeah, you've got two top-notch entomologists dealing with it, so I believe you're in good hands." I was about to say, "There's always prayer," but it would've come across way too sarcastic.

"Tell me," I asked. "What will happen to all of you if Arnold Mowen's will doesn't name the Holy Sepulcher Convent as a beneficiary?"

Sister Gloria Mae paused and crinkled her nose. "Same as what happens to other small convents that dissolve. We'll get absorbed into larger orders in Syracuse, Rochester, or maybe even Albany. Albany seems to have some thriving orders still."

"I hope that doesn't happen," I said. "And thanks. I appreciate what you're doing."

"Miss Ellington, can you tell me why you're so intent on finding out who killed Mr. Mowen? Even the most dedicated sleuths wouldn't creep around an insect-infested convent for answers."

I chuckled. "His body was found on the adjoining property between our winery and our neighbors'. And it wasn't the first time something like this happened. This sort of thing is never good for business."

She grimaced. "I suppose not."

"Sister Gloria," I said, "do you mind answering one more question?" Before she could respond, I blurted out "What's the real reason your convent is convinced Arnold Mowen left his fortune to you?"

She paused and pressed her lips together. Finally, she spoke. "There is no delicate way to put this. Suffice it to say, some of us in the Triumvirate had colorful past lives before we became nuns. Thankfully the Lord forgives all."

I knew that little schoolboy tale about a letter Arnold wrote wouldn't hold a can of beans. "You said Triumvirate. Not the other nuns in the order?"

"Our other Sisters came to us as postulants directly from Catholic schools and seminaries."

Okay. I'll cross them off my list.

The screenwriter part of my brain went into overdrive and in a flash, I was conjuring up all kinds of sordid details regarding the past lives of Sisters Mary Katherine, Gloria Mae, and Celeste.

"I see. I mean, I understand."

"Good."

She motioned for me that it was time to leave the room. We stepped back into the corridor and stood there for an uncomfortable second until Godfrey emerged from behind one of the doors. He and Sister Gloria locked gazes for a second.

"Hi, Sister Gloria. It won't be much longer, and you'll be rid of these pests. Next year, please don't put any pumpkins close to the building."

"You won't have to worry about that. And thank you. I'd best be getting downstairs."

Sister Gloria and I exchanged nods and she mouthed, "I'll send the email" when Godfrey turned his head.

"I guess you must've met her on your first visit," I said to Godfrey once Sister Gloria was out of earshot.

"Uh-huh. She's the fun one of the group. So, any luck with your sleuthing?"

"More than you can imagine. And that's the problem."

"What do you mean?"

"I think Arnold Mowen's death might've had something to do with one of the nun's pasts."

"You're not implying—"

"Not them, but maybe someone else who had something to gain."

Godfrey put his hand on his chin and smiled. "Do you remember the scientific method?"

"Vaguely. Why?"

"Because you'll need it. You're already on step two—poised for a hypothesis."

"When Sister Gloria emails me the blueprints and I find out who the architects are, I might be able to make some headway."

"Why didn't you ask her?"

"Because I didn't want her to know it was the architect information I needed. Right now, she thinks I want to see the scope of the project. Besides, when I contact those architects, she won't take the fall for it. It's the funding I'm curious about. It seems like there are so many little secrets hidden in these walls."

"Yeah. Along with the boxelders. At least we can tackle our problem with pheromones and a decent vacuum cleaner."

"Now what?" I asked.

"Alex should be back here any minute. We'll put the pheromone lures in the other rooms. The nuns understand that all they need to do at this point is vacuum up the pests, secure the bags, and dispose of them. Come on. Let's check the progress in the kitchen."

Sister Gloria Mae was right. I heard a voice that had to be Sister Celeste's bellowing all the way out into the foyer.

"Point that nozzle away from you and give it a good spray. A little Clorox cleaner never hurt anyone!"

"You go first," I said to Godfrey. "She's liable to hand me a soapy bucket and some rubber gloves."

The Holy Sepulcher's industrial kitchen wasn't much different from the one we had at the winery. Granted, it was larger and, instead of posters depicting wine bottles on the walls, there were crucifixes, along with a gigantic calendar and a whiteboard that listed the cheesecake and tart varieties. Three young nuns were scrubbing cabinets busily, and another two were on their hands and knees cleaning the baseboards.

"This is so Dickensian," I whispered to Godfrey. "Like something out of *Hard Times.*"

He stifled a laugh and walked directly over to Sister Celeste.

Her hands were on her hips and she was facing the interior of a large pantry. I imagined the scowl on her face. Suddenly, she spun around. She ignored Godfrey and me, and instead, directed her attention to the nuns in the kitchen. "All of the contents in this pantry need to be removed and put on the counters so we can wipe everything down before Vespers."

"Vespers? But that's hours away, Sister," one of the nuns said.

"At the rate you're all moving, we'll be lucky if we finish by tomorrow's Lauds."

"Oh, I think you're moving along quite well," Godfrey said.

Sister Celeste glared at him. "We will after these cursed insects have been removed once and for all."

I'd never met Sister Celeste, but the minute I saw her face, I swore I recognized it. The trouble was, I couldn't link it to a time, place, or distant memory. The fact that her hair was concealed by a plain beige head covering didn't help. Her pale complexion made her look washed-out, a stark contrast from the black-rimmed glasses she wore.

"Don't worry," Godfrey said. "That's why we're here."

Chapter 16

"I've come across drill sergeants who were less intimidating than Sister Celeste," I said to Godfrey and Alex once we were back in the car and on our way home.

Alex turned around and gave me a nod. "I know what you mean. She gave me the willies, too. I was glad most of my work was in the chapel."

"You think they're going to be okay with that infestation?" I asked.

Godfrey answered immediately. "Absolutely. You know, the overwintering pests aren't dangerous, they're just well...pests. With the pheromone treatment and the vacuuming, the Sisters should be fine."

"Is anyone hungry?" Alex asked. "We can stop at a fast-food place and get a burger. Usually I'm famished at lunchtime, but I wanted to get the whole deal over with so I didn't bother to see if either of you wanted to take a break."

"Same here," Godfrey said. "Oh, I'm sorry, Norrie. I never even stopped to see if you were hungry."

"Don't worry. I wasn't. And if you don't mind, we're not that far from Geneva and Penn Yan. I'd just as soon go straight home."

Alex laughed. "I'll tell my stomach to hold off and spare us the grumbling."

The men spent the rest of the ride home discussing various infestations and experimental treatments for tackling them. Neither Godfrey nor I mentioned the real reason for my impromptu visit. It was only when we reached the Experiment Station that Alex asked if I'd like to accompany them to a roach-infested apartment building in Ithaca's Collegetown to observe the insects' movement patterns.

God no! Not on your life! "As fascinating as that sounds, I've got a full plate at the winery. Not to mention a strict deadline for my screenplay. I was lucky I could squeeze today's venture into my schedule."

I swore I heard Godfrey choking under his breath, but I ignored it. I thanked them both and took off for my car before Alex offered up another equally disturbing fieldtrip.

I snapped the Toyota's seatbelt, started the engine, and headed to Tim Horton's. I picked up dinner—a roast beef wrap and a chipotle chicken, in case I got hungry later. It was almost seven and a wet snow had begun to fall. At least it waited until I was back in my neck of the woods.

Charlie almost knocked me over the second I walked in the door. Feeling guilty for leaving him all day, I shredded little pieces of my roast beef and put it in his kibble. I devoured my meal as if it was going to be my last. I seriously doubted Sister Gloria Mae had sent the email, but I was anxious to have a look.

Sure enough, it was there. A brief sentence with an attachment. "Thank you for your interest in our convent."

Talk about covering one's bases. I imagined Sister Gloria's emails weren't exactly private. I wrote back, "It was a pleasure learning about your order."

I tore into the attachment like a wild woman. It was eighteen pages long and consisted of detailed blueprints—none of which I could understand. I was, however, able to locate the architect's information. An overlapping triangle logo on the lower left-hand corner had the initials AMA. Below the logo, I found the name Aiden McGovern Architects, with their address on Clinton Square in Syracuse. Bingo! I was home free.

From email to Google search in record time, I had the firm's phone number and fax. The only trouble was, I had no idea how I was going to get the information I needed. I couldn't very well call them and say, "Do you mind telling me how the Sisters of the Holy Sepulcher paid for your in-depth architectural designs for a new school and residence when they can barely cough up the money to heat their existing one?"

I shoved the laptop away and groaned. I was overtired and overwired. Maybe I'd have an epiphany by morning. Outside, the wet snow had turned to real snow and the winds were kicking up. Charlie enjoyed his few moments outdoors before coming in for the night. I was frozen, but glad the house had a decent furnace and solid insulation. I put on warm pajamas and spent the rest of the night watching reruns and the Weather Channel.

Calling it a night at a little before eleven, I drifted off into a mindless sleep. When the phone rang and jolted me awake, I had no idea if it was minutes or hours later. I sat up, rubbed my eyes, and read the digital numbers on the alarm clock by the bed—12:53. My brain had programmed itself to respond to late night calls with the only two options it knew—a winery emergency or the possibility that a jaguar had attacked Francine or Jason.

"Hello?" I mumbled into the receiver. *Francine and Jason really need to get an unlisted number for the house phone. And it's still listed under my parents' name—Ellington.*

"Someone's trying to kill me and don't tell me to call the county sheriff because I already did, and they won't listen."

"Lavettia?" *Dear God. Why the heck was Lavettia calling me? When did I win the prize?*

"It's because they know I'm about to inherit a fortune and they want me out of the way."

"Lavettia, it's almost one in the morning. Who wants you out of the way? Did something happen? And why on earth are you calling me?"

"Too many questions. You're asking too many questions. I'm positive Miller Holtz and that weasel of a secretary, Clayton LeVine, have teamed up to put me in an early grave."

Either Lavettia was really coming unhinged or she had reason to believe her life was in jeopardy.

"Okay, tell me what brought you to that conclusion." *And be succinct, I'm already sleep deprived.*

"Tonight was the giant pre-holiday sale at the outlet mall in Waterloo. All the stores were open until midnight. Between Chico's and Ann Taylor, I couldn't fit another bag in my car. I left the mall a few minutes before midnight and drove straight home. At least I tried to. I swore someone was following me on Route 318 so I went south on Nine Foot Road. The headlights were practically on top of me. I was about a mile from State Route 96 when they ran me off the road. I careened into some bushes and they took off. Imagine if it was the highway. I would've hit a guardrail and who knows what could've happened."

"Um, so that's it? You got sideswiped off the road?"

"I could've been killed! In case you haven't looked outside, we've had a lousy wet snow for hours before the real stuff kicked in. That and the winds turned the roads into death traps."

Not that deadly as to cancel a trip to the outlet mall. "Lavettia, maybe whoever ran you off the road was a drunk driver or someone who was in a hurry to get home. Just because they took Route 318 and turned south doesn't mean they were tailing you. Did you see their license plate? Or the make of the car?"

"My God! You sound just like the sheriff's deputy. And no, all I saw were headlights."

"At least you're home safe and sound. Maybe you can revisit this with the sheriff's office in the morning."

"Revisit? There's nothing to revisit. He told me to use caution when driving in inclement weather."

In a way, I felt sorry for Lavettia. It must've been frightening for her, but I was convinced she had a propensity for overreacting. I was about to say something when I realized she hadn't stopped talking.

"...like I'm not equipped to drive in the snow? I was driving in the snow when that deputy was still in diapers."

"Um, yeah."

"Drunk driver my you-know-what. I'll tell you who was behind that wheel—Clayton LeVine. It had to be him. He knew I was going to the outlet mall. I was in Arnold's office earlier in the day and I might've let it slip."

Okay, Lavettia, now you've got my attention. "What were you doing in Arnold's office?"

"Sometimes Arnold and I used his office for...well, shall we say, our afternoon delights or early evening—"

Ew! "I get it. I get it. But, um, er...Arnold's gone now."

"Don't you think I know that? I went there to pick up a few of my things. A lady has to be discreet about her personal items."

"Uh-huh. I still don't understand why you called me."

"My life is in danger and you're the only one I trust. I think one of those two men is going to make an attempt on my life during the reading of the will."

"That would be a tad difficult with all of us in the room. And besides, what gives you that idea in the first place?"

"I pulled the death card, La Morte, when I did a Tarot reading on myself a few days ago. Norrie, you simply have to put a stop to Arnold's little charade or whatever that midnight reading of the will is supposed to be. Tell them your winery is booked for the night. Tell them you have roaches. Tell them anything but get his lawyer to read the damn will in the office like normal people."

"I think it's a bit late for that, but don't worry. I honestly don't believe you'll be in any danger that night in our winery."

What the hell am I saying? For all I know, Clayton LeVine could be a psychopathic killer and Miller Holtz could suffer from borderline personality disorder. Maybe Lavettia isn't all that far off.

"First thing in the morning, I intend to buy a gris-gris," she went on. "If Arnold had been wearing one of those talismans, he might still be alive today."

For a second I wasn't so sure it was Lavettia speaking. She sounded more like Glenda. And a gris-gris. Wasn't that some New Orleans voodoo thing?

"Um, good," I said. "Whatever you need to do."

"All I want to do is claim my inheritance and move on with my life. And if that means acquiring Arnold's business, so be it. Businesses are bought and sold every day."

"Right. Well, I hope it works out for you."

"What do you mean 'hope'? Do you know something I don't?"

"It's after one, Lavettia. I'm not sure I know anything at this late hour."

"Oh dear. I really *did* wake you, didn't I? Well, I'll be in touch."

With that, the phone line went dead and I put the receiver back in its cradle. My mind was a jumble as I tried to get back to sleep. Gris-gris charms, Tarot cards, wet snow, mega sales at outlet malls, and drunk drivers all danced around my mind until I finally fell asleep. Then another call woke me—this time at the obscene hour of 8:49.

"Norrie, you sound groggy. Thought you'd be up by now."

"Theo?"

"Who else? Listen, Don and I caught the news a few minutes ago. There were two smash-and-grabs at wineries on our side of the lake. Farther down, but still in Yates County. The owners discovered the damage this morning. And before you say anything, I'll spare you the guesswork—all bottles of Pinot Noir that were set for distribution. Whoever did this knew exactly what they were looking for. The bottles weren't out in the open in the sales areas. They were in the store rooms."

"How many robberies or sabotage attempts does that make? And why haven't those sheriff's departments gotten anywhere?"

"I don't have an answer for either of those questions. But I'll tell you this much—whoever's the culprit in this, they know exactly what they're doing and frankly, I wouldn't put it past Miller Holtz if he was behind the scheme. With Arnold out of the picture, and Miller poised to take the reins, well…at least according to Miller…he'd ensure a mighty nice profit on the sale of the Pinot Noir. Heck, we've got panicked customers already thinking there's going to be a shortage."

"Why Pinot Noir? Why pick that grape?" I asked.

"Because the yield is iffy enough without tampering."

"What do you mean?"

"Aargh. One of these days I'm going to sign you up for a course in viniculture. Okay, here goes. It's a really sensitive plant. And I do mean sensitive. It has issues with wind and frost, more than other varieties and if that isn't enough, it's really fussy about how it's pruned."

"Seriously?"

"Oh yeah. And wait—I didn't get to the best part. Pinot Noir has a really thin skin and that makes it downright susceptible to things like fungal diseases and bunch rot. And please don't tell me you don't know what bunch rot is."

"Isn't that what makes dessert wines?"

"Yeesh. No! That's botrytis—the noble rot. Bunch rot turns the grapes grey and moldy."

"Oh. I don't know how you can keep this all in your head. And speaking of things in people's heads, Lavettia is convinced someone's trying to murder her. She woke me up from a sound sleep at one in the morning to tell me as much."

"You? Why'd she call you?"

"She wants me to cancel that midnight reading of Arnold's will. She's convinced herself Miller and/or Clayton will try to kill her so they can inherit the money and the business."

"I take it she doesn't know about the nuns."

"You've got that right. Far be it from me to be the one to mention it. She's likely to go off on a rampage. Marvin Souza and Bradley Jamison can deal with it when the time comes. I'm sure they must have some experience with that sort of family drama."

Theo laughed. "No one's had that kind of experience. Trust me. Best you can do is sell tickets."

"Very funny. Between you and me, I don't think Lavettia has a thing to worry about regarding her life. Her future finances maybe, but not her life."

"If you say so. Catch you later, Norrie. And make sure your alarm system is on at the winery. We're not off the hook, yet."

Terrific. In a little over a week, a cadre of unbalanced people would descend on our winery for the reading of a will that was penned by an even more unhinged person. If that wasn't enough, an insidious plot to undermine the small Seneca Lake Wineries by gradually diminishing their supply of next year's Pinot Noir was fast underway. I was desperate for an answer, but it would have to wait its turn.

It seemed, after all, that Lavettia had been right all along.

Chapter 17

Twenty-four hours later, Bradley Jamison called. At least I was awake, fully dressed, and in complete control of my faculties, thanks to a decent night's sleep. I was savoring the last bite of a toasted English muffin with jam when my cell phone made that annoying buzz. I meant to change the ringtone but, like so many other miniscule things in my life, I forgot.

"Norrie? It's Bradley. I hope I'm not taking you away from anything important, but I thought I'd better give you the news before you hear about it elsewhere."

"News? What news?"

"Lavettia Lawrence was found dead in her condo this morning. The cleaning lady discovered the body when she let herself inside. When she called the Seneca County Sheriff's Office and they showed up, they found our number. Believe it or not, they didn't have far to search. Lavettia had it written on a small whiteboard in her kitchen next to her financial advisor's information. No family members were listed, only professional contacts."

Bradley was going on and on as if he was describing a soccer match. I hadn't gotten beyond the first sentence. "Dead? Lavettia? Are you sure? Of course, you're sure. What am I saying? Oh my God! Lavettia was convinced Miller Holtz, with or without Clayton LeVine's help, was going to kill her."

"Huh? When did all of that happen?"

"Two nights ago. She woke me up out of a sound sleep to tell me. Oh my God! Lavettia's dead! I tossed it off and told her she was overreacting."

"To what?"

"Someone tried to run her off the road during that mini snowstorm. She left the outlet mall after midnight. Pre-holiday sale and all that. Bradley, what else do you know? What happened?"

"The sheriff's deputy didn't go into too many details, but he told my boss it appeared as if Lavettia had been shot in the back of the neck. Same as Arnold. The cleaning lady found her slumped over the kitchen table. At first, she thought Lavettia might've fallen asleep, but then she saw the blood that had saturated into the sweater she was wearing."

"Sweater? Not PJs or a robe? A sweater?"

"That's what Marvin said. Why?"

"Because it's nine o'clock now and Lavettia wasn't an early riser. If she was wearing a sweater, then someone had to have killed her the day before or the night before. Did those deputies tell Marvin anything else?"

"Nothing about the body. You know how that goes. Until the coroner gives a report, it's mums the word."

"What about her condo? Did it look like a break-in? A struggle?"

"No sign of a struggle. Not even so much as an overturned glass."

"You said the cleaning lady found Lavettia slumped over the kitchen table. Was it set up for two people? You know, two glasses, two plates…"

"Calm down, Norrie. I know what two means. And no, the table was empty and there were no signs Lavettia had been entertaining anyone."

"What else do you know?" I was beginning to sound like a broken record. "What else did they tell Marvin?"

"Like I said, the sheriff's deputy contacted us because our number was listed. They're sending someone over here to question Marvin, but I doubt he'll have a whole lot to tell them. All he knows is that Lavettia was Arnold's Mowen's girlfriend and a possible beneficiary to his estate."

"I understand client privilege and all that, but Arnold's dead. Lavettia too, for that matter. Come on, Marvin drew up Arnold's will. It's not a trade secret. Can't you please tell me who's about to inherit that whole kit and caboodle? It could be Lavettia's killer."

"Lavettia's death hasn't been ruled a homicide."

"Good grief! You said she was shot in the back of the neck. What do you think happened? She reached behind her head with a gun and killed herself? It's Lavettia we're talking about, not a contortionist. Of course, she was murdered. Probably by the same lunatic who killed Arnold. Did anyone mention anything about the gun? I'll bet it was a twenty-two, same as last time."

"The coroner hasn't even performed an autopsy. And, as for the forensics, I'm pretty certain the crime scene investigators are pouring over the evidence in her condo."

"Fine. Fine. What about the other thing? Arnold's beneficiary. Please don't hold out on me."

"I'm not. That's the truth, Norrie. I really don't know. Marvin drew up Arnold's will and the memorandum that went with it. He hasn't divulged a word to me or anyone else in this office, for that matter. Not even our secretary. Believe it or not, he handled all of the paperwork himself."

"So, come midnight a few days from now, it's anyone's guess. Hey, what happens if it turns out Arnold left everything to Lavettia, then what?"

"Last wills and testaments usually stipulate a secondary beneficiary, should the primary beneficiary be deceased. It's more cost efficient that way. People can't keep going around writing and rewriting their wills, and they certainly can't predict who'll still be alive at the time of their own demise."

"Makes sense, I suppose."

"Arnold was a savvy businessman. He wasn't about to risk having any portion of his estate go to our illustrious Empire State because there was no next of kin and a proper beneficiary wasn't named."

"This sounds really awful, but I take it Lavettia Lawrence is no longer a suspect in Arnold's murder, huh?"

"Yep. Scratch that name off. Listen, once this debacle is over, what do you say we get together and go out again? Things have been so hectic, we've hardly had time together. If you don't want to eat out, we can always take in a sappy holiday movie."

"I'm game. Oh, one more thing. Did Marvin get the name of the cleaning woman?"

"I knew you'd ask. You're worse than a bloodhound. And I mean that in the nicest way. Wish I had a name to give you, but I don't. It wasn't information that was shared with my boss. Listen, whoever committed these murders is dangerous. I don't need to be telling you that. Let the Seneca and Yates County sheriffs do their business. I'll see you for the reading of the will. Come hell or high water."

"Sure you don't mean rain or snow?"

"Yeah, that too."

When the call ended, my stomach felt as if a lead sinker had landed on it and had no intention of leaving. I felt awful. Way beyond anything physical. I hadn't taken Lavettia's call seriously and now she was dead. I looked at the clock on the microwave—9:14 a.m. Too early for Cammy to be in the tasting room, but not too early for Theo and Don to be at the Grey Egret.

My finger tapped out their number in record time, and I began to babble the second Theo answered. "Lavettia Lawrence is dead. Probably murdered in her condo. Bradley called."

"Whoa! What? Slow down and try to be coherent."

"This is as coherent as I can get, Theo. I poo-pooed a person who told me she was in danger of being killed and then she was killed. I should have believed her."

"Even if you believed her, there was nothing you could've done. You said she called the sheriff's department about that road incident. What more could've been done? Slow down and tell me what Bradley told you."

I took a breath and reiterated what little I'd gleaned from my brief conversation with Bradley Jamison. "Whoever murdered Lavettia had to believe she was going to inherit Lake-to-Lake Wine Distributors and everything that went along with it. Most likely we're looking at the second or third person on the totem pole. What do you think? Miller or Clayton? Somehow, I can't bring myself to name those nuns, but they're players, too."

"No kidding. Look, I don't know much about Clayton, but Miller's sure been acting like the Big Kahuna."

"What do you mean?"

"Don had to run a few errands in Penn Yan and stopped by the liquor store to see if our wines were moving. Curiosity, really. Anyway, the owner told him Miller had been in not too long before and said there'd be some changes when the business officially became his."

"Really? Does Deputy Hickman know about this?"

"Don made it a point to relay that information."

"And?"

"And nothing. Deputy Hickman spouted off about people putting horses before carts and told Don the sheriff's department had a good handle on the investigation. I imagine he was referring to Miller."

"Hmm, I have two possible leads to follow and neither is going to be easy. I need to find out who Lavettia's cleaning lady is, and I'm dying to learn how the Sisters of the Holy Sepulcher were able to pay an architectural firm to draw up the blueprints for their new residence and school."

"Architectural firm? What did I miss?"

"Yikes—the boxelders or were they stinkbugs?"

"Huh?"

It took me five minutes to relay everything that happened during my "field trip" with Godfrey and Alex.

"I think I have a way to get what I need from AMA. That's Aiden McGovern Architects in Syracuse. When Penn Yan had that school building project years ago, they got bids from three different firms. It was a major big deal with lots of community meetings. Each firm gave a presentation that included a rough sketch proposal of what they had in mind. Ultimately, the school board selected the company they wanted and entered into a contract."

"Please don't tell me you're going to—"

"Call and tell them we're considering a substantial building project for our winery and find out what it entails to have architectural plans drawn up. Somehow I'll reference the Convent of the Holy Sepulcher and see if I can wheedle an answer from them about how those nuns were able to fund their detailed designs."

"Hold up a second, will you. Just because an architectural firm did business with a school or a convent doesn't mean they're familiar with wineries. Those companies stick to their specialties. You've got commercial, industrial, and institutional. AMA might not have any idea about building or renovating a winery. Maybe focusing on your second lead might be the better choice—the cleaning woman. If that doesn't pan out, then circle back."

"Circle back? You must be watching too many westerns."

"I'll ignore that. You said Lavettia had a condo. Maybe her association would know. Or at the very least, a neighbor."

"That place is probably sealed as tight as Fort Knox by now, but you've given me an idea. Lavettia was a rep for The Essential Life Company, and I know exactly who to ask. Thanks, Theo. I couldn't've done this without you. I've got to hurry. I'll be in touch."

"Be careful, Norrie. And if you do decide to call those architects, call Don or me first. And whatever you do, don't sign anything. Okay?"

"Yeesh. It's like having two big brothers. You have nothing to worry about."

"Like hell."

I laughed when the call ended and then glanced at the microwave clock. Our tasting room was opening for business in less than thirty minutes, and I was positive the person I needed to see, absolutely *had* to see, would be making her entrance. I rinsed my knife and plate in the sink, put them in the dish drainer, and raced upstairs to dab on some eyeliner and fix my hair.

In keeping with the holiday spirit, I put on a Two Witches festive sweatshirt, grabbed my all-weather jacket, and raced out the door. The damp winter air, coupled with a light snow, made my trek down to the tasting room miserable. Still, it wasn't worth starting up the Toyota to go a few yards.

A handful of cars was already in the parking lot when I got there and that didn't include the ones that belonged to our staff. Good. The tasters and shoppers were out and about early. I all but knocked into Lizzie when I raced inside the building.

"Norrie! You look as if you're running from the mob!"

Instinctively, I spun my head around. "What? No. Sorry, Lizzie. No time to talk. Have you seen Glenda? Is she here yet?"

Lizzie pointed to the kitchen. "She's in there with Cammy. They're setting up a few more tasting tables and went to get pitchers of water. Sure everything's okay?"

I shrugged. "Sort of. I'll explain later."

I must've taken Cammy and Glenda by surprise, because the minute I flung the door open it hit the side wall and they both jumped.

"Talk about entrances," Cammy said. "Good morning, Norrie."

"Hi! I'd like to talk but I don't have time. This is really important." I walked over to the sink where Glenda was filling up the water pitchers. "Glenda, can you call your friend Zenora from The Essential Life Company and ask her if she knows who Lavettia's cleaning woman is? Now. I need you to find out right away."

Cammy gave me a sideways glance and grimaced. "What happened? Did you decide to make a home-cooked meal and trash the kitchen?"

Before I could answer, Glenda turned off the water and put the pitcher on the counter. "Um, wouldn't it make more sense for you to call Lavettia and ask her?"

I bit my lip and grimaced. "I would, except Lavettia's dead—shot in the back of the neck like her boyfriend. The cleaning woman found her this morning, and I need to find the cleaning woman. Lavettia called me Tuesday night convinced someone had tried to kill her. And now they have. So, I need you to call Zenora right away. Those women must've talked about something other than essential oils."

Glenda looked at Cammy then me. "What do I tell Zenora? Do I act as if nothing's happened, or can I tell her another soul is about to enter the spirit world?"

"Good point." Cammy eyeballed me. "And how exactly do you know all of this?"

I gave them the abbreviated version of Bradley's phone call and went on to explain I felt guilty as all get-out because I didn't take Lavettia seriously.

Glenda made an unsettling hum and clasped her palms together, placing them under her chin. "This could be bad for you, Norrie. You do realize Lavettia's restless spirit could fixate on you. You might have been one of the last people she spoke with."

"You're scaring the crap out of her!" Cammy shouted.

"I'm fine, ladies. Really, I am. I just need to find out who that cleaning woman is. Glenda, we can talk about spirits and cleansings and all sorts of ephemeral stuff after I get a name and a phone number. So, please—go call Zenora."

Glenda walked to the door. "I have her on speed dial. Give me a few minutes. My bag is under my tasting room table."

She thundered out of the room, her purplish-green hair flying all over her face. If I wasn't so freaked out about Lavettia's death, I would've said something about Glenda's latest color choice.

"Lavettia was wearing a sweater. Not a nightgown, not pajamas. A sweater. She must have been stone-cold dead when her cleaning lady arrived."

Cammy crossed her arms over her chest. "So, how is finding her cleaning lady going to help you?"

"Lavettia might not have been able to speak, but maybe her condo did."

"Holy Heck, Norrie, you sound worse than Glenda!"

Chapter 18

"Hold on, hold on, and think about it. The cleaning woman might've noticed something those sheriff's deputies ignored. That's why I must speak with her. I can't have Lavettia's murder hanging over my head. And it's not because of all that mumbo-jumbo with the spirit world, it's because my own conscience won't stop plaguing me. I'll always wonder what would've happened had I done something differently when she called me."

"You've got to stop beating yourself up," Cammy said. "You aren't the responsible party."

"No, the responsible party may be gunning for someone else we know."

Just then, Glenda raced back into the kitchen, out of breath and holding her palm over her heart, as if she was about to recite the Pledge of Allegiance. "Lavettia doesn't have a cleaning lady."

"What?" I felt as if the wind had been knocked out of me.

"Zenora and Lavettia got pretty chummy from attending so many essential oil conferences and workshops together. Zenora said Lavettia never would have paid anyone to do the housecleaning. She didn't want 'other people's hands' all over her things, especially her personal and private possessions."

"Then who the hell tipped off the sheriff's department?" I asked. "Bradley insisted a cleaning lady called the authorities when she let herself in and discovered Lavettia's lifeless body. In fact, they took a statement from her."

"Maybe Lavettia changed her mind and hired someone," Cammy said to Glenda.

"Not according to Zenora. Lavettia was convinced that if anyone touched her things or moved them, the positive energy she had built around those objects would be compromised."

Cammy let out a sigh. "Oh brother. What a bunch of malarkey."

"That's precisely why smudging and aura cleansing are so important," Glenda replied. "Too bad I never counseled Lavettia."

"Well, cleaning lady or no cleaning lady, *someone* opened that darn door and made the grim discovery. Then they opened the door a second time for the sheriff's deputies. I've got to call Bradley back and let him know what I learned. Thanks, Glenda, and please, keep this to yourself until there's an official statement."

Cammy glanced at her wristwatch. "I'd give it another hour and a half. It'll be on the noon news. Trust me. Unless some local councilman had an affair with the governor's wife or something equally scandalous, it'll be on the noon news. I'm not telling you what to do, Norrie, but if I were you, I'd wait for the news first and then make that call. Maybe those reporters will beat you to it as far as the cleaning lady is concerned."

"Aargh. You're probably right, but I'll be chewing my fingernails for the next ninety minutes. Oh, and will someone please tell Lizzie and the rest of the crew what's going on? I really should hightail it back home and get some work done. I'll stop back later whether I find out anything or not."

By twelve twenty-three on the nose, the entire Finger Lakes Region and most likely the Southern Tier and Western Corridor of the state were all privy to the shocking news about one of The Essential Life Company's most valued employees, Lavettia Lawrence from the Waterloo-Seneca Falls area. Who knew essential oils were such a hot commodity?

Not only did the newscasters expound on Lavettia's recent demise, but they reran their original story about Arnold Mowen's murder, showing footage of our winery and the Grey Egret. Just what we needed. In addition, they flashed photos across the screen showing Lavettia arm-in-arm with Arnold Mowen. One reporter even speculated the two deaths might somehow be linked. *Way ahead of you on that one, people.*

Unfortunately, there was no mention of a cleaning lady, so I felt completely within my bounds to have another conversation with Bradley. In fact, he didn't seem all that surprised to hear from me so soon.

"Norrie! Hi! I imagine you caught the news. That was fast. Must be Lavettia didn't have any next of kin or they wouldn't have released the information to the public so quickly."

"Um, not all the information. I found out Lavettia doesn't have a cleaning lady. So that begs the question, who made the call and let the sheriff's deputies into her condo?"

The line went quiet for a moment until Bradley found his voice. "Are you sure? Marvin distinctly told me it was a cleaning woman and he got that straight from the lead deputy."

"Then can he get the name? They questioned her, didn't they?"

"Give me some time. I'll get back to you. Marvin's in a meeting right now and I can't interrupt, but I promise, I'll call you one way or the other. If what you're saying has any validity, then the sheriff's department might be one step closer to solving Lavettia's murder."

There was no word from Bradley by three when I went down to the tasting room bistro to grab an extremely late lunch.

"This is so frustrating," I whined to Cammy. "Deputy Hickman refuses to keep us apprised of the investigation's progress, even though Arnold's body was found on our property. Well, ours and the Grey Egret's. And now, as if that isn't bad enough, Lavettia gets murdered and the Seneca County Deputy Sheriffs are equally close-lipped."

"I think they have to be, to conduct a thorough investigation. They have to play by the rules. You don't."

"Meaning?"

"If this was your screenplay, what would you write next?"

I thought about it for a second and remembered something. Clayton LeVine had an entire Pinterest board devoted to his passion—disguises with wigs. I'd pushed that information to the back of my mind, but it was beginning to make sense. If I was writing that kind of screenplay, it wouldn't be implausible for Clayton to be second in line for Arnold's throne. He simply needed to knock off the person who was first in line in order to inherit.

"I know I'm going to kick myself in the rump for doing this, but I need to pay Clayton a little visit. Whatever you do, don't tell Theo or Don if they call and ask for me."

"Arnold's secretary, right?"

"And quite possibly his and Lavettia's killer."

The look of shock registered immediately on Cammy's face and I didn't give her a chance to respond. "Don't worry. It's not as if I'm meeting him in some dark alley. I'll drop by Lake-to-Lake Wine Distributors to see if they've had any updates about all those thefts and sabotages. While I'm at it, I'll see if I can't get a sense of whether Clayton is our guy."

"Boy, if that isn't a well-thought out plan, I don't know what is. You'd better be careful. If he is the murderer, he could snap, you know. Wait! Hold on!"

Cammy rushed out of the room and was back in a few seconds. She handed me a small aerosol can. "It's anti-wasp lemongrass spray—handheld size. I keep it with me because there are some nests near my garage. If that man makes a move toward you, aim for his eyes. Got it?"

"Um, yeah, sure, but I don't think it will come to that."

I wasn't about to sit around and wait for Marvin Souza to come out of his meeting—or whatever else he was doing that prevented him from conferring with Bradley. If I hurried, I could be at Lake-to-Lake Wine Distributors before they closed at five. It was only twenty minutes to four and since it was a clear day, the drive would be a half hour at most.

The complex consisted of a retail office and storage, and was located on the north end of Seneca Lake by the intersection of Routes 5 & 20 and Route 96A. I'd passed by the place numerous times when my family went out to eat in Auburn, but I never gave it much thought. Now, I wondered exactly what I'd say to Clayton LeVine when I made my impromptu visit.

There was only one car in the parking lot, and it had to belong to Clayton. It was an older white Mazda3 in dire need of a wash. A haze of brownish dirt covered the vehicle, making it appear ancient. If there were dings and nicks, the dirt hid them.

It was five fifteen on the nose when I opened the door to the office and stepped inside. I'd only seen one photo of Clayton, and that was on his Pinterest board. At least I thought the snapshot was of Clayton, wearing a green wig that resembled a dragonfly head. The man seated at the front desk had a horrible brown comb-over and the chubbiest cheeks I'd ever seen. On a cherub they'd be adorable, but for someone in his late thirties or early forties, it had the opposite effect.

"Hi." I extended my hand across the desk and accidently moved his computer monitor. "Er, sorry about that." I immediately straightened the monitor, but not before tilting it my way to sneak a peek at the screen—the official Mazda website. "I'm Norrie Ellington, co-owner of Two Witches Winery in Penn Yan. I was on my way back from shopping in Auburn when I realized how close I was to your office. Sorry it's so late. I really should've called first, but I'll only keep you for a few minutes."

Clayton leaned forward as if he was about to push himself up from his seat. "Have the plans changed for the midnight reading of Arnold's will at your winery? No one told me."

"What? No. The plans haven't changed."

"Oh. Forgive me. How rude of me. How totally unacceptable. Please pull up a chair. It's nice to meet you, Miss Ellington. I'm familiar with your winery on paper, but it's our reps who really get to know the clients. Let me say this is indeed an unexpected pleasure."

Unexpected yes, but pleasure? My ass!

I forced a smile and sat down while Clayton continued to talk.

"I imagine you're here because of the current instability in management. Please let me assure you Mr. Mowen's business plan ensured a clear transition to whomever is named his successor."

Clayton was short and squat and, with the appropriate wig, makeup, and attire, he could've easily passed for a nondescript cleaning woman. I tried to picture him feigning the role of a hysterical housekeeper who'd made a grim discovery. That part was quite possible. In fact, the whole scenario was feasible. Perhaps Clayton knocked on Lavettia's door and she, immediately recognizing his voice, let him in.

The fact that the kitchen table was empty, according to Bradley, didn't mean anything. For all we knew, Lavettia could've served him a four-course meal, and he could've cleaned up after he did away with her. I was so engrossed in visualizing the scene, I didn't hear Clayton's question.

"Miss Ellington?"

"Huh?"

"I asked, was that your reason for the visit?"

Suddenly, I was yanked back to reality, and I thought fast. "Partially. I'm more concerned about the widespread thefts and sabotage of this year's Pinot Noir. I'd be remiss if I didn't mention the shock I felt when the afternoon news reported Lavettia Lawrence's murder."

"Her murder? When?" The words caught in his throat. Either he was Academy Awards material, or he really didn't have a clue. "How? I've been cooped up here all day. Didn't even take a break for lunch. Brought my own salad and fruit bars. Did this happen at your winery, too?"

Yeesh. Our reputation for murders is going to supersede the one we have for wine. "Uh, no. Her condo. I probably shouldn't have used the word 'murder.' It was on the noon news. They referred to it as a 'suspicious death.' Her cleaning lady discovered the body early in the day."

Clayton remained poker-faced, but I noticed he kept folding and unfolding his hands. I decided to use a bit of old dialogue from one of my screenplays and tweak it a bit.

"All I can say is, thank goodness for DNA evidence. Her killer might've thought he scoured the place, but I wager the one spot he missed was under the chairs. People sometimes press their fingers underneath their chairs when they sit or stand. Someone's bound to figure it out. Did you know her well?"

By now, Clayton had stopped the hand folding and instead, rubbed his hands together. The sound was audible. "Not that well. She was a real presence, though. Hard to miss. Other than that figure of hers, I always wondered what Arnold saw in her."

"Probably enough to name her the beneficiary of his will."

"I doubt it. She was eye candy for him. He would've named someone who had a deeper and more meaningful relationship with him."

"Business or personal?"

"It was all business with Arnold. Now, the rest of us will have to wait until Saturday to see how it all pans out. If you don't mind, Miss Ellington, I really do need to finish up and be on my way. Oh, you asked about those thefts...the Pinot Noir...Listen, three county sheriff departments are dealing with it, not to mention the state police. I'm sure they're conducting a thorough investigation and they will apprehend the culprits."

"Let's hope so. It's the wineries who'll suffer. Your company and the restaurants will come out unscathed."

"Not if we lose your business. We're all in this together. By the way, did that news report say anything else about Lavettia Lawrence?"

"Like what?"

"Never mind. It doesn't matter."

I think the little tidbit I'd contrived about the DNA evidence might've hit a nerve with Clayton. Quite possibly he was the killer. Lavettia didn't have kind words to say about him, but I wasn't sure she had kind words to say about anyone. If it was Clayton who knocked off Lavettia so he'd be next in line for the moolah, especially if he was in the market for a new Mazda, then my guess was he'd head over to her condo to wipe his prints off the undersides of the chairs.

If he shot her, the assumption that he'd at least rummage through her bag to take the house key in case he had to make a return visit was a no-brainer. Or...perhaps he'd plant the key on someone else. I was tempted to tail him to Lavettia's condo, but I didn't. Cammy's lemongrass wasp spray wasn't much of a defense against, say, a loaded .22 caliber gun.

Nope. I did the sensible thing once I made my exit from Lake-to-Lake Wine Distributors. I called the Seneca County Sheriff's Department from the nearest convenience store parking lot and insisted the deputy send a car to Lavettia's address to see if Clayton was there.

"You said your name is Norrie Ellington?" the deputy at the other end asked.

"That's right. From Two Witches Winery in Penn Yan."

"Will you hold the line for a moment, please?"

"You need to hurry," I said. "A killer could literally be getting away with murder."

"Please hold the line."

I had parked off to the side of the building where I wouldn't be readily noticed.

"Miss Ellington?"

"Yes?"

"Thank you for your concern. We will take this under advisement."

"That's it? Advisement? It's not like you're reviewing a proposal or something. Clayton LeVine had motive, means, and opportunity to kill Lavettia Lawrence."

"Before we send deputies to a scene, the evidence would need to be stronger than someone's hunch."

Oh my God! I've heard those words before. Those exact words, and they came out of Deputy Hickman's mouth last month. "Deputy Hickman from the Yates County Sheriff's Department spoke with you, didn't he?"

"I'm not at liberty to discuss our internal and/or external communications."

"Fine. All I can say is you missed an opportunity to catch a killer." Fuming, I ended the call before he could utter another word. When I got home, I was more than exasperated. The red light was blinking on the landline, and the thought of returning a call annoyed me even more. I decided it could wait and made myself and the dog a bite to eat.

An hour or so later, after I calmed down, I played the message.

"Hey, Norrie! You're probably not up for this, but on the off–chance you might be, I'm going back to the convent tomorrow morning to check on the eradication progress. Just me. Alex drew the short straw and will be studying the travel patterns of those roaches in Ithaca. I wasn't sure if you still needed to snoop around. Give me a call."

I wasn't quite sure what I'd discover at the convent if I took Godfrey up on his offer. I'd gotten what I needed from Sister Gloria Mae, and I seriously doubted she'd tell me how they paid for those comprehensive blueprints. Still, I wouldn't get another opportunity like the one that was right under my nose.

Lavettia had told me she thought Clayton was holding something over Arnold's head. Not quite blackmail, but close enough. What if the Sisters of the Holy Sepulcher had something on him as well? Something so damaging he'd been forced to make a deal with them?

"I'll go," I practically shouted into the phone when I returned Godfrey's call.

"Terrific. Since it's only me, I can pick you up if you'd like. No sense leaving your car in our parking lot all day."

"Okay. Sure. What time?"

"How about eight?"

"I'll be ready."

"Dress warm. That place is worse than a tomb. By the way, I saw the news over the internet about Arnold Mowen's girlfriend. Horrible, huh?"

For the next five minutes, Godfrey was forced to listen to my theory about Clayton, my suspicions about the nuns, and my impression of Miller Holtz.

The poor guy couldn't wait to get off the phone. "I've read epic novels that had less intrigue."

When I hung up, I was buzzing with energy. It was only seven thirty-nine. Plenty of time to bring Theo and Don into the loop. By now, I assumed they had eaten dinner and were hanging out.

"Don! Theo! Whoever this is at the other end, I'm pretty sure Clayton LeVine is the cleaning lady and the killer. That draconian sheriff's office in Seneca Falls refused to believe me and missed the chance to nail him."

"I think I missed the first act," Don said. "Start from the beginning, will you?"

I took a deep breath, complete with a few moans, and told him about Glenda's conversation with Zenora, which led to my revelation about Clayton and my subsequent drive over to Lake-to-Lake Wine Distributors.

"I've got to hand it to you," Don said, "you'll stop at nothing."

"Bradley Jamison told me the same thing, in a roundabout way. So...do you think I'm right about Clayton? Could he be our guy? He was practically drooling over the new Mazdas on his computer screen when I walked in to Arnold's office unannounced this afternoon."

"I'm not so sure—"

"That's not all. According to his Pinterest board, he's a mastermind at disguises with wigs. He could've easily pretended to be the cleaning lady. I hinted about DNA evidence at Lavettia's and, all of a sudden, he was in a hurry to get out of work. What absolutely galls me is that I practically handed the killer to Seneca County on a platter, and they refused to stake out Lavettia's condo and catch him in the act."

"I think that's because—"

"Ugh. I know. All those sheriff departments are the same. If they don't have iron-clad evidence in front of them, they don't make a move. As far as I'm concerned, no one understands the ins and outs of that business better than the secretary. He runs everything behind the scenes. Clayton could've gotten tired of working for Arnold or maybe he was just plain greedy. With Lavettia out of the way, it was probably a shoo-in for him to become the next owner."

"We've still got Miller Holtz to think about."

"Miller Holtz doesn't monkey around with wigs and disguises. Aargh. This is so frustrating."

"What about those nuns? Maybe one of them got a little too overly zealous."

"I'm suspicious about where they got the money to pay for all that architectural planning, but the two nuns I spoke with couldn't even bring themselves to kill stinkbugs."

"What about the third nun? You said it was a Triumvirate that ran the place."

"Oh yeah. Sister Celeste. I didn't actually speak with her, but now that you mention it, I could picture her wielding an axe or blowing off a shotgun. You should've seen her in that kitchen. She was terrifying. Still, I don't think she's Arnold's killer. Or Lavettia's, for that matter. No means or opportunity, even if she had the same motive everyone else did—money."

Chapter 19

"I know how frustrating that must be," Godfrey said, "about the sheriff's department refusing to send someone to Lavettia's place. I once had a department head who adamantly refused to consider a joint venture with Texas A&M's entomology department. The end result teamed them up with UC Davis. Together, they produced a groundbreaking study on the Tatuidris, better known as the Armadillo ant. You know, Jason and Francine might come across some of them in Costa Rica, although they are quite rare."

We were in his car headed over to the Holy Sepulcher Convent and, for some reason, I couldn't stop complaining about yesterday's disaster.

"They had nothing to lose," I moaned. "Absolutely nothing. And they might've caught Clayton in the act of tampering with evidence. Or, in his case, removing it entirely."

Godfrey glanced my way and then quickly turned his attention back to the road. At least it wasn't raining or snowing, but it was windy and overcast. That meant things could change without much warning. "If Clayton is the killer, he'll slip one way or another. So, tell me, what exactly are you hoping to uncover today? Those nuns aren't the most gregarious."

"Sister Gloria implied that one of the Triumvirate had a not-so-pristine past life that involved Arnold Mowen. I need to find out more. Maybe that Sister was blackmailing him—and that's how the convent got its money for the architects."

"I don't know, Norrie. I'm not so sure Sister Gloria is going to be willing to tell-all. And as far as approaching the other two—"

"I know. In a way, it's like that three-headed dog from the first Harry Potter book."

"Fluffy?"

"Was that his name?"

"Uh-huh. Hagrid's dog."

I gave Godfrey a sideways stare. Maybe we had more in common than I thought. "Sister Gloria is certainly the most approachable of the three, but is she the most reliable? I got the feeling she and Sister Celeste weren't exactly chummy."

"I think that's the nature of the profession," he said. "Do you want to stop for coffee or anything? We're almost there."

"No, I'm okay."

"This shouldn't take all day. Not like last time. A few hours at most. Then we can get something to eat."

"Sounds good. I'll probably be ravenous by then."

The traffic was light, and we made it to Lodi without any delays. The convent's long driveway, shrouded by barren trees, gave the place an ominous look. The dreary, overcast day didn't help much. We were partially down the drive when we noticed a Seneca County Sheriff's car in front of the residence.

Godfrey was the first to comment. "This can't be good."

"I don't see any emergency vehicles or yellow tape. Maybe it's a routine thing. A safety check or something."

"Doubtful, but let's give the door a knock."

Three taps on the brass doorknocker and nothing.

"They *do* know we're coming, don't they?" I asked.

"Of course. I even confirmed it with Sister Mary Katherine a few minutes before I left to pick you up."

"Try again. Maybe they're all in the kitchen, too terrified to escape from Sister Celeste."

Godfrey laughed and gave the door another knock. Then four raps. We waited a few more seconds and he tried again. Finally, a young nun, who I hadn't noticed before, opened the door.

"Please come in. Sister Mary Katherine said you'd be arriving this morning but she's in the garage with two deputy sheriffs. Sister Gloria is there, too."

"Is anything wrong?" Godfrey asked as we stepped inside.

The nun pressed her lips together and swallowed. "I'm not sure. Something about our delivery van. For the cheesecake deliveries. You know."

Suddenly the words I had been thinking flew out of my mouth nonstop. "Is it missing? Stolen? Wrecked?"

The nun shook her head. "Our van is here. Today's not a delivery day. But we do have deliveries lined up for tomorrow morning. Since tomorrow's Saturday, lots of restaurants want cheesecakes on hand for Sunday. I wish I could tell you more about the van, but I don't know."

"That's all right," Godfrey said. "It's really none of our business unless, of course, unwanted, overwintering pests are inhabiting the interior. Anyway, I'm sure Sister Celeste will shed some light on the subject when we see her."

The nun shook her head vehemently. "She's not in the kitchen. She's not well. A dreadful headache. She's been incapacitated since Wednesday night. It must be a really terrible migraine because she won't allow anyone in her room and insists we leave her food trays at the door."

"That's horrible," I said. "Does she suffer from them often?"

The nun gave a nod. "From time to time, but never this bad. It must be the change in barometric pressure or something."

Godfrey and I walked through the foyer and into the kitchen, where four or five nuns were working.

"I'll try not to disturb you," he said, "but I need to open cabinets and drawers to check our progress with the Boisea trivittata. I'll try to be inconspicuous. I'll have Miss Ellington head over to your garage to inform Sisters Mary Katherine and Gloria."

"That would be fine," one of the nuns said, but I couldn't tell which one. Godfrey motioned for me to step into the small pantry area, where he was shining a light on one of the shelves.

"Now's your chance," he whispered. "That sheriff's deputy didn't stop over to check their tire pressure. Good luck."

"Thanks. You, too."

I walked out of the kitchen and exited by the front door. The large Morton garage was equidistant from the residence and the chapel. At least a quarter of a mile. I wondered why the sheriff's deputies decided to hoof it rather than take their car the rest of the way. It actually felt warmer outside than in the convent's kitchen—and that was with the ovens on, too.

It was too short a distance for me to rehearse a decent scenario that would necessitate my reason for the visit. I'd have to wing it. I took a few steps and got the uncanny feeling that I was being followed. I turned my head but nothing—no one in sight. Probably my imagination. I picked up the pace and kept moving. There *was* someone behind me, and they were gaining ground. I was half-walking, half-running at this point, and my legs felt as if they were going to give out. *Damn it! I really need a better exercise routine. I'm not even thirty and I'm getting winded.*

Out of nowhere, I felt a shooting pain that ran from my hip to my ankle. *This really stinks!* I forced myself to keep moving. The garage was only yards away, and all I needed was one last burst of speed to make it. I spotted a small toe-path off to my right that would shave off some of the distance. I veered toward it but knew the moment I reached the uneven flagstone that I'd made a mistake—too easy to jam a foot into a crevice and stumble. I tried not to dwell on it and kept moving. Whoever was behind me was either one hell of an athlete or in incredible shape. In a flash, they latched on to my shoulder blades from behind and pressed them so hard I winced and doubled over from the pain. Then, if that wasn't enough, they gave me a good shove. I fell face down on the grass a few inches from the toe-path. My head grazed something hard, a rock maybe, and a small trickle of blood made its way from my forehead to my cheek.

Unlike my screenplays, where the heroine leaps from the ground to encounter her assailant, I pitched forward and when I stood my eyes filled with moisture. It was impossible to focus. Not that it mattered. Whoever pushed me was long gone.

I reached into my pocket and pulled out a crumpled napkin that was left over from a donut I had eaten the day before. I meant to toss the napkin yesterday, but was glad I hadn't. My forehead had only suffered a slight graze, but there was blood on the napkin. I took a few minutes and wiped the sticky residue from my face. Then, I steadied myself and continued my walk to the garage.

Either one of those nuns was totally off her rocker, or someone else didn't want me snooping around. It didn't matter. In fact, whoever shoved me gave me more reason to do exactly what I was doing—sleuthing.

When I approached the garage, a second sheriff's vehicle was parked in front. If I ever I needed to inhale an antacid, it was at that moment. The print and logo were unmistakable—Yates County Sheriff's Department. Apparently, the two counties were collaborating on whatever they thought happened at the Sisters of the Holy Sepulcher. I brushed my loose bangs over the scrape on my forehead, making sure I wiped clean all dirt and residue, and walked inside the garage as if I was an invited guest.

I should have snapped a photo of Deputy Hickman's face when he saw me. It would've boosted the LIKE status on my website to new heights. He was standing next to two other sheriff's deputies, who, I presumed, were from Seneca County. Across from him were Sister Mary Katherine and Sister Gloria. The only thing separating them was the hood of a white cargo van with a dented Chevy logo.

Sister Gloria gave me a quick wink and I smiled.

"I'm here with entomologist Godfrey Klein from Cornell's Experiment Station. All of us in the wineries are concerned about overwintering pests that inhabit our residences and wineries. I was invited to watch the eradication process."

"Nothing is being eradicated in this garage," Deputy Hickman said. "We're here on another matter."

"I, um, er..."

Sister Gloria must have sensed I was at a loss for words and broke in with an over-the-top act that was almost comical, had it not been for the audience.

"Our van! Our cheesecake delivery van might have been used for those terrible hijackings and robberies all over Seneca Lake. Dear Lord above, we're a peaceful order, not a bunch of criminals."

Then, if that wasn't enough, she began to sob. Really sob. Sister Mary Katherine turned to the three sheriff's deputies and shook her head. "There. See what you've done. You've tormented a kind and gentle soul."

As she stepped closer to the deputies, Sister Gloria turned to me and mouthed, "Pretty good, huh?"

I tried not to laugh.

Seemingly oblivious to the charade, Deputy Hickman continued his conversation with me. "If I find out, Miss Ellington, that you're here on any circumstance that doesn't involve insects, I will issue you a citation for interfering in an investigation."

"Which one? Mr. Mowen's death, Miss Lawrence's death, or—"

"You know very well what I'm talking about. The winery sabotage and the related wine thefts, including the recent smash and grabs in Yates and Seneca Counties. The homicide investigations are another matter entirely, and I can assure you, we'll be making an arrest soon."

"I don't suppose—"

"Don't even ask."

"Oh my gosh! Am I looking at the robbery vehicle? Is Sister Gloria right?" *Yep, I can go for the dramatic, too.*

At that point, one of the Seneca County deputies stepped forward and shook his head. "Deputy Holm, and before anyone jumps to conclusions, we were sent to this address as part of a routine check. Since the winery thefts involved two counties, we notified our counterpart."

"It seems," Deputy Hickman said, "a van matching the description of the one sighted in the first hijacking was observed making a delivery to the Tri-Lake Diner in Seneca Falls yesterday. We were able to obtain the license and track the van down to this convent."

Sister Mary Katherine rested her hand on the hood and gave it a tap. "Our van couldn't possibly be the one in question. You can check our delivery logs if you'd like. You'll find we were nowhere near where those awful things took place."

"How can you be so sure?" Deputy Holm asked. "According to what you told us before, your deliverymen make stops all over Seneca Lake."

"Not on the west side. Our businesses are at the tip of the lake, in Waterloo, Geneva, Seneca Falls..."

"We'd like to have a good look at that log, Sister, if you don't mind," the deputy continued. "Since we don't have a warrant to remove it, we'd ask if you would be so kind as to make us a copy."

"I'll do it," Sister Gloria offered. "The log's in the glove compartment. I review it monthly, not weekly. I'll head back to the office and make the copy."

She opened the passenger door and reached inside. "Here. See for yourself. It's a detailed list of all the stops made each day. It's a template I made with time, date, location, and items delivered." With that, she scurried out of the garage before the deputies had a chance to press her further.

"We'll pick it up at the residence," Deputy Holm shouted. "No need for you to walk back."

Then he turned to Sister Mary Katherine. "We'll need the names, addresses, and phone numbers of your delivery personnel. For questioning."

Sister Katherine gasped. "That's unthinkable. I already opened the van for you and there was no evidence of anything belonging to a winery. No wine bottles, nothing. I didn't have to do that, you know. I could have insisted on a search warrant."

The third deputy, who had been quiet up to that point, finally spoke. "Believe me, Sister, we appreciate it. At this juncture, we're merely following up on all leads. To make things easier, I can leave you my card and you can email me the personnel information."

Sister Mary Katherine sighed. More like a sigh of annoyance than anything else. "As long as you're stopping by the residence for the delivery log, you might as well wait, and I'll secure that information for you."

Suddenly, she turned and looked at me. "Miss Ellington, forgive me for not addressing you. Was there a reason you walked to the garage?"

"I came to notify you that entomologist Godfrey Klein is on the premises checking the eradication process. I'm on my way back there, now."

"Five people can fit comfortably in the sheriff's van," Deputy Hickman said. "You can ride back with us."

Talk about a long five minutes. No one said a word until we all exited the vehicle in front of the Tudor structure. When we got to the front steps, Sister Mary Katherine uttered three words to the deputies, "Follow me, please." I tagged along, but only until I reached the foyer. Then I muttered something about having to confer with Godfrey and took off toward the kitchen. Meanwhile, Sister Mary Katherine ushered the deputies into her tight little office.

A few seconds later, before I reached the kitchen, Sister Gloria appeared with a photocopy of the delivery log. "I had just gotten in the door when all of you walked in. I should've waited for a ride. Did they go into Sister Mary Katherine's office?"

"Yes. But can you hold on for a minute? I need to ask you something."

"Better be quick or they're likely to send the cavalry."

I chuckled and made it as quick as I could. I told Sister Gloria about my encounter with an assailant and asked if she had any idea who might have a reason for not wanting me to snoop around.

"I'm clueless. Totally clueless. No one even knew you were coming."

"I was on my way to the garage. Why try to stop me when three sheriff deputies were there already?"

"Maybe whoever it was thinks you know too much."

Chapter 20

The look on Sister Gloria's face told me she was serious.

"How could I possibly know too much," I asked, "when I don't know anything? I've got a ton of hunches but nothing viable and certainly nothing that could be substantiated by evidence."

Sister Gloria shrugged. "Are we talking about our conversation from the other day? You know, I can't divulge anything about the Sisters when it comes to who they were before they took their vows. But I can tell you that not everything is as it seems."

"What's that supposed to mean?"

"If you're really intent on finding out who killed your wine distributor, you'll have to look much deeper than the surface."

Oh brother. I think the Cheshire Cat was more helpful than that.

"And, by the way," she continued, "were those blueprints any help?"

"In a way. Someone had a great deal of foresight to commission a project of that scope and size without any indication there would be monies to oversee it."

"Ah hah! That's what I mean about looking further. Every move around here is calculated and that includes the expansion."

I took a step closer and kept my voice low. "Am I hearing you right? Because if I am, you're implicating the Sisters of the Holy Sepulcher in Arnold Mowen's death. Get him out of the way and the money will come rolling in."

"That's not what I meant, but I agree, it does look bad. When I said, 'every move,' I was referring to nurturing the contacts we've established over the years. You know, wealthy patrons and families who either attended our school or whose children did. Certainly not some diabolical murder scheme. Lord, save us!"

"Um, speaking of murder, were you aware Arnold Mowen's girlfriend, Lavettia Lawrence, was found dead in her condo yesterday morning? Shot in the neck, same as her boss."

Sister Gloria crossed herself and took a breath. "Rest her soul. I'm sorry. I really must go."

Then, without warning, she pressed a folded piece of paper into my hand and whispered, "I made a copy for you as well."

I unfolded the paper and when I looked up, she had gone into Sister Mary Katherine's office. I looked at the paper again and pursed my lips. I was staring at the delivery log.

With Deputies Hickman, Holm, and the guy who didn't give his name, plus Sisters Mary Katherine and Gloria behind closed doors, I figured maybe I'd be better off seeing if I could glean anything from the conversations in the kitchen. With Sister Celeste out of the way, and out of commission for the time being, the kitchen was bound to be much cheerier.

Aromas of vanilla and cinnamon permeated the room the second I stepped inside. Cheesecakes in various stages of production were all over the place. At least a dozen of them were on cooling racks near a window, while others were waiting on the counter for their turn in the oven. Bowls with assorted mixtures took up every conceivable space.

Each of the five nuns seemed to have her own space and no one was talking. It was like watching one of those futuristic shows where the robots performed the household chores. In this case, however, there was nothing futuristic about anything. Except for one large blender, all cooking utensils were straight out of the 1950s. Wooden spoons, hand graters, even old baking tins.

"Hi! Remember me? I'm Norrie Ellington from the other day. I'm here with Godfrey Klein from the entomology department to see if you've made any progress removing those stinkbugs."

A slender olive-skinned nun, who couldn't have been much older than eighteen or nineteen, stepped forward. "I think we've weathered the storm. The combination of elbow grease and prayer has really helped."

"And whatever it was Dr. Klein used to coax those dreadful things out of their hiding spots," another nun added.

I wasn't used to hearing Godfrey referred to as Dr. Klein, but he did have a PhD in entomology, same as Jason. And like Jason, he didn't flaunt it.

146

J.C. Eaton

"I'm glad to hear that," I said. "Dr. Klein is checking the rest of the residence. I'm sure Sister Celeste will be pleased to know the kitchen is back to normal. I do hope she feels better soon."

The olive-skinned nun reached for a pot holder and walked toward one of the ovens. "Yes, that was surprising. Up until now, Sister Celeste's migraines have never been this bad and have never taken her by surprise, but I understand they can appear suddenly—without warning."

I nodded. "So, I imagine tomorrow's a big delivery day from the looks of the kitchen. I've never seen so many cheesecakes in one place."

"Saturday's a major delivery day for us," she said. "Well, the morning is, anyway. By eleven, the men should be finished with their route. Of course, they're here by five and on the road by five thirty."

"The same men who make all the deliveries?" I asked.

"Yes. We only have two deliverymen for local patrons, and the guys don't work every day. I think one of them works for another company when he's not handling our baked goods. Thankfully, we contract out for our New York City deliveries."

I tried not to sound overly exuberant, but this was the closest I was going to get to a lead. "Would you happen to know their names?"

The Sister took the browned cheesecake from the oven and put it on a cooling rack. "Only their first names—Rob and Derek."

Suddenly, one of the Sisters who was at the sink with her back to us, spoke. "I do. But I'm not sure which is which. I heard Sister Celeste speaking with them once and she used formal titles, Mr. Tapscott and Mr. Lungren."

"Um, thank you," I said. "It's really none of my business. I was just curious. Especially since sheriff's deputies from two counties are concerned the van might have been used for nefarious purposes."

I heard a thud and turned my head sideways to see one of the nuns grab a wooden rolling pin that had dropped from her grip onto the counter. It landed inches from the pile of graham crackers she was pulverizing.

"Weren't all of you aware of that?" I asked.

At that instant, the room came alive with a chorus of "No."

The nun who had let Godfrey and me in on our first day here gave a short cough. "We've been working in the kitchen since breakfast and early morning prayers. We had no idea. Sister Mary Katherine or Sister Gloria must have answered the door. Does this mean there won't be anyone to deliver our cheesecakes and tarts tomorrow? We were getting ready to begin the chocolate swirl variety."

I brushed a bit of hair out of my eyes. "I think your delivery will go as planned. My understanding is the official visit was more of a fact-finding one. Your van matches the description of the one that was used in those wine hijackings."

All movement in the room ceased and a few nuns crossed their chests. I stood there, not sure of what I was going to say next when Godfrey walked in. He had obviously overheard me.

"I'm sure nothing will come of that visit. There are scads of white delivery vans in this area. Anyway, the good news is we've managed to stave off the Boisea trivittata. But that doesn't mean you're out of the woods. You've got to be vigilant. At the first sign of them, vacuum the entire area and wipe it down with Clorox. Understood?"

The nuns nodded their heads in unison and Godfrey went on.

"I was unable to check Sister Celeste's room, but I don't think it's a concern. Again, let her know what I said. All right?"

Again, the nodding in unison. Godfrey took me by the arm and ushered me toward the door leading out to the foyer. "I'll have one last minute look-see and we'll let Sister Mary Katherine know we've completed our check of the premises," he said to the Sisters. "Should anything come up, please don't hesitant to contact the Experiment Station."

"You should've asked to sample the cheesecake," I muttered when we were clear of the kitchen. "It smelled heavenly. No pun intended."

"Maybe they'll send us one. I wanted us to hustle out of there and go back upstairs for a minute. Hurry up. A second sheriff's car is out front. Do you know what's going on?"

"Yeah. Did you take a close look? It's Deputy Hickman's. It was parked by the garage. Long story. They're all in Sister Mary Katherine's office."

"All?"

"Deputy Hickman, two deputies from Seneca County, Sister Mary Katherine, and Sister Gloria. What is it you want to show me upstairs?"

"Not show. Smell. Come on."

"Ew. Is this going to be one of those disgusting bug things?"

Godfrey shook his head and smiled. It was the first time I'd actually seen his smile up close and I had to admit, it was adorable. Perfect teeth and all. My God! What was getting into me? Here I was, dating a hunk-of-the-year and practically salivating over another guy's mouth. I needed to rein myself in.

"No, hurry up."

We raced up the stairs, all the while trying not to make much noise. When we reached the corridor, Godfrey tiptoed a few feet down and whispered, "What do you smell?"

Okay. So, I wasn't losing my mind. It was the same cloying smell I'd noticed on my first visit, only this time it seemed a bit stronger.

"Stale perfume?"

"I thought so, too," he said, "but I wasn't sure. That's why I had you come up here. You caught a whiff of that odor, too. Perfume could cause a problem. Some insects are attracted to perfumes, lotions, and even certain laundry detergents. The scent is heaviest near Sister Celeste's room, and there's no tactful way of putting it—she needs to stop using body scents if she expects this place to remain insect free."

"Since when do nuns douse themselves in perfume?" I asked.

"Now that you mention it, maybe it's not perfume. It could be any number of things. Like one of those air sprays. Glade, Febreze... Face it, left to its own devises, this place smells like a 1940s schoolhouse. Anything would be better. Still, the Sisters in this convent need to understand the risks involved if they get overly indulgent with sprays and perfumes. I'll mention it to Sister Mary Katherine on our way out the door."

Our timing couldn't have been better. When we reached the bottom of the stairwell, Sister Mary Katherine was closing the front door.

I gave Godfrey a nudge. "Whew! Glad I didn't have another encounter with Grizzly Gary."

Sister Mary Katherine spun around and walked toward us. "How did everything go? Are we in the clear?"

Godfrey reiterated everything he had told the Sisters in the kitchen and advised that they refrain from using perfumes and the like.

"I would find it odd that one of our Sisters would be indulging in body scents," Sister Mary Katherine said, "but as far as aerosol sprays are concerned, I'm afraid we're all at fault. This building is quite old, and I'm afraid it's retained the scent of old wood and stale air. It wasn't built with airflow in mind. Hopefully, we'll be able to proceed with our renovation and expansion plan. Then old lingering scents will no longer trouble us."

Before Godfrey could reply, I spoke. "Uh, speaking of trouble, I hope everything works out as far as your van is concerned. I can imagine what a shock that must have been."

"I'm not worried," the Sister said. "I'm sure once they're done investigating, they'll realize how mistaken they were. Thank you, Dr. Klein and Miss Ellington, for all your help with those stinkbugs. I suppose the next time I see you will be at the reading of Mr. Mowen's will. Strange request, the reading. I don't like driving at night and neither do the other Sisters. We'll figure something out. Maybe we'll have one of our delivery men drive us to your winery. Anyway, I look forward to our next meeting."

Godfrey extended his hand and they shook. "I'm afraid it will be Miss Ellington at the reading of the will. I really have no part in that."

Like a burp, the words escaped my mouth. "You're more than welcome to listen in. Who knows? Maybe the Experiment Station will turn out to be one of the beneficiaries."

Godfrey and Sister Mary Katherine stared at me as if I'd lost my mind.

I remember uttering some inconsequential pleasantries before Godfrey escorted me out of the place.

"You weren't serious," he said, "about having me attend the reading of Arnold's will?"

It dawned on me, at that very instant, I was indeed serious. "Your presence would make those nuns more comfortable. Like a common denominator."

"Holy cow! I've been called lots of things, but common denominator really takes the cake!"

We laughed and I brushed the bangs from my face as I approached the car.

Godfrey immediately noticed. "Hey! How'd you get that cut? It wasn't there this morning. I've got some Neosporin in the glove compartment and some Band-Aids. In my line of work, they come in handy."

I told him about the assault, even though "assault" seemed like a pretty strong word for what it really was—a shoulder blade pinch and a shove.

"Good grief, Norrie. That's really troubling. But it does make something clear."

"What's that?"

"Someone in that convent doesn't want you snooping around."

"That's exactly what Sister Gloria said. More or less."

"Hmm, with those nuns poised to inherit a serious amount of money and the fact their van may indeed have been used in those heists, I'm beginning to wonder if—"

"I know. I'm wondering the same thing—which one of them is orchestrating this charade."

Chapter 21

"I keep going over it again and again in my mind," I said to Cammy the next morning when I stopped by the tasting room. It was twenty minutes to ten and everyone had arrived, except for Sam and Lizzie.

Cammy poured me a hot cup of coffee while I recounted yesterday's events.

"For the life of me, I can't figure out who threw me to the ground. Certainly not one of those neophyte nuns slaving away in the kitchen. And definitely not Sister Katherine. She was in the garage being grilled by deputies from two counties. And as far as Sister Gloria is concerned, she'd be the last person I'd accuse. Besides, she was already in the garage when I arrived."

"Wasn't there a third nun?"

"Oh yeah. Sister Celeste. But she was sequestered in her room upstairs with a bad migraine. Everyone was tiptoeing around so as not to make a noise that would disturb her."

Cammy reached under her table for a box of crackers and added more to the small bowl wedged between the water pitcher and the tasting sheets. "Maybe there's another player you don't know about."

"Like who?"

"What about one of those cheesecake delivery guys? Could be they have had something to hide."

"Oh my gosh. I all but forgot. I have their names. First and second, but not necessarily connected."

"Huh?"

"One of the nuns knew the first names and another knew the last. Kind of like a mix and match thing. No biggie."

"It's a start. If they're locals, someone around this area is bound to know them."

"I'm sure Deputy Hickman and his Seneca County cronies will do an official search for criminal records and all that, but I've got social media. I can ask the wineries at our end of the lake if either name rings a bell."

Just then Lizzie walked in and rushed over to us. "You can thank me later, but I did a little of my own Nancy Drew sleuthing. I've been far too demanding of you, Norrie, expecting you to follow up on every lead, so I tracked one down for you."

"Uh...thanks. What lead?"

"Remember that woman you told me about who paid for Pinot Noir by credit card the night before Thanksgiving? The one whose friend's son, Scottie, is supposedly a hotshot in the wine business? Well, I tracked her down and lo and behold! She's my dentist's receptionist. Small world, don't you think? I decided it had been a while since I had my teeth cleaned so I drove over there to make an appointment. I wanted to find out what this Scottie guy knows about the wine market. Especially since he encouraged his mother's friends to buy out the Pinot Noir."

"And? What did you find out?"

"He has about as much validity as Alvin, our goat."

Cammy and I both laughed, and Lizzie continued. "Turns out, the son is a part-time limousine driver for Finger Lakes Winery Tours, and he supplements his income making deliveries for smaller companies. That doesn't make him an industry professional. Although the woman did say Scottie had an uncle who was 'higher up in the business.' Goodness. That's probably someone who worked stocking wine in a warehouse."

"Oh brother." I rubbed the back of my neck and shook my head. "At least that's one lead we can cross off the chart."

"Quite true," Lizzie said. "Nancy Drew solved many a mystery by the process of elimination."

At that moment, Sam came through the door and shouted, "Hey! Did you catch the news? They just arrested some bigwig from Seneca Lake Communities Bank for certain account discrepancies. Isn't that a euphemism for embezzlement?"

"Not necessarily," Cammy said. "It could be anything."

Lizzie tilted her head and furrowed her brow. "Seneca Lake Communities Bank? That's the bank Arnold Mowen did business with until he transferred his accounts to First Liberty Federal. I was told Mr. Mowen had a falling out with one of the higher-ups."

"Falling out or not paying out?" I turned to Sam, "Did they give the name of the guy who was arrested? I'd be curious if it turned out to be the one Arnold had trouble with. In fact..."

Cammy cut in before Sam could respond. "Are you thinking what I'm thinking? That maybe the man they arrested might've done more than 'cook the books' or whatever it's called these days?"

Sam gave her a nudge. "Aw, why don't you come out and say it? You're thinking our banker guy could also be Arnold's killer."

"Oh my God! I exclaimed. "Who didn't want Arnold Mowen dead? The list of suspects keeps growing exponentially. By the time we get to the reading of his will, it won't be a legal procedure, it'll be a who's who of suspects."

"Goodness," Lizzie said. "It's almost ten and we're about to open. We'll have to revisit this later."

With that, she walked directly over to her spot at the cash register/ computer. Sam hightailed it to his table, which was adjacent to Roger's and Glenda's spots. Thankfully, those two were busy unloading wine bottles so we were spared long diatribes about the French and Indian War and God knows whatever unearthly scenario Glenda would dredge up.

"Have a good morning, everyone!" I called and then, for reasons I still couldn't explain, I walked over to Cammy and whispered, "Have you ever noticed Godfrey Klein's teeth? His smile is like...perfect."

She shot me a look that stayed in my head for hours. I left the tasting room and walked back to the house, determined to do two things—work on my screenplay and continue my sleuthing.

At a little past two, Rosalee Marbleton called and I was totally unprepared for what she told me.

"Your plan worked, Norrie! Leandre is ecstatic! He filled the oak barrel with water but used the numbering sheet as if it was wine. He also used that transparency paper you suggested, and we got fingerprints! The culprits poured lots of calcium carbonate into the water thinking they were tampering with our Pinot Noir. The surprise will be on them when an arrest is made. I called the sheriff's department and they sent someone over first thing in the morning. I wanted to call you sooner, but I've been inundated."

"No problem. I understand. That's fantastic news. Keep me posted, okay?"

"Of course."

"If you don't mind, I'm going to let Theo and Don know."

"Thank you. I was going to call them myself, so this is really a time saver for me. I'm going to send an email to our WOW group and let them know."

"Good idea. Talk to you later."

For the first time in days, I felt as if the muddled mess we were dealing with might actually clear up. As it turned out, I was wrong. Theo burst my bubble within seconds of picking up my call.

"Yeah, of course it's good news. Great news, really, except…well, for one thing. The fingerprints they pull must be in a database. The sheriff's department will start with the criminal database and then move on to federal and state files…Department of Education, Armed Forces… If our wine vandal isn't in a known database, finding the prints isn't going to help. Still, we might have a fighting chance."

As things turned out, we didn't. Not a fighting chance, or any chance at all. Whoever tampered with our wines didn't have a criminal record, hadn't served in the Armed Forces, and hadn't been employed by any federal or state agencies. Still, as Deputy Hickman put it when he gave Rosalee the bad news a few days later, "There are lots of individual businesses that require fingerprinting of their employees. This isn't over yet."

I wondered if he coined the phrase from the Starship song, "It's Not Over 'til It's Over," but I doubted it.

That week moved slowly with nothing new to report. No more instances of vandalism or wine theft that we were aware of and, mercifully, no one else claimed rights to Arnold Mowen's inheritance.

Strangely enough, three or four days before the reading of Arnold's will, I got a call from Henderson's Funeral Home in Seneca Falls regarding Lavettia's final wishes. She had designated me, of all people, as a contact and they had nowhere else to turn.

"Me?" I shouted over the line. "Me? I hardly knew the woman. I think I met her on two occasions. I don't understand."

"It's not a matter of money, Miss Ellington. Everything has been paid in full. It's simply a matter of signing off on her wishes," the woman at the other end of the line explained.

"Fine. Fine. Whatever has to be signed, I'll do it, but please don't expect me to handle the particulars. I know she has an attorney."

"She did, but she let him go due to a conflict of interest. Anyway, the state will intervene regarding her property and that sort of thing."

When I got off the phone, I felt miserable. I felt guilty enough for not taking Lavettia seriously when she thought someone was trying to kill her, and now, I shrugged off the disposal of her estate, as if it was something I could toss into a trash compactor. I pushed the caller ID to find her number and then placed the call before I had a chance to change my mind.

"Forget the state intervention," I said. "I'll do whatever is necessary to settle her estate."

When I told Theo and Don about my decision, they said I needed a permanent guardian. It was Taco Tuesday at Abuelos Restaurant in Geneva and a few days shy of the midnight madness we were all dreading.

"Lavettia's estate? This is worse than that Declan Roth fiasco," Don said.

"Or that crazy bank impersonator scheme you wanted to pull," Theo added.

"It'll be fine. Paperwork, that's all."

I figured, once we got past Arnold's will, everything else would fall in place. We could devote our entire attention to finding his killer. Logically, it made sense, but logic and reality, as I learned, were eons apart.

When I got home after stuffing myself full of tacos and enchiladas, I noticed the answering machine light blinking. *Now what? Can't I enjoy one peaceful evening?* I tapped the machine and waited for the message.

"Norrie, hi! The message on your cell phone said the voice mail was full. You have to empty those messages once in a while. It affects the storage. Heck, I don't mean to be lecturing you. It's Godfrey. In case you don't recognize my voice. Call me at home. It's important. It's half past nine right now, and I'll stay up until you return my call. Okay, bye."

There was only one reason Godfrey would want me to call him back no matter how late it was. Something awful must've happened to Francine and Jason. A deadly snake bite? A puma attack? A swarm of flesh eating insects? Or…yikes…one of those adorable poisonous frogs that paralyzed your body in seconds. I glanced at the entomology phone numbers Francine had written on one of her wall charts and dialed Godfrey's home. He picked up on the second ring.

"What happened?" I gasped into the phone. "Are Francine and Jason still alive?"

"Oh my gosh, Norrie, I didn't mean to scare you. This has nothing to do with your sister and brother-in-law. They're fine."

The tension in my back slowly evaporated as Godfrey continued speaking.

"I called because you'll never guess what Alex Bollinger found in that cockroach-infested apartment building in Ithaca. He phoned me once he got back to Geneva. You'll never guess."

"Geez, I don't know. A really, really big cockroach?"

"Nope. Alex located the stolen wines from Seneca Lake. Mostly Pinot Noir but a few bottles of Merlot and Cabernet Sauvignon. They were in the basement of a building on Buffalo Street. Whoever stashed them there thought they were well-hidden under some tarps, but Alex was tracking insect movement and naturally those tarps weren't going to get in his way. When he realized what was under the tarps, he notified the Ithaca Police Department. I imagine they're conferring with the county sheriff's departments and the state police. Boy is that going to be a long process. Sorry to scare you with my phone message, but I thought you'd want to know." "I do. I mean, I did. Wow. I can't even think straight. How did Alex know the wines were stolen and not someone's secret stash for a party?" "He didn't. Not until he called the police and they tallied the cases. Can you believe it? They were stored in separate piles, each one from a different theft. What idiots! The Ithaca Police obtained the information from the state police regarding that delivery truck hijacking and the subsequent thefts the counties reported to them. It was a perfect match. Of course, it took lots of time away from poor Alex, who now has to return tomorrow to finish his study."

"I don't suppose they'll be able to dust for fingerprints or anything, huh?" "They might, but it's a longshot. According to Alex, who spoke with them for a while, they're going to be canvasing the tenants in that building. They already notified the landlord who, again according to what Alex overheard, is being cooperative. The landlord doesn't live there."

"Of course not. Who in their right mind would live in a cockroach-infested building unless it was a college student?"

Godfrey laughed. "Good point. This'll be on all the news stations tomorrow. I guarantee it. And if those wineries think they're about to get their pricy wines back, they'll be in for a surprise. Those cases are now evidence."

"True, but once the thieves are caught, the wine will be returned. Those are cases of reds, and they're good for years. Too bad it doesn't help the rest of us whose wines were tampered with or spilled all over the place. I hope our combined law enforcement catches those dirty rats."

"Yeah, me too. Say, were you really serious about having me attend the reading of Arnold Mowen's will? That's what? Three days from now?"

"Uh-huh. And yes. I was serious. With you there, the nuns will feel more relaxed and might let down their guard. If they're hiding anything, it might slip."

"I've got to admit, this is a first, but sure, I'll come. I've been leading a very organized and predictable life. It's about time I did something different."

"Oh, it'll be different, all right. And about as far from predictable as they get."

I thought I was being clever and snappy with my response. Little did I know, I was right on the money.

Chapter 22

I called Theo and Don the second I got off the phone with Godfrey. They were incredulous.

"Oh my God!" Don said. "What a coincidence! One minute the guy's looking for roaches and the next he stumbles on stolen property. I hope the police or whatever agency is taking the lead does a thorough background check on the building's owner. Then again, it could be one of the tenants... maybe a college student trying to earn a few extra bucks."

Just then I heard Theo in the background. "If he or she wanted to earn some extra bucks, they should work at a fast-food counter, not rob the local wineries."

"Shh," Don said. "I won't be able to hear Norrie."

"That's okay," I replied. "It's getting late and I'm exhausted. I'll catch you tomorrow. After all of this, maybe Pinot No-More can go back to being Pinot Noir."

Don let out a slight chuckle. "You know what I wonder? Where were the thieves planning to offload the wine? Guess we'll have to wait until the perpetrators are caught. *If* they're caught."

"At least the police have a starting point for those guys. What about Arnold and Lavettia's killer? Too bad the sheriff's department hasn't made any progress. Clayton LeVine is still in the running as far as I'm concerned, and what are we supposed to do? Exchange pleasantries with him at the reading of the will? I almost wish we had a metal detector to check for a gun when he steps through the door."

"Killer or no killer, he's not going to brandish a gun in front of everyone."

"We can only hope. Say good night to Theo. Talk to you tomorrow."

I seriously thought about calling Bradley, but it was already ten forty and I didn't want to come across as the gossip-mongering screenwriter from Two Witches Winery. Instead, I changed into comfy flannel pajamas and settled on the couch, channel surfing until I couldn't keep my eyes open. At one point, I thought I heard a noise, but it turned out to be the dog. He bumped the coffee table on his way upstairs, beat me to the bed, and refused to budge an inch.

* * * *

A few inches of snow fell overnight, but nothing that made anyone around here bat an eyelash. I defrosted some raisin bread, popped in a K-cup of Dunkin' Donuts coffee, and poured Charlie his kibble. I opened the fridge to grab some milk and the phone rang. I figured maybe it was Godfrey calling with more news, or Don and Theo calling to see if I'd heard any more tidbits. Instead, it was Bradley.

"I was going to call you last night," I said, "but it got too late."

"I've been meaning to call you for days, but it seems as if I'm yanked around with one thing or another. I promise, Norrie, after this will-reading debacle, we're going to enjoy a leisurely gourmet dinner, even if it means driving out of state to get away."

"Hey, you don't have to apologize. I've been just as busy as you. I have a screenplay hanging over my head and a zillion winery things to worry about. Not to mention those unsolved murders. But there's one good thing—the stolen wines were found. That's why I was going to call you last night."

"When? Where?"

In that instant, I figured it hadn't made the news yet or Bradley was too preoccupied to turn on his TV or push one of his news app icons.

"Yesterday. In Ithaca. The cellar of an apartment building in Collegetown. Buffalo Street, to be exact."

I went on to give him the details about Alex Bollinger's cockroach study and his subsequent discovery in the basement.

"Do you know the address?" Bradley asked.

"Not offhand but I can get it for you. Why?"

"It's probably nothing, but one of our clients owns apartment buildings there. Real slums, if you ask me, but no code violations so he stays in business. Listen, the reason I called was to make sure you were all set for Saturday night. You know, the food, the drinks…"

"The crazy lunatics who'll be scratching each other's eyes out if they're not the beneficiary to Arnold's will?"

"Yeah, them, too."

"Don't worry. We're all set. By the way, I asked Theo and Don to join us since Arnold's body was found on their property, too."

"No problem."

"Oh, and Godfrey Klein from the entomology department at Cornell. He's acquainted with the nuns."

A short silence followed by, "Sure, why not? Actually, Norrie, if I could invite the Marx Brothers, I would. From what Marvin told me, this week is shaping up to be a real sideshow."

"What do you mean?"

"Remember a while back when you pestered me for the name of the VIP whose plane was met by Deputy Hickman? I wondered how you even knew about that. Anyway, it's no secret now. It's been all over the news. The VIP happens to be the CEO for a large community bank operation that includes Penn Yan and Seneca counties."

"The embezzlement. I *did* hear about that from one of my employees. But only the headline, so to speak. I don't know anything else. Your firm is handling that?"

"No. We're family law, but our clients seem to think we're Johnnie Cochran, Alan Dershowitz, and Gloria Allred combined. Marvin's in the process of securing a topnotch defense lawyer for our banker."

"Banker or murderer? I heard Arnold Mowen had a falling out with one of the bigwigs at that community bank. Maybe things went too far..."

"Um, about that...oh, never mind. I'd really love to stay on the line and talk with you, but Marvin will have my head on a plate if I'm even a second late for his nine o'clock briefing. Let me know if you need anything for Saturday's will reading. I'm bracing myself for anything, including a damn PowerPoint presentation. Thank God Arnold didn't leave us an old VHS tape to show."

"If Marvin does go high tech, we have Wi-Fi. See you Saturday."

I poured milk in my coffee while I waited for my raisin bread to toast. At least two mysteries were solved—the identity of the VIP whose plane landed in Penn Yan the night of my date with Bradley and the whereabouts of the stolen wine. If this was a puzzle, I'd still be looking at missing edges and a giant gap in the middle. It felt as if I had everything I needed to solve the murders and yet everything was as cloudy as my coffee after I stirred the milk.

With the screenplay deadline looming, I knew I should boot up my laptop and go directly to the file. Instead, I pulled out the delivery log Sister Gloria had slipped me and stared at it. Granted, Deputy Hickman had probably reviewed it looking for a connection between the wine thefts and the cheesecake deliveries, but he certainly wasn't about to share his findings with me.

I'd scrawled the dates of the winery incidents on the wall calendar, beginning with the first hijacking. I worried the thieves would target us next. And yeah, we were hit, but not with a hijacking. From that point on, I noted everything. Not quite as detailed as Francine would have, but thorough enough for me. The first heist took place on a Tuesday in mid-November. Theo called to tell me it was on the news and the delivery truck was on its way to our side of the lake.

Immediately, I looked at the convent's delivery log to see if there was a match. Hard to tell. They made one delivery to a restaurant in Seneca Falls, followed by two others in Geneva. Impossible to pinpoint anything. I grabbed the calendar off the wall and transferred the incident dates to scrap paper. No sense jumping up and down to look at the calendar every few seconds.

Next to every incident date, I noted where the delivery van stopped. Each stop was in the range of possibilities, but, while I had the time of each delivery, I didn't have the exact time for each incident. I did note something of interest, though, and I kept my fingers crossed Deputy Hickman would notice it too. The van made deliveries to upscale restaurants in Ithaca. It didn't necessarily translate to unloading stolen wine at a cockroach-infested apartment building, but given the addresses of those restaurants, it did put the drivers coincidentally close.

Knowing that if I were to share my theory with Deputy Hickman he would admonish me beyond belief for my sleuthing, I took another approach—the back door. Aka Gladys Pipp. Before I had time to talk myself out of it, I grabbed my cell phone and called her.

"Gladys? It's me, Norrie Ellington. Is Deputy Hickman anywhere within earshot?"

"No, why? What's going on?"

"I may have a lead on those winery thefts, but I can't tell him. He has to believe he's the one who thought of it."

"Good grief. How are you going to do that?"

"Um, well, er…actually…I was kind of hoping you would. Just tell him you liked that idea of his about the delivery van from the convent in Lodi hiding stolen wine in a nearby apartment building. When he tells you he doesn't remember saying anything about it, tell him he said something like that after the Ithaca Police Department got in touch. Trust me. I know they would have gotten in touch and I know his ego will take it from there."

"I hope you're right, Norrie, or he'll think I'm the one who's touched!"

"So you'll do it?"

"If it can get him closer to solving all these crimes, I sure will."

"Thanks, Gladys. You're the best."

I had enough on my mind with the upcoming reading of the will and my determination to ferret out Arnold and Lavettia's killer. All Deputy Hickman needed to do was follow the clues and catch some thieves. So what if I gave him a little push? And while I was doing the pushing, something else occurred to me—Bradley wasn't the only one who could benefit from getting the address of that cockroach-laden building. If Deputy Hickman didn't grab the bull by the horns on this one, I'd need to be prepared as well. Drat! So much for screenwriting deadlines.

I was right next to the phone, so I called Godfrey Klein at his office.

"Hi! It's me. Norrie. Sorry to bother you again so soon, but I wondered if you could give me the address of that building Alex was working in."

"Sure. Hold on a second, will you? It's in our field work files. Don't tell me you plan on snooping around over there since that's where the stolen wine was discovered."

"Ew! Not on your life. The attorneys handling Arnold's will have a client who owns lots of those buildings in Collegetown. It might turn out to be him."

"Okay. Give me a second."

I held the phone and glanced out the window. With the light snowfall on the ground and the seasonal decorations surrounding our tasting room building, it really was beginning to feel like the holidays. That thought gave me a pit in my stomach. I hadn't gotten back to Godfrey's invitation to join him and his entomology crew for Christmas.

It wasn't the thought of bugs that held me back, or the fact I had an open invitation with Theo and Don. It was something else and I couldn't quite figure it out. Just then, Godfrey got back on the line.

"Here you go—567 East Buffalo Street. I'd love to stay on the line and chat, but I have to finish a field study report regarding the pheromone treatment on the Boisea trivittata. Say, is there anything I should be bringing to Arnold Mowen's will reading?"

"Yeah. Aspirin and a big bottle of Tums."

Godfrey laughed, and I thanked him for the address. I was certain Deputy Hickman would take the bait and look for a correlation between the convent delivery van drivers and the list of tenants occupying that building. I knew sheriff departments had access to all sorts of databases, but there was one database I could tap into and I didn't waste any time. City and county tax records were available to anyone and everyone, but it was a nightmare to navigate through the web of information the assessor's office provided. All I really wanted to find was who owned the damn place. Two hours and countless websites later, I got my answer. When I saw the name staring me in the face, I almost choked. It was the last person I expected. And now, the first on my list as the mastermind for the wine sabotage.

Having secured that information without leaving my kitchen table, I felt kind of ashamed for sending Deputy Hickman on a wild goose chase. Then again, there was absolutely nothing linking the owner of that building to the cheesecake guys, Rob and Derek. My pulse raced with the latest discovery, and there was no way I could keep it to myself.

The faster I tried to tap Theo and Don's number into my cell phone, the more mistakes I made. I forced myself to slow down, take a breath, and move my fingers slowly.

"Don? Theo? Whoever you are, you won't believe this!"

"It's Don, and what won't I believe?"

"I found out who the owner of that roach-infested building is, and it's none other than Miller Holtz. It *must* be our Miller Holtz. How many Miller Holtzes can there be?"

"Holy Cow! That would explain a whole heck of a lot. Who better than a wine rep to manipulate the market by removing the wines that carry the highest price tags. Tell me everything you know."

"I just did. Except for the fact I found out by doing a hellishly long internet search on city and county tax files. No wonder real estate attorneys get paid so much."

"Do you think Miller's the murderer, too?"

"Nope. Not at all. I'm totally convinced Clayton LeVine deserves all the credit for that. Listen, we only have three days until all hell breaks loose over Arnold's will. We have to act fast."

"We?"

"You don't expect me to do this alone."

"I'm afraid to ask," Don said.

"A plan. We need a plan that will force Clayton to confess."

"Even the most ruthless governments have some sort of trial before they convict someone of murder. How can you be so sure?"

"Lavettia was convinced Clayton had something on Arnold. Whatever it was, Arnold had to keep Clayton satiated for fear of being found out. Lavettia was petrified Arnold was going to leave everything to him. Let's be honest. Clayton had motive, means, and opportunity."

"So did everyone else in Arnold's circle."

"True, but no one could come up with disguises the way Clayton could. You should see his Pinterest site. It's spectacular. That absolutely *had* to be him pretending to be Lavettia's cleaning woman."

"So, what are you proposing?" Don asked.

"It's really quite simple. When Clayton arrives for the reading of the will, someone mentions that the Seneca County Sheriff's Department has a surveillance tape of him sneaking into Lavettia's apartment to wipe his fingerprints from the chairs. They called our winery to let us know that a Yates County Deputy was on his way to arrest Clayton."

"And which lucky person gets to break the news to Clayton?"

"Not to Clayton. That's way too obvious. No, we make sure Clayton is within hearing range, and you and Theo have that conversation. Or…if you prefer, you and me. Or Theo and me. It doesn't matter."

"All right. Suppose we agree to this one-act show. Then what?"

"Sit back and watch. Clayton will have no choice but to make some flimsy excuse and bolt out of there. If he's smart, he'll head for the nearest airport. We'll call our county sheriff for real this time."

Don groaned. "Before or after the reading of the will?"

"Before. If we wait until after the will is read, his disappearance could be attributed to sour grapes if he wasn't the beneficiary or sheer, unadulterated bliss if he was. No question about it—we have to enact this little charade before Marvin sits everyone down for the grand finale. So, do you think Theo will buy it?"

"Oh yeah. He'll buy it, all right. He's just as kooky as you are when it comes to these little schemes."

"You won't be sorry. Everything will work out."

If I could've erased those last four words from my vocabulary, I would have. How was I supposed to know that my little plan would take a back seat to one over which I had absolutely no control, beginning with an idiotic storm named "Brutus" that was brewing somewhere on the West Coast.

Chapter 23

I woke up Thursday morning prepared for a productive day of screenwriting and that was exactly how the morning *began*. However, everything changed when I got a call from Theo a little after nine.

"Want to share a ride over to the WOW meeting? I can pick you up if you want."

"The WOW meeting? That's today? When did that happen?"

"When they announced it at the last meeting. Honestly, Norrie, you need to start writing stuff down or get one of those Amazon Echo things to remind you."

"Yeesh. I've been so preoccupied with everything else, I totally forgot about the meeting. Is anything important on the agenda?"

"The official agenda items that Madeline Martinez emailed include updates on 'Deck the Halls around the Lake,' and some sort of charity benefit for the Humane Society. But you know how it'll go. Everyone will talk about the stash of stolen wine that was found. Did you plan on dropping the Miller Holtz bombshell on them? Don told me about it. Of course, once you do that, there's no turning back. They'll spout off theories like nobody's business. Should be one hell of a meeting."

"Well, I didn't plan to go that far. Look, I identified Miller Holtz as the owner of that building and I only had access to public records and the slow internet access around here, so the sheriff's department should already be aware of it. In fact, they're probably questioning him right this minute. I know this sounds terrible, but truthfully, Miller Holtz is the last of my concerns right now. True, if it turns out he was the one who stole that wine to manipulate market profits and all that, he deserves everything coming his way. Especially Deputy Hickman and any WOW gossip that follows.

But my gut tells me Miller's not our killer, Clayton is. So, did Don talk to you about my plan to get the little weasel to snap and run on Saturday?"

"He did. Were you planning to provide us with scripts or do we wing it?"

"I can give you an entire screenplay if you want. I'm just glad you're going to do it."

"Yeah. You'll be way too busy with everything else. Besides, it might be fun to see if I have any acting talent."

"Don't overdo it. Try to sound nonchalant but focused. Intent but not too driven."

"Okay, Mr. Coppola. Or are you more the Steven Spielberg type?"

"Very funny. Hey, Catherine mentioned something about trading recipes for holiday cookies if I remember the last meeting."

"The only thing they'll be trading are rumors but, what the heck, it should be interesting. I'll pick you up at nine forty. Okay?"

"Works for me."

* * * *

Much as I hated to admit it, Theo had summed up the meeting before it even started. A dull headache had formed in the back of my skull and morphed into a real pounder by the time the women had run out of things to say. I really couldn't blame my headache on the WOW get-together, as annoying as it was. Given the pressure on my temples and the relentless hammering at the base of my neck, it was a bona fide tension headache. It would most likely disappear after the reading of Arnold Mowen's will. At least I hoped it would. Meanwhile, I resigned myself to limping along with Tylenol or whatever other over-the-counter pain reliever I could find.

"We're keeping our fingers crossed, Norrie," Catherine said, as Theo and I put on our jackets and headed to Madeline's front door. "If all goes well, Steven will be here in plenty of time for the next 'Deck the Halls around the Lake' and the two of you can finally meet up."

Theo balled up my woolen scarf and thrust it at me, trying not to laugh.

"Um, yeah," I said to Catherine, "uh, that would be something."

Next thing I knew, Theo all but shoved me out the door and shouted, "See you later" to anyone within hearing range.

"It never stops," I whined when we got in his car. "Personally, I'm hoping Steven Trobert will have a revelation he's on your team and will break the news to his mother."

"Don't count on it, but we're always glad to welcome new members."

I wasn't hungry when I got back from the meeting. I attributed it to my headache and the lemon cake and streusel I had eaten. I was, however, freezing cold. The temperature had dropped into the high twenties and, unless snow was in the forecast, which usually meant temps above freezing, I had to resign myself to thermal underwear and lots of scarves.

The Weather Channel had predicted some sort of a snow event, but it wasn't supposed to materialize until Sunday. I didn't bother to check out the details. When they used the word "event," it was their way of saying, "Who knows what to expect? Rain? Snow? Sleet? Wind? More snow?" When I used the word "event" to describe the gathering of money-hungry vultures at our establishment for the reading of some narcissist's will, I envisioned a scenario so replete with lunatics and crackpots, it left little to the imagination: unlike The Weather Channel.

I popped into the tasting room late in the day to make sure Cammy had all the arrangements made for midnight Saturday. Last thing I needed was a snafu regarding the food. She reassured me it would be a simple, yet plentiful, canape menu that wouldn't feature any spicy or weird food combinations that might make anyone nauseous at such a late hour. No, the reading of the will was bound to do that.

"Relax," she said when I asked her. "Fred has an assortment of lovely finger foods lined up, plus muffins in every conceivable variety with flavored butters and cheeses. Not to mention jams. We also have fruit cups, sherbet cups, and three different flavors of mousse. We'll have our wine, of course, plus juices and coffee/tea service. It'll be fine, Norrie. Take a breath."

Cammy tidied up her tasting room table and didn't notice Glenda rushing toward us. She practically ran into Cammy's backside.

"Norrie! I wasn't going to tell you this because I thought it might upset you. Then I realized I would be doing you a disservice if I didn't."

"Didn't tell me what?"

Glenda took a long, deep breath and when she let out the air, it sounded like a moan. "I had the most dreadful premonition about Saturday night. So throat-clutching I called my friend Zenora. You know, the one who works for Essential Oils like Lavettia does. I mean, *did.* Anyway, Zenora suggested I have dinner at her place on Saturday and we could conduct aura cleansings on each other. That way, when I arrive for the will reading, my body and mind will be clear of all unwanted outside influences."

"Um, sure." *Personally, I plan to take a quick shower and the hell with it.*

Glenda grabbed my wrist and gave it a slight squeeze. "If you'd care to join us, you are more than welcome."

"Gee, thanks. That's very kind of you, but I think I'll be fine. I think we'll all be fine."

"I'll be sure to recite a protective earth, air, and water spell on the winery just in case."

"Good. Good idea. As long as it doesn't involve lighting anything."

"Wonderful." Glenda gave my wrist another squeeze and went back to her table in time to greet three women who walked in while we were talking.

Cammy, who'd been pretty quiet up until then, whispered, "She's a dear soul but, frankly, some of her stuff scares the daylights out of me. By the way, did you want the banquet room set up in any particular fashion? I figured we'd use one of our long rectangular tables for the attorneys and arrange the chairs in a semi-circle around them. The outlets would be right behind the table if they wanted to go all high-tech."

"That sounds about right. I'll shoot off an email to Bradley and if they want anything different, he'll let me know."

"We'll have rectangular tables set up against the long wall. That's where the food and drinks will be. Sam and Roger will pour the wines and take care of coffee/tea service. Am I missing anything?"

"If you are, we'll figure it out when they get here. By the way, the banquet room looked pretty good with all the lights and holiday decorations."

"Yeah, I thought so, too. You can thank Lizzie for all that. She really went overboard this year."

"I appreciate it. I mean, even though everyone's getting paid, it's a major inconvenience—midnight of all times. At least that storm they keep talking about won't get here until Sunday. If it's really bad, the county will close the roads and we can all stay home."

Cammy shook her head. "I don't think it'll be that bad. Those news stations love getting us hyped up only to disappoint us later. Fred and Emma will be here before ten. They'll get the food ready. The rest of us will arrive between ten-thirty and eleven."

"I'm good with whatever you worked out. Oh, and one more thing—if you see a man with a wretched comb-over and chubby cheeks suddenly get up before the will is read and race for the nearest exit, call the sheriff's office and yell for me."

"Huh? What did I miss?"

While Cammy knew all about my suspicions regarding Clayton, I hadn't had the time to fill her in on the little drama Don and Theo planned to stage. She listened wordlessly until I was done. Then she clasped her hands together and stretched them out in front of her. "And you think Glenda is wacky? Why don't you just tell someone at the sheriff's department?"

"Because, if you haven't noticed, I'm on their 'Do Not Believe' call list."

Just then, the phone in my pocket buzzed. I took it out to answer.

"Catch you later," Cammy said.

I walked toward a quiet corner of the room, so I could hear whoever was on the line.

"Norrie? It's Bradley. Listen, there's been a change of plans. Well, not plans exactly, more like attendees. You can add one more to your list—the CEO of Seneca Lake Communities Bank. He's out on bail and will be attending the reading of Arnold's will, along with everyone else. Hope that doesn't put a dent in your food and drink menu."

"No, unless there's something about his appetite you're not telling me. But why invite a bank CEO who's being charged with a crime? What was his relationship with Arnold? Was he the reason Arnold switched to another bank?"

"He was the reason Arnold had money to put in a bank in the first place. Long story. No time to get into it right now. Marvin's driving all of us crazy. Got to run. See you Saturday. If I make it through the rest of this afternoon and tomorrow."

"That bad?"

"Times ten!"

The next day was as uneventful as could be. Weather-wise, the air was cold and still. Winery-wise, based on what I could see when I looked through the window to the tasting room parking lot, there was a steady stream of shoppers. Storm predictions do that in the Finger Lakes. People either rush off to the nearest supermarket and stock up on goods, as if they were facing Armageddon, or they flock to the wineries and buy wine as if Armageddon awaited them at home in the form of cooped-up family members.

For me, Armageddon meant a blissful day spent finalizing my screenplay. Another read through and I'd be able to send it to Renee. Charlie was having a decent day, too—trips in and out of the doggie door, followed by hours-long naps. I phoned Cammy in the afternoon to make sure she didn't need anything last minute, although we had a full day ahead of us before midnight tomorrow rolled around.

Henderson's Funeral Home called to inform me that Lavettia had been cremated as per her wishes and, in lieu of any memorial service, she simply requested the placement of her obituary, which she herself had penned, in the local newspapers.

"Uh, did she leave any instructions for her ashes?" I asked. "Some people want them scattered all over or they have a burial spot."

"Lavettia requested that hers be scattered into Seneca Lake next spring. We arranged to store them until then. You might want to hold a small gathering of her friends. It's up to you."

Gathering of her friends? I didn't know she had any. After all, why am I doing this? "Um, yeah. Of course."

It was one of those creepy phone calls that left me feeling numb. I nuked a frozen cheese and kale lasagna that Francine had made and defrosted a bagel to go with it. Not the most exciting meal I'd eaten, but it got stars for being convenient.

By four thirty I was getting twitchy, so I rustled Charlie out of his doggie bed and forced him to take a brisk walk around the place. We snaked through the vineyard rows, crisscrossed the property a few times, and semi-jogged back to the house. When we got home, I pulled up the file for my screenplay one more time for a "quick look."

The "quick look" lasted over two hours. I made tiny, yet significant dialogue changes. Satisfied it was ready for Renee's eyes, I sent it to her as an email attachment, even though I knew she wouldn't get to it until Monday. At least it was off my plate for the time being.

Paramour Productions had given Renee a wish list of movie themes they were interested in acquiring and she, naturally, had passed it to me, along with a brief note that made me laugh—"Same you-know-what, different day."

I did, however, notice a subtle shift from contemporary and modern romance to Victorian and post-World War I romance. I'd give Renee a call next week to talk about it.

Finally, I settled on the couch with a bowl of nachos and a Coke. I caught the end of a sitcom and the nine o'clock news. Nothing exciting to report. The storm wouldn't make it here until Sunday, if it showed up at all...something about a discrepancy between the United States and European computer models.

My eyes closed as the news anchors talked about possible wind shift directions. I fell asleep on the couch and woke up to find Charlie licking nacho crumbs from my chest.

"Guess that's my hint, huh boy?"

We traipsed upstairs. I knew I'd fall asleep in minutes. I didn't. For some inexplicable reason, my mind latched on to Saturday's reading of the will. All sorts of hideous scenarios came to mind, including, but not limited to, Miller and Clayton getting into a brawl and the nuns threatening everyone with eternal damnation if they weren't named the beneficiaries.

Finally, I gave up and decided to focus on a new tactic. Instead of counting sheep, I'd count attendees, beginning with Arnold's employees and branching out from there. Over and over again, I said the names in my mind—Miller Holtz, Clayton LeVine, Sister Mary Katherine, Sister Gloria Mae, Sister Celeste, the CEO who had dealings with Arnold…I also added our employees to the mix, followed by Theo, Don, and Godfrey.

It must have worked because I didn't wake up until the next morning.

Chapter 24

Bradley had assured me the reading of the will would be conducted in a formal, businesslike manner, despite any interruptions that may or may not emanate from the audience. I pictured something entirely different— something more akin to a piñata party. Instead of waving a giant stick, Marvin would be holding Arnold's will, waving it in the air. Suddenly the term "midnight madness" took on a new meaning for me.

I was downright twitchy all day, stopping in and out of the tasting room so often I was making everyone nervous. At one point, Cammy approached me and begged me to go home and "write something mushy."

The colorless sky gave no indication a storm would be heading our way the next day. It was downright frigid and void of any moisture. I figured that had to be a good thing. At a little before three, Theo called to ask if there were any last minute things we needed since he had to make a run to Wegmans for some bottled water and batteries.

"I'm playing it safe," he said. "If I stock up on emergency supplies, the storm will bypass us. Happens all the time. Sure you don't want anything?"

"Nah. Thanks anyway. We're all set. John even made sure to put lots of extra hay in Alvin's little house in case it gets brutal out there. Are you and Don prepared to launch into your dialogue as planned?"

"Geez, I don't think Cecile B. DeMille prepped as much when he filmed *Cleopatra*."

"Only checking. Honestly, my mind keeps flitting from one thing to the next. Weird stuff, too, like how are those nuns going to get here? Sister Gloria told me they have a sedan at their disposal, but none of them drive at night."

"They probably made arrangements for one of their delivery guys to bring them."

"Unless they've been arrested for stashing stolen wine in Miller Holtz's apartment building. Remember, they had cheesecake deliveries in that area. If Miller wasn't behind the thefts, one of those two men could have been responsible."

"We would have heard about it by now. Try to relax. Showtime begins in less than nine hours, and I'm not counting the prep time. See you around midnight."

With my screenplay sitting in Renee's inbox and everything under control at the winery, I did something I probably should have done weeks ago, and I did it with such determination and attention to detail, I felt as if I deserved a commendation. I cleaned the house. Not just a simple dust and sweep but a genuine deep cleaning or whatever the heck it was called. I even crawled on my hands and knees to get some stubborn dust bunnies (more like full-grown rabbits) out from under the beds. Ew! I also cleaned the gunky sink drains.

My music teacher, Mr. Howard, once told the class that the true sign of being an adult was when you were the person who cleaned the gunk in the sink drain. Ugh! No wonder Peter Pan refused to grow up.

It was a little past eight when I took a shower and made myself an egg salad sandwich. Charlie went out the doggie door for a quick turnaround before settling in his bed. I pulled the plastic cover over the door because the last thing I needed was for him to go outside and howl.

"I'm driving down there," I said to the dog, who barely lifted his head, "because it's cold and it's dark." *My God! I'm now justifying my moves to the dog.*

When I stepped into the tasting room foyer, Cammy was already there, along with Fred and Emma. The huge gas fireplace was blazing, giving the place a homey, ski lodge look. The holiday tea lights that we had strung in the main and banquet rooms looked welcoming and tasteful, although I wasn't quite sure if they were appropriate for the reading of a person's final wishes.

"Something smells fantastic," I said.

"It's the braised pork loin Fred and Emma marinated in honey and soy sauce. I sampled that as well as the bacon-wrapped shrimp skewers. The banquet room's all set. Make sure the chairs are where you want them."

"Um, think we should assign seats?"

Cammy gave her head a shake. "That might make people uncomfortable."

"Theo and Don absolutely *have* to be seated behind Clayton."

"They'll figure it out. Stop worrying."

At that moment, Sam came through the doorway, followed by Lizzie and Glenda. "Roger's parking his car," he said, "When we saw him pull in, we made a mad dive for the door. Guy's been on a roll all day about pivotal moments in the French and Indian War. Lizzie got him started when she mentioned tonight being a pivotal moment regarding the direction the lake's wine distribution is about to go." Then he turned to Lizzie. "Thanks a heap. Roger will be citing battles all night. Maybe if we're lucky, Arnold's spirit will rise from the dead and shut him up."

At that point, Glenda gasped. "Don't even go there! This place hasn't been appropriately cleansed for that sort of thing."

"Yeesh," I groaned. "Enough with spirits and war stories. If things go poorly with Arnold's will, our banquet room could turn out to be the next battlefield. Come on, let's get set-up. The attorneys should be here any minute."

As if on cue, the front door opened and Marvin Souza walked in, a large briefcase tucked under his arm. He was tall and had a medium build, and a full head of white hair. If I didn't know any better, I would have sworn I was looking at a younger Hal Holbrook sans the Mark Twain mustache. Bradley stood a few feet behind him, also carrying a briefcase and looking as serious and pokerfaced as I'd ever seen him. I immediately walked over to introduce myself to Marvin, but Bradley did it for me.

"Mr. Souza, I'd like you to meet our hostess for this evening, Norrie Ellington. She's one of the owners of Two Witches Winery."

He held out his hand. "A pleasure to meet you, Miss Ellington. We genuinely appreciate you opening your winery at such a peculiar hour to accommodate the wishes of the late Arnold Mowen."

"Glad we could help out," I said.

Another gentleman, whom I hadn't noticed at first, barreled toward us. He was tall, like Marvin, but that was where the similarities ended. He appeared to be in his early fifties, with broad shoulders, thick eyebrows, and wavy brown hair. This time, Marvin Souza made the introduction.

"We've brought another attendee for tonight's reading of the will. Allow me to introduce Thane Eldridge, the CEO of Seneca Lakes Communities Bank."

"Nice to meet you, Mr. Eldridge." I extended my hand once again.

"Likewise."

Thane Eldridge's voice was really deep, and I could have sworn I'd heard it before.

"We've got a table set up for you, Mr. Souza." I pointed in the direction of the banquet room. "Will you need a computer set up as well?"

"If the late Mr. Mowen had his way, we would have needed a film-screening room, but as it stands, all I'll require is additional table space for some framed photos of him that he wanted on display tonight."

"No problem. I'll get one of our employees to set one up. Meanwhile, make yourselves comfortable. We'll have coffee service and drinks available in a few minutes. Everything will be ready to go by midnight." *Including myself.*

"Good. Good. I'd like to be done with this affair by one thirty—two at the latest. It's starting to get nasty out there, and I don't trust the forecast. A late Sunday storm could very well turn out to be an early morning surprise."

"Yeeks. Let's hope not."

The last thing I needed was for a gaggle of money-hungry vultures to be snowed in.

Bradley led his boss and Thane Eldridge into the banquet room while I rushed off to find Sam or Roger to move that table.

"No problem," Sam said when I told him what I needed. "I've got it covered."

White skirted tables hugged the walls and Cammy had already set up three large carafes with hot beverages. Pitchers of juice and ice water were visible too. It was a little past eleven and the countdown was on. Out of nowhere, I developed an annoying twitch in my right eye, and it felt as if my entire face contorted every few seconds.

I rushed over to the wall mirror by the main doors to get a better look just as Theo and Don walked in. Their coats were covered with white specks, and I hoped it was only a light snow and not "Brutus" making an early entrance.

"Look at my face, will you?" I said. "What do you see?"

Don and Theo moved their heads closer and stared.

"What are we supposed to see?" Don asked. "If this is one of those questions about 'how do you like my new eye shadow or lipstick,' you can forget it. I'm terrible with those things."

"No! It's a twitch. In my right eye. Look carefully. Does it resemble Quasimodo?"

"I don't see anything," Theo said.

Don leaned in even closer. "Yeah, me either. If it's any consolation, eye twitches always feel far more dramatic than they appear. Must be nerves, huh?"

I grimaced. "You can say that. Anyway, our entire crew is here and they're busy getting all the food ready. The lawyers are here, too, and they brought Thane Eldridge with them." I looked around to make sure no one could hear us. "He's that bank CEO who's been arrested for some sort of discrepancy. You know the one I'm talking about—the bigwig who had a falling out with Arnold."

"Looks like we might be in for some surprises tonight," Theo said. "We'll go to the kitchen and see if anyone needs any help with anything. If not, we'll gossip."

I laughed as the two of them took off their coats and headed to the kitchen. I was standing by the hallway mirror when the door opened again, and Godfrey Klein stepped in.

"Whoa, Norrie! I almost bumped into you. I've got to admit, this is, by far, one of the strangest event invitations I've ever received and that includes my cousin Heidi's gender reveal party for her first child. As party favors, we all got copies of her latest sonogram. By the way, the baby was a boy...if you were wondering."

"Huh? What? Um, thanks for coming. The lawyers are here as well as Don and Theo from the Grey Egret and, of course, our employees. So far, none of the other attendees have made it. Oh wait, let me rephrase that. The lawyers brought Thane Eldridge with them. He's the CEO from Seneca Lake Communities Bank who was recently arrested but is now out on bail. White collar crime, not some lunatic."

"Terrific. That's always reassuring. So, is there anything you want me to do? I mean, other than find a seat and watch the...the, er...proceedings?"

"That's about it. Make yourself comfortable. You can put your coat in the office or use the rack near the door. I probably should have mentioned this earlier, but if a guy with chubby cheeks and a bad comb-over tries to make a run for it, he's the killer. Don't worry—I have a plan in place."

Godfrey rubbed the back of his neck. "Oh brother."

He headed to the banquet room where Marvin and Bradley were setting up their visual shrine to Arnold.

Figuring I should pop into the kitchen to give Fred and Emma a quick "hello," I took off as well. That was when I heard the door open behind me, followed by Miller Holtz's voice.

"Damn sand and salt trucks. They're all over the place slowing down traffic. Impossible to pass one of them. What's the matter with those morons at the highway department? It's hardly snowing and look at all the taxpayer resources they're wasting. That storm isn't supposed to get here for hours."

Immediately, I doubled back and ushered Miller Holtz inside. "Hi, Mr. Holtz. Come on in. I guess the county's just taking precautions. Usually they wait awhile." *Just like the deputy sheriffs around here who haven't arrested you yet.*

"Morons," he muttered. "Where is everyone?"

"Mr. Souza's in the banquet room, along with his partner and some other guests."

"Don't tell me they dredged up long-lost relatives of Arnold's."

"Nope, nothing like that."

"I better not have missed anything."

"You haven't. We're just waiting for a few more attendees to arrive. Non-relatives. Feel free to make yourself comfortable. We have drinks, coffee service, and a midnight buffet."

"Hmm, haven't been to one of those in years. Damn cruise ships stopped holding them."

With that, Miller tossed his coat on the rack near the door and walked straightaway to the banquet room. Only four guests remained to arrive—the nuns and Clayton LeVine.

I had told Theo and Don to make sure they seated themselves behind Clayton, even if it meant trading places with someone.

"Tell whoever you're ousting you want a better view," I said when we first discussed the plan. "Tell them you're considering going into law and you need to familiarize yourselves with the procedures."

"How about we shove them out of their seats and tell them we've had a bad day?" Theo replied, at which point, I dropped the subject.

I took out my cell phone and glanced at the time—11:43. We still had time. I went into my office and looked out the window. Miller was right. It was snowing outside but there was still plenty of visibility. I could make out my house and the south side lights from across the lake. I blinked for a moment and looked out the window again. Headlights. Hallelujah! It had to be Clayton's car or the one bringing the nuns.

I prayed Clayton wouldn't show up at the last minute and ruin everything. It appeared as if Marvin wanted to get the whole will-reading nightmare over with as quickly as possible, and I figured he'd launch right into it the minute everyone was accounted for. I needed, or I should say, *Theo and Don needed* the time to run their little dialogue past Clayton.

The headlight beams looked too high up to be a car or even an SUV. I all but pressed my nose to the window. It was a minivan. Not one of those sleek family vans that tout adventurous living, but a long, boxy van that schools used to transport children during field trips. Unless Clayton had traded in his Mazda for this contraption, it had to be the nuns. But why a minivan for only three people?

Chapter 25

I remained glued to the window, watching as the van pulled into our parking lot and drove straight up to the front entrance. Thankfully, our outdoor lighting gave off enough illumination for me to get a good look at the passengers as they approached our building. It also gave off plenty of light for me to read the faded banner on the side of the vehicle—Holy Sepulcher Convent and School. They must have kept their old field trip van.

Sister Mary Katherine exited first from the side of the van, followed by Sister Gloria and a third nun, who I assumed was Sister Celeste. All three of them were wearing ankle-length black coats and, heaven help me, traditional black head coverings.

Maybe the reading of the will was more formal than I realized.

I watched as the three Sisters followed each other in a single line and wondered if they invited their driver inside. If not, I was going to do so. No one should have to wait in a cold vehicle for hours. All of a sudden, more nuns exited the van. I stopped counting at five and rushed into the kitchen.

"Fred! Emma! Cammy!" I shouted. "Brace yourselves. Looks like the entire Convent of the Holy Sepulcher came. We weren't planning on that many people. Do we have enough food for eight or nine more?"

Fred handed a spatula to his wife and walked over to the doorway where I was standing. "It'll be fine. Absolutely fine. You're only talking eight or nine more people, not eighty or ninety. We've got more than enough food, thanks to the late Mr. Mowen's wishes for something extravagant, plus we've got lots of things we can defrost and prepare at the last minute."

My pulse was racing, but at least I wasn't hyperventilating. I looked at Cammy. "Chairs. We're going to need more chairs. Set up lots of rows."

I wasn't sure if she gave me a wave or a salute, but she took off for the small storeroom where we kept the extra folding chairs. Fred and Emma told me to calm down and that everything was totally under control.

In my mind, I was the epitome of "grace under pressure," but Theo, who caught sight of me on his way to the restroom, later told me I looked like Hermione Granger after she fought off the troll. Somehow, I managed to open the front door and welcome the nuns inside.

The Triumvirate had opted for formal black veils that concealed a good portion of their faces, while the younger nuns dressed in the same plain, beige attire I had seen them wear on the two occasions I had visited their convent.

"Welcome," I said. "Please make yourselves comfortable in our banquet room. We have coffee service, cold drinks, and a variety of canapes and light foods. Mr. Souza will begin the reading once everyone has arrived. We're still expecting one more person." *And darn it all! Where the heck is that conniving Clayton? He's going to get here so late it'll be impossible to rat him out.*

I caught a whiff of that familiar cloying smell as I ushered the nuns into the banquet room. Maybe it was their soap. Or shampoo…I wondered if they all had to use the same brand.

The additional table was set up and covered with one of our fancy brocade tablecloths. Off-white from having been laundered so many times. Still, it looked lovely. Except for one thing. Make it five things. There were four framed 8 x 12 photos of Arnold and one larger gold-leaf framed photo—at least 18 x 24—that faced the audience.

"The many faces of Arnold Mowen" glared at the attendees like something out of a macabre movie. I shuddered and took a step toward the buffet table. Miller Holtz piled enough food on his plate to feed a football team, while Thane Eldridge and Marvin Souza went straight for the wines. Maybe they'd already tasted the food.

"I feel as if this is a sentencing and not a reading of someone's will," Bradley whispered from behind.

I spun around. "Sorry. I didn't realize you were right behind me."

"Didn't mean to catch you off guard. Cripes. I can't wait till this is over. Once Marvin gets a drink in him, he'll be ready to start."

"Not yet. He can't!"

Bradley narrowed his eyes and shrugged. "Why not?"

"Clayton's not here."

"Maybe he decided not to come. Those things happen, you know."

Then, from a few feet away, I heard "Psst" and turned to see Don motioning to me.

"Excuse me," I said to Bradley. "I need to go. If you can, try to keep Marvin occupied until Clayton walks in."

I hurried over to Don and held both palms out in front of me. "What? What's the matter?"

"In case you haven't noticed, your man-of-the-hour hasn't arrived yet, and it's two minutes to midnight. Theo keeps running in and out of the restroom to practice his lines. He's driving me nuts. What's with Clayton? It's snowing a bit, but I checked my county road app and the roads aren't bad. Maybe he changed his mind."

"Geez, that's just what Bradley said a minute ago."

I glanced at the buffet table again. This time, it was overtaken by a flurry of nuns. Well, the young ones anyway. Sisters Mary Katherine, Gloria Mae, and Celeste were huddled together off to the side in the front row, facing the large rectangular table where Marvin would be addressing the audience.

"By the way," Don asked, "Who's the guy standing next to Miller Holtz? He looks like he's still in high school."

"Yikes. He better not be or we'll be in trouble for serving alcohol to minors. I better go check."

By now everyone seemed to be milling around the room as if it was a cocktail party. I felt a tap on my arm and turned to see Sister Gloria Mae. Somehow she must have escaped from the clutches of the other two.

"He's pretty good looking, huh?" she said.

"Who?"

"Our delivery driver. Don't act coy. You've been staring at him. Can't say I blame you, but he's probably a few years younger than you."

"I wasn't…I mean, okay, I was, but not what you think. I was hoping he didn't turn out to be an underage drinker." *And I'm glad he's not sacked out in your van.*

"He's not underage. I can assure you of that. That's Rob Tapscott, one of our delivery guys. When Sister Katherine asked if he'd be willing to drive us here tonight in our old school van, he agreed. He even put on the snow tires and made sure the van was in decent condition since it hadn't been driven in eons. We're hopeful, you know. About things going well tonight so we can expand and start up our school again."

I swallowed and bit the bottom of my lip, not knowing quite what to say. At that second, Glenda and Lizzie walked past us, each carrying a tray of appetizers. One whiff and I excused myself from Sister Gloria Mae.

No way was I about to let Miller Holtz pile on the skewered scallops and bacon without trying a few myself.

Like a homing pigeon, Miller moved from the end of the table that featured the sausage stuffed mushrooms directly toward the spot where Glenda and Lizzie placed their trays. Rob Tapscott was behind him.

"You've got a decent spread here," Miller said to me. "Think I'll try a few of those scallop things and get another glass of wine. You need to tell your employees over there that this is a drinking, not a tasting."

"I'm sure they'll be happy to refill anything you'd like," I replied, turning my head slightly so I could read Sam and Roger's faces. Both of them snarled.

Out of nowhere, Marvin Souza cleared his throat. He followed by picking up a wineglass and tapping it with a spoon. "I'd like to get this evening's reading of Arnold Mowen's will started if you don't mind. Please, everyone, be seated."

"Yes!" I exclaimed trying to buy more time for Clayton to arrive. "Be seated, but make sure you've filled your plates with our delectable canapes. If you'd like more wine or coffee, our staff is at your service. Oh look! Is that a new tray of beef with roasted chestnuts?"

Marvin stormed over to Bradley and I imagine he told his partner to help hurry things along. Meanwhile, I left the banquet room to look out the window again. Dammit! Where the heck was Clayton? And, for that matter, where was Theo?

With my gaze fixed on Marvin and Bradley, I didn't notice Miller brush past me until I spotted him a few feet away, his voice booming. "Don't start the revolution without me! Got to visit the little boys' room for a minute."

He was followed by Rob Tapscott, who looked as if he had been holding it since he and the nuns left Lodi. Marvin and Bradley had seated themselves at the front table and were shuffling some documents around. Then, in a flash, Clayton LeVine marched into the room, shook the damp snowflakes from his jacket, and looked around. His chubby cheeks had turned a bright crimson, and I half-expected smoke and fire to flare from his nostrils.

"I would've been here an hour ago if it wasn't for the fact I had to follow Ma and Pa Kettle all the way from Seneca County to Route 14, where I could finally go the speed limit. And for those of you who don't know who Ma and Pa Kettle are, go rent an old black and white movie! Honestly, fifteen miles an hour because they saw one snowflake. Why don't they move to Florida with the rest of the geezers? Those old coots who drive below the speed limit are more of a hazard than the ones who hammer hard on the gas pedal. Oh, before I forget, this needs to go on the table with the other photos of Arnold."

Clayton reached into a briefcase he was carrying and took out a framed 8 x 12 photo of the two of them. Arnold's arm was around Clayton's shoulder. It looked like some sort of celebration, although neither of them appeared to be smiling. He plunked it on the table, upstaging the other photos.

"Mr. Mowen and I were like this." Clayton held up two crossed fingers and waved his hand in front of the people who were seated.

Thane Eldridge, still holding a glass of wine, was off to the side near the buffet. He cleared his throat. "The only thing that man was close to was money and, in his case, it was mine. I expect that will be reconciled in his will."

The last thing I needed was a confrontation between Clayton and Thane. I grabbed Clayton by the arm and waved my hand at the buffet. "You must be hungry. Especially after such a miserable drive. Why don't you take a seat and have some food? Food always helps. Here, looks like the second row is wide open. Take a seat. I'll bring you a plate of canapes."

Clayton didn't need any prodding. Don immediately took the seat right behind him and gave me a wink. Still no sign of Theo.

How long does that guy need to rehearse one line?

A few of the nuns were still at the buffet table, and I could tell Marvin was getting edgy because he kept tapping the table with his pen and taking deep breaths. Finally, after what seemed like hours, but in reality was only a few seconds, Miller and Rob returned to the room, followed by Theo.

I was about to hand Clayton a plate of skewered shrimp and scallops when Theo almost knocked me over. "I overheard a conversation in the restroom. It's very—"

"Later. It'll have to wait, Theo. We're about to get started. Quick! Go sit next to Don and break a leg!"

I handed Clayton the plate and rubbed the back of my neck. It was killing me from pent-up nerves. I must've grimaced because Godfrey noticed.

"Are you all right? I was just about to sit down when I saw you. Did you move suddenly and wind up with a stiff neck?"

"Huh? What? No. I'm fine. Only stretching, that's all."

"I don't know about you, but from where I'm standing, the tension in this room is palpable."

I looked at the audience and began to think Godfrey was right. Miller and Rob, for reasons unbeknownst to me, appeared to be arguing, but at least they kept their voices down as they took seats next to each other in the third row, opposite from Don and Theo.

Sister Mary Katherine was devoid of all expression, but Sister Gloria Mae looked as if she had paid admission to a feature film. As for Sister Celeste, it was anyone's guess. Her veil covered most of her face, unlike the head coverings the other Sisters were wearing. Maybe she ordered a size too large.

I walked to the edge of the rows and leaned in next to Theo and Don. "Now!" I mouthed. "Now!"

Don leaned forward, so he was only a few inches from Clayton's neck. "I'm not kidding," I heard Don say. "I got this from a buddy of mine who works for the Seneca County Sheriff's Department. They've got a tape of some guy breaking into that Lavettia woman's place and wiping down chair bottoms. Probably removing his fingerprints. Has to be the killer. It's just a matter of time until they catch him."

Then Theo added his two cents. "They'll probably have it on the news tomorrow morning. Did they give a description?"

"Yeah. A really detailed one. You know what they say about criminals not being too bright. This guy didn't realize he was staring right into the camera. It was one of those nanny cams on a shelf in the kitchen."

"If I was that dude," Theo said, "I'd be heading for the nearest airport and not looking back."

I held my breath, expecting Clayton to have some sort of reaction but he didn't. So I mouthed the words, "Do it again" to Don and Theo.

Theo furrowed his brow and gave me a weird look. Then he poked Don and shrugged.

"Again," I mouthed, hoping no one noticed.

"Yeah," Don said. "They'll have this wrapped up like a Christmas turkey. Once that video's made public, Lavettia's killer will be behind bars. He's probably the same guy who killed Arnold. Talk about timing. Right at the reading of the will."

I stepped away, trying to appear nonchalant while, all the time, I was eyeballing Clayton. Not a move. Not a reaction. Not anything. Then the moment I was waiting for. Clayton shifted in his seat as if he was about to make a run for it. I tapped my teeth and reached in my pocket for my cell phone.

Phooey! Instead of bolting out of there like a fugitive on the run, Clayton turned to Don and Theo and asked them something. By now I was out of range and didn't want to appear too obvious.

Theo stretched out both arms. "I need to get a drink," he said, loud enough for everyone to hear him. "Looks like this will be a long night after all."

He walked toward the coffee service, making sure he would be inches from where I had planted myself. "It's not him," Theo whispered. "Miller's a different story."

Chapter 26

"Now that everyone has had sufficient time for food, drink, and potty breaks, may we *please* begin the reading of my client's last will and testament?" Marvin asked in a voice that sounded more like a demand than a question.

Muted voices echoed their agreement, and I took a seat at the end of the last row. I honestly didn't know how I could've misread the situation, but I had. By eliminating Clayton as the person responsible for killing Lavettia and Arnold, we were back to where we started. And what did Theo mean by "Miller"? I glanced around the room, but all I could see were the backs of peoples' heads. I pinched my shoulder blades together, stretched my arms, and walked to the side of the room so that I could see their faces.

Unlike my screenplays, where the characters always give themselves away, this room was full of would-be poker players. The guests, that was, not my staff. Cammy, Glenda, and Lizzie stood in the back, adjacent to the food tables. Sam and Roger were inches from the drinks in case someone got up for more wine. Fred and Emma were still in the kitchen. They had a dessert menu to present once the will had been read.

The younger nuns took up the entire fourth row, except for the seat I originally grabbed. The Triumvirate planted themselves down front. Thane sat a few seats over from Clayton and diagonal from Sister Celeste. Godfrey sat one seat over from Thane, his view partially obstructed by the nuns' veils, but I didn't think he cared.

Marvin introduced himself and Bradley. He cleared his throat, planted his palms on the table, and leaned toward the audience. "Good evening, or should I say morning, because it's already a few minutes past midnight. Thank you all for coming. I realize this is a most unusual venue, but my client, Arnold Mowen, had his reasons. According to his wishes, the reading of his last will and testament will begin with the sharing of fond memories. Who would like to speak first?"

"Isn't that something they do at the funeral?" Sam leaned toward Roger. Everyone heard his question, including Marvin.

Marvin turned his head slightly. "True, true, but Mr. Mowen wasn't certain there'd be a funeral, so he left explicit directions for me to allow the mourners to speak."

I wasn't so sure there were any real mourners, but I kept my mouth shut and returned to my seat. Marvin stared directly at the audience and didn't say a word.

Finally, Clayton stood and clasped his hands together. "Arnold once picked up the tab for both of us when we ate at Emile's Restaurant. We were on our way back to the office after a routine IRS audit. Those of you who knew Arnold, knew how he hated to part with a dime, so paying for my meal was really, really over the top. All seven dollars and ninety-nine cents for the meatball special." Clayton sat down and leaned back in his chair.

"Who else would like to share?" Marvin asked.

Sister Mary Katherine stood and folded her hands together. "Mr. Mowen never forgot us at Christmas. He always sent us a card. 'Holiday Greetings from Lake-to-Lake Wine Distributors.'"

By now, I was doing mental eye rolls like crazy. There was an uncomfortable silence in the room and if I could have thought of something to say, I would have. Instead, I locked gazes with Miller Holtz and then widened my eyes, hoping he'd get the hint and say something. Instead, he looked down, as if he'd forgotten to zip up his fly. I immediately turned the other way.

"If there are no more fond recollections of Mr. Mowen," Marvin said, "we shall proceed with his last will and testament."

That was when Miller opened his mouth. "Finally!"

Marvin reached for the legal-size manila folder on the table and removed some papers. He turned to Bradley and began to read.

"'I, Arnold Stanley Mowen, being of sound mind and memory, do hereby make, publish, and declare this to be my last will and testament, hereby revoking all prior wills and codicils. I hereby name and appoint Marvin Leroy Souza as personal representative to administer my estate. Mr. Souza shall be paid reasonable compensation for serving in this capacity. I repeat, reasonable. Do you hear that, Marvin?'"

At that point, the audience gasped, and Marvin took a deep breath. "Mr. Mowen believed in specificity. Now then, I need to continue."

"'I direct my personal representative to pay any debt or claim which he deems legally enforceable against my estate. Legally enforceable, Marvin, not anecdotal.'"

With that, Thane Eldridge stood and bellowed, "He wants legally enforceable, he'll get it."

Meanwhile, the temperature outside must have dropped considerably because the fans from our furnace kicked on full strength, loosening some of the cottony snow clusters from the mantels in the banquet room. A few wisps of fake snow floated around the room. At that very second, the front door banged open and what at first appeared to be a specter draped in billowy layers of mauve, purple, and black, turned out to be a middle-aged woman who rushed into the banquet room. Her waist-long hair, in shades of blue and black, covered the front of the cloak she had on. The last time I'd seen anyone wear anything of its kind was during a documentary I watched on the Brontë sisters.

Her sudden entrance caught all of us by surprise, especially Marvin, who dropped the papers he was holding, and Bradley, who bent down to pick them up from the floor. They had scattered all over the place.

"Glenda!" the woman shrieked, charging over to the buffet. "Thank goodness I'm not too late."

Glenda toppled backward into the table, shaking some of the double-tiered food trays. "Zenora, what on earth are you doing here?"

Zenora! Glenda's wacky friend who also dabbled in the occult. And yes, why in heaven's name did she drive over here in the middle of the night?

Upon close inspection, Zenora looked as if she had just come from the set of a Johnny Depp movie. She reached out and took Glenda by both wrists. "I read your tea leaves after you left my house and I knew, beyond any doubt, I had to warn you. Even if it meant driving over here with those terrible winds. I'm lucky a tree didn't fall over or, worse yet, one of those utility poles."

Damn it! That storm better hold off until tomorrow like the news anchors said.

Zenora shook Glenda's arms and kept talking. "I would've come sooner, but your cup was in the sink with the dirty dishes. I didn't start the dishes right after you left, and it was only when I started to pour the dishwashing liquid and run the water that I saw the bottom of your cup. You're in danger, Glenda. Dark, evil spirits are surrounding you. They're in this room. Hurry! We can cast a purifying spell. Let me light the sage sticks I brought."

With that, Zenora proceeded to take something out of a large brown satchel.

"No!" I shouted. I left my seat and raced toward her. "No sage sticks. No purifying. Can't you and Glenda work it out in the kitchen? Please. We have to finish reading a will."

Zenora turned to face me but instead, looked past my shoulder to the three Sisters in the front row. She reached an arm to the table, where Marvin and Bradley were still hunched over, picking up papers and, as if steadying herself for a launch, pressed against the table before charging in front of Sister Celeste.

"Lavettia, why the hell are you dressed like that?" she screamed. "Halloween was two months ago! I thought you looked like a corpse at the essential oils symposium, but I can see I was wrong. And you're still dosing yourself with that wretched perfume. What's it called? Oh yes, 'Amor Propre.' Every time I catch a whiff of it, I think I've walked into a bordello. Honey, I don't know what's up, but you're really overdoing it tonight."

Sister Mary Katherine, who was seated one spot over from Sister Celeste, came to attention, her arms crossed in front of her chest. "I'm afraid you're sadly mistaken. This is Sister Celeste from the Convent of the Holy Sepulcher."

"Yeah, and I'm Mother Teresa." Then Zenora went eye-to-eye with Sister Celeste. "What's with the charade? You might be able to fool everyone else, but not me."

Sister Celeste crossed herself as if she was about to lead everyone in prayer. "This poor misguided woman needs all of our prayers."

Zenora latched on to one of Sister Celeste's hands and waved it in the air. "Since when do nuns have such perfectly manicured nails? You might've removed the polish, but there's always a little bit that remains along the cuticle. I take it you're still sporting Malice by Chanel?"

At that point, Sisters Mary Katherine and Gloria Mae gasped. I looked around the room and everyone, including Marvin and Bradley, had turned their attention to Sister Celeste.

"Dear Lord," Sister Gloria Mae said, "If this woman isn't our dear Sister Celeste, then where *is* she?"

Before anyone could respond, I let it slip. "Henderson's Funeral Home if I'm not mistaken."

It was as if I had shouted "Fire!" in a movie theater. Sisters Mary Katherine and Gloria Mae were on Sister Celeste like Dobermans on steak tartare. The three of them were screaming at each other and, at one point, it looked as if Sister Mary Katherine was about to pull Sister Celeste's veil from her head.

"I say we light the sage sticks now!" Zenora bellowed from another part of the room. Apparently, after the two nuns converged on their peer, Zenora had taken safe refuge next to the buffet table.

"No lighting of anything!" I bleated, but I didn't think anyone heard me.

Sister Mary Katherine gave Sister Celeste's veil, coif, and wimple a good yank and, at that moment, Sister Celeste shoved her away and stood. She reached into the folds of her skirt and pulled out a gun. "This was supposed to be a quiet little matter between Mr. Souza and me, but unfortunately, it doesn't appear as if that's possible."

I felt as if I'd been kicked in the shins. "Lavettia? My God! It *is* you. What the heck? I was beating myself up over your death, thinking I was somehow responsible for not taking you seriously. Oh my God!"

"Sorry, Norrie. I always liked you. I'm sorry I paid one of those novice nuns to jump you if you returned to the convent. You were becoming too much of a snoop." With a sudden move, her veil was off, revealing her platinum blond hair. She brandished the gun, but not before she turned around and threatened everyone who was seated behind her.

"If any of you gets a crazy idea to stop me, think again. I know how to shoot this thing and I'm not afraid to do it."

Wonderful. With my luck, the winery will need new sheetrock.

The winds sounded as if they'd level the building. Windows were rattling and I felt an occasional shake. I was so stunned by the fact I had gotten it all wrong regarding Clayton that I couldn't think clearly. I tried to get words to form in my mouth, but I stood there tongue-tied.

Marvin held out his palms and rose slowly from the table. "There's no need to overreact, Miss Lawrence. Drop the gun and we can discuss whatever is concerning you like civilized human beings."

"What's concerning me? Are you looney?" Lavettia shrieked. "You know damn well what's concerning me. Arnold's money! Now, listen carefully, because I'm only going to say this once. My late sister, Luella Lawrence, whom some of you know as the dear departed Sister Celeste, was once Arnold's business partner in New Jersey, back when they were handling real estate. They got into some shady business, and Luella decided becoming a nun was better than becoming an inmate."

At that point, one of the younger nuns in the back row whispered, "Dear God, preserve us," but because the room was so still, her whisper was audible.

Lavettia paid no attention and kept the gun fixed on Marvin's table. "Arnold was going to rat her out and let her take the fall. That's when we came up with a plan. She'd do the nun thing and I'd seduce the ratfink. Then, at the opportune time, we'd find a way to get even. I was always more the femme fatale than Luella. Once I hitched up my skirt to adjust my garter, Arnold didn't stand a chance."

"So you lured him into a relationship and killed him?" Bradley asked.

"Please! That makes it sound so crass. This was a carefully crafted plot. My sister, who by then was Sister Celeste, was fortuitous enough to come across indisputable evidence that proved Arnold was responsible for that real estate scheme. She told him that if she and I, along with that convent of hers, weren't named the beneficiaries in his will, she'd go straight to the police with that information."

"So *she* killed him?" Bradley asked again.

"Just listen, will you?" Lavettia hissed. "Luella made sure all of us were named the beneficiaries. *And,* she had a legal document drawn up that stated she was to receive any and all copies of any new wills or they would be considered null and void."

"Is that even legal?" I asked, but no one responded and Lavettia went on. I had to admit that, by this time, I was getting more than a tad edgy about the pointed gun, which wavered between Marvin's table and where I stood.

"Wouldn't you know it? That lousy lowlife changed the will. When Luella got the new copy, she was enraged. All the money was going to go to that mealy-mouthed secretary of his. But, time was on our side. The new will hadn't been filed yet. That's when Luella and I pulled a switch. She managed to get out of that convent for the day with one excuse or another, so she could pretend to be me at the essential oils symposium."

"I knew it!" Zenora shouted. "Even on a bad day, your makeup was never in the neutral zone."

"And, well… Poor Arnold had to be sent to his final resting place before the new will could be filed."

"I was right," Bradley exclaimed. "It *was* you who killed him. Cold-blooded murder."

"The skunk had it coming," Lavettia replied. "And so did my precious sister, who was about to turn me in to the police for murder. Can you imagine? After the deed was done, the guilt got to her. Too many years of being in a convent, I suppose. I had to get her out of the picture as well."

I clasped my hands together and took a step back. "So, that was you? Pretending to be the cleaning lady who discovered Lavettia. Only it was Luella dressed to appear like you."

"You catch on quick, Norrie."

Not quick enough. I almost had Clayton carted away for killing Lavettia so he'd get Arnold's money.

"Listen," Lavettia went on, "even a fifty-fifty split of the old coot's money was better than nothing. The nuns would get their new school, maybe even erect a statue for my sister, and I'd go off and live the good life in Belize."

Belize? What is it with these people and Central America?

"That's hardly going to happen now," Marvin said. "What do you expect to accomplish? Murder all of us?"

Oh, for God's sake, don't give her any ideas. She's as nuts as they come.

I tried to text the sheriff's department but couldn't. The wind storm interfered with the reception. Too bad we had a goat instead of trained carrier pigeons. Lavettia lowered her voice and remained calm, but the gun was still at the ready. "I expect the eminent Mr. Souza to get on his iPad, or even one of those winery computers, log on to his business account, and transfer a tidy little sum of his money into my bank account. Don't worry, once Arnold's monies come through, I'll be sure to reimburse Mr. Souza. And if you were wondering, I've got a private plane waiting for me at the Penn Yan airport. Isn't that so, Mr. Eldridge?"

"I'm afraid it is, folks," Thane Eldridge replied, "Looks like Miss Lawrence is calling the shots from now on."

Again, that deep voice of his. Where did I hear it? Where did I hear it? I closed my eyes and tried to think. Not so much a conversation as a blip, a phrase, a…that voice! It came to me. That was the voice I'd heard in the background at Lavettia's house when I called to tell her I'd found Arnold's wallet.

Thane puffed out his chest as if he'd won a prize. "Oh, and we'll be borrowing the convent van for a quick jaunt to the airport. Sorry for the inconvenience."

"Didn't I mention," Lavettia said, "Thane Eldridge happens to be the man Arnold swindled in that real estate deal."

Chapter 27

"Prissy little coward, too, that Arnold," Thane Eldridge said. "When I took over as the CEO for Seneca Lake Communities Bank, he couldn't get his monies out of there fast enough. Got news for you, Arnold. You can't take it with you, but we can. We'll be on that plane long before Yates County decides to send a sheriff's car to this location. What will be it be, Marvin? That iPad you've got in your briefcase or do I need to make Miss Ellington boot up the winery computer?"

Marvin didn't get a chance to respond. Clayton stood up, put his hands on his hips, and stomped his foot. "This is so unfair! Unfair I tell you! I was supposed to get that inheritance. Do you mean to tell me we're all bound to that old will?"

"I'm afraid so," Marvin said.

Then, out of the blue, Rob Tapscott lit into Miller Holtz. "I thought you said you were getting the money Uncle Miller. You had it all planned. The wine manipulation...the money...the..."

"Shh, now's not the time, Scottie."

Scottie? Scottie? Where did I hear that name before? Oh my gosh—Tapscott!

It all began to make sense. Too bad there was a nutcase with a gun pointed our way. Scottie, aka Rob Tapscott, not only made cheesecake deliveries for the nuns, but he was also the part-time limousine driver responsible for telling his mother's friend about the Pinot Noir scarcity. *Was that what Theo had been trying to tell me?* And to think our own rep was responsible for that diabolical plot and his nephew was the one who used the nuns' van for the stolen wine. *Hope you enjoy your jail time, Miller. Absorb our losses, my butt!*

"You have three seconds to get your hands on your iPad." Lavettia pointed one finger at Marvin while aiming the gun with her other hand.

Just then, one of those little wispy pieces of fake snow landed on her neck and she moved her finger-pointing hand to that spot.

"STOP!" Godfrey yelled. "DON'T MAKE A MOVE. THAT'S A BROWN RECLUSE SPIDER ON YOUR NECK. I SHOULD KNOW. I'M AN ENTOMOLOGIST FROM CORNELL. DON'T MAKE A MOVE!"

Lavettia remained perfectly still, but everyone else in the vicinity began to back away, moving their chairs or, in Sister Gloria Mae's case, making a dead run for it.

Godfrey, who was directly behind Lavettia, lowered his voice, but not his tone. "The brown recluse from the Loxoscelidae family is a highly venomous spider. Don't move. Whatever you do, don't move. One bite and it'll produce a necrotic skin lesion. That is, if you're lucky. Otherwise, it will result in a viscerocutaneous reaction in the bloodstream. Whoa! Don't want to go there."

The high-pitched scream practically shattered the windows. It was followed by shrieks of "Get it off! Get it off! Get it off!"

No one dared make a move. Except Godfrey. He took a step closer to Lavettia and held both hands out in front. "Stay still. I'm going to find a broom or something so that I can get the spider off your neck. Oh, I forgot to mention. If you're nervous, the brown recluse will sense it and begin to bite like crazy!"

No sooner did he say that than Lavettia lost all control and waved her arms in the air, forgetting momentarily she had a gun in one of them. It thudded on the floor at the very second the power went out. I figured the winds must have downed a power pole somewhere along the road.

"Help me!" she shouted. "Will someone please help me!"

At first, it seemed as if the room went totally black, but as my eyes adjusted to the absence of light, I realized the battery-operated tea lights on the mantels gave off enough hazy illumination for the chaos that ensued. Lavettia was still screaming her lungs out but thankfully, without the gun.

The gun was somewhere on the floor. Godfrey and Bradley were on all fours, desperately trying to retrieve it. Two seconds later, they were joined by Sam and Roger.

"Does this place have a back-up generator?" Thane Eldridge demanded.

"No," I said, "only the winery lab."

"Get a flashlight," Clayton yowled. "That damn spider could've gotten off of Lavettia and jumped to one of our shoulders."

His remark was followed by screams, shrieks, and howls.

"I tried to warn you, Glenda," Zenora announced. "The tea leaves told me a dark spirit would descend on this place. It's not too late. I have matches."

The words came bellowing out of my mouth as I tried to locate Zenora. "No matches! You'll burn the place down. I don't care how many brown recluse spiders are holed up in here for the winter."

"Spiders? You mean there's more than one?"

I wasn't sure which one of the nuns asked that, but the minute she did, the screaming reached an entirely new decibel.

"It's still on me," Lavettia shouted. "Get it off! Get it off! I can feel it biting me. It's biting me. I'm going to die of blood poisoning."

At that point, the crowd was all over the place and a few of our folding chairs were knocked to the ground. Oddly enough, I didn't hear a word from Cammy, Glenda, or Lizzie. I glanced at the back corner, where they were standing, and not one of them made a move. I figured they were too petrified to budge.

"Got it!" Sam exclaimed. "I've got the gun! Oh crap! Now my fingerprints are on the damn thing! Hey! What the hell? Get your foot off my hand! Someone's stepping on me!"

"If you know what's good for you, you'll hand me that gun." Thane's voice was oddly devoid of any emotion.

"Can't hand someone a gun with broken fingers," Sam replied. "Besides, I'm not that stupid."

Thane bent down to reach for the gun and, in a flash, Sam used his free hand to land a nasty punch to the guy's groin. I didn't know which was worse, Lavettia's screams to get the spider off her or Thane's primordial howl. In seconds, Bradley, Theo, and Don had wrestled Thane to the ground while Sam's shaky hand held the gun.

"Don't point it at anyone," I said. "And, for heaven's sake, whoever has a cell phone, call the sheriff's office. Maybe the reception is back."

"Good for you!" Lizzie cheered. "Safety first. That's one of Nancy Drew's basic tenets."

I felt like punching Nancy Drew in the face.

Then, like something out of a bad horror movie, Lavettia kicked over the nearest chair and started to tear her clothes off. The coif and wimple surrounding her neck and chest came off first. Her platinum wig got caught up in the fabric and it, too, came off, revealing her naturally curly brown hair.

"I'm…going…to…die…of…that…necrotic…blood thing…" she sobbed, gasping for breath, "and no one's helping me."

Godfrey covered his mouth and turned away.

"It will be a fast, gruesome death, won't it?" Lavettia asked between sobs.

"I can't let this continue," Godfrey said before bursting out laughing.

"You think it's funny?" Lavettia shot back at him. "You're a horrible, sick individual to watch someone die in front of you!"

And look what the pot's calling the kettle!

"You're not going to die," Godfrey said. "That wasn't a brown recluse spider on your neck. It was a piece of that cottony snow from those mantel decorations. In fact, the brown recluse spider isn't even native to this part of the country. They're mainly down south and in the western states."

I'd heard of people going ballistic but, up until that minute, I never really knew what that meant. Lavettia picked up the nearest folding chair, held it over her head, and made a mad dive at Godfrey. The Wildlings from *Game of Thrones* had nothing on her.

Fortunately, Godfrey stepped aside, but the chair came plummeting down on the rectangular table that housed the framed homage to Arnold Mowen. Broken glass from the picture frames scattered all over the floor.

Still, that didn't stop Lavettia's rampage. The only thing that did was when Sister Gloria Mae crawled on the ground and grabbed Lavettia's ankle, causing her to tumble over a few more chairs before she landed between Marvin Souza and the buffet table.

Suddenly, the lights flickered and the power came back on. The banquet room looked like it was last used for a fraternity party and not the reading of someone's will. Bradley, Theo, and Don were still restraining Thane Eldridge, but at least they no longer had him in a headlock.

Sam was a few feet away, the gun still firmly in his grip. As for Lavettia, Sister Gloria Mae was standing over her, one foot on her back. The young nuns were out of their seats and huddled together near Sister Mary Katherine, while my employees and Godfrey Klein were doubled over laughing.

I gave them a quick shrug, to which Cammy replied, "We knew it was the fake snow all along. Your buddy gave us a wink before he caught Lavettia's attention with that spider ruse."

Behind me, I heard Clayton and Marvin arguing.

"Arnold meant for the new will to go to me," Clayton said. "I'm the real beneficiary."

"Not according to the state of New York," was Marvin's reply.

"I'll contest it. I'll fight it. I'll…"

I stepped away and scanned the room. Everyone was accounted for, except for two people—Miller Holtz and Rob Tapscott. I was about to ask if anyone had seen them when Fred and Emma came into the room, followed by Deputy Hickman and a female deputy sheriff, who looked to be my age. Fred charged toward me and grabbed my arm.

"When we heard a ruckus in here, I took a peek and saw the nuns fighting. Then one of them pulled out a gun, so I phoned the sheriff's office and gave them a blow-by-blow description of what I saw. Looked like total chaos."

"It was," I answered. "Did you tell them Lavettia was the killer? Did you hear her confess?"

"Oh, yeah. She's got a voice like a longshoreman."

Emma quickly caught up to her husband. "They've got Miller Holtz and that other guy in one of the sheriff's cars out front. What the heck did *they* do? Yates county sent two cars, and another showed up from Seneca County."

"Wine theft," I replied. "But how did they know? Miller only let it slip a few minutes ago, before Lavettia had a meltdown."

"Fred's was the second phone call," Theo shouted. "Hey, will someone please cart this guy away? My hands are getting tired."

"Second phone call?" I asked, as the female deputy zip-tied Thane's wrists and took him into custody.

Deputy Hickman walked toward me and gave Theo a glance. "Mr. Buchman phoned our office about a suspicious conversation he overheard in your restroom. Normally we wouldn't respond to that sort of thing, but apparently, Mr. Buchman recorded it."

"Huh?" I was flabbergasted. *So that's what he was trying to tell me.* "Recorded it? How?"

"With some sort of an app on his phone. We've got enough evidence to book him for those wine thefts and the wine sabotage. Seems Mr. Miller had quite the plan to manipulate wine prices by tightening the supply and hyping the demand."

"Lavettia Lawrence is alive and well." My voice rose to a fever pitch. "She's the one who murdered Arnold Mowen and then pretended to be her sister, a nun at the Convent of the Holy Sepulcher. Did I mention she killed her sister? It was all about money. Money and revenge. Oh, and she had a cohort, too. Thane Eldridge, the guy your partner handcuffed."

Meanwhile, Sam was still holding Lavettia's gun when Deputy Hickman's partner drew out her own weapon and pointed it at him. "Drop it before I shoot!"

"I'm the good guy!" Sam exclaimed. "You want to arrest someone, go for the fake nun on the floor." He dropped Lavettia's .22 and kicked it toward the deputies. "That's a hell of a thanks!"

Deputy Hickman pulled Lavettia up and read her the Miranda Rights. She, in turn, threatened to sue Godfrey for misrepresentation. Meanwhile Marvin and Bradley were head-to-head, and I imagined they were trying to figure out whether they should continue with the reading of the will.

As it turned out, they did. It was at a little past two, after the Seneca County deputies took Miller and Rob (aka Scottie) into custody and Deputy Hickman and his partner did the same with Lavettia and Thane.

"Dessert anyone?" Fred asked, once the Sisters of the Holy Sepulcher were informed that God had indeed answered their prayers, and everything had been left to them. Clayton, however, was totally bereft. It was only when Sister Mary Katherine informed him they would pay him generously to run the Lake-to-Lake Wine Distribution business that he perked up.

With Rob Tapscott under arrest, Sister Gloria Mae volunteered to drive the school bus back to Lodi. "Don't worry," she said. "I drove camp buses during the summers when I was in college."

The winds were still in full force, but, as predicted, the snow held off until the next day. Marvin and Bradley headed out with the nuns. Bradley pulled me aside in the foyer and gave me a kiss on the cheek. "Dinner Friday?"

"You bet."

Theo, Don, and the Two Witches Winery crew, along with Godfrey, cleaned the kitchen and straightened out the banquet room. Theo swept up the broken glass from Arnold's picture frames. Even Zenora helped.

"You'd enjoy working at this winery," I overheard Glenda telling her. "Much better than selling those essential oils. That business is becoming too bourgeois."

I gritted my teeth and shuddered. If both of them worked here, it wouldn't be Two Witches. More like Two Wackos. Then, I suddenly realized what Arnold had meant by insisting his will be read at our winery. He told Marvin "It was all in the name."

That was when I realized what, or should I say, *whom,* he was referring to—Lavettia and Luella Lawrence. They were his two witches. Reading his will here was definitely apropos, if not unsettling.

Chapter 28

Fred and Emma made all of us "care packages" from the leftover food on the off-chance the major snow event that was predicted actually happened.

As the entourage walked to the front door, I said "Turn on your radios tomorrow. Oh my gosh. It *is* tomorrow. Yikes. It's past three. Anyway, check the forecast. If that storm arrives early, we may need to open late. I'll post it on our website and Facebook page."

"Do you want us to wait while you set the alarm and lock up?" Theo asked.

From behind me, I heard Godfrey. "I can do that. You folks go ahead."

Theo gave the door a pull and it latched behind him. I turned to Godfrey, who was standing a few feet away. "Thanks. I just need to set the alarm and turn off the lights."

"That was one hell of a show. No one in their right mind would ever believe me."

"You're not going to say anything to Jason and Francine when you get them on the satellite phone, are you?"

"Of course not. The Satphone can be used only for official research station business and updates on the global invasive species map."

"Um, about species…that was really clever of you to pull that stunt. I seriously thought Lavettia was going to wind up shooting one of us."

"Yeah, that thought crossed my mind, too. Hey, do you need a ride back up to your house?"

"No, I parked my car near Alvin's pen. Goat's got enough hay to last through the storm, if we get one. So far, it's only wind and some light flakes."

"It could've been worse, you know. That storm could've arrived early and trapped all of us in here."

"Aargh. Perish the thought."

Godfrey walked me to my car and even held the door open for me. "This probably isn't the best time to ask, but have you given any thought to my invitation for Christmas? It's at Alex's place this year, so you already know the host."

"I, er, I…"

And then, he offered up that smile of his. Call it an impulse or a sudden lapse in judgment, but I leaned toward him and brushed his cheek with a quick kiss. "Wouldn't miss it."

* * * *

The winds continued all night, but the light snowflakes turned to rain, and the rain got heavier. Then the temperature dropped. When I turned on the radio in the morning, I heard the following announcement:

"Expect damaging winds and some power outages. All roads in Yates, Ontario, and Seneca Counties are closed. Repeat. All roads in Yates, Ontario, and Seneca Counties are closed."

I poured out some kibble for Charlie and made myself a cup of coffee. "It was all about greed and money," I said to the dog. "But there's one bit of good news. If we ever decide to hold a costume party at Two Witches, I know just the guy to call."

Sneak Peek

While waiting for Norrie Ellington's next adventure in the
fourth book of THE WINE TRAIL MYSTERIES (March 2019)
don't miss J.C. Eaton's bestselling
The Sophie Kimble Mysteries!
STAGED 4 MURDER
by J.C. Eaton is available now from your
favorite bookseller or e-retailer

Turn the page for a quick peek!

Chapter 1

The wet sponge that hung over the Valley of the Sun, sapping my energy and making my life a misery for the past three months, wrung itself dry and left by the end of September. Unfortunately, it was immediately replaced by something far more aggravating than monsoon weather—my mother's book club announcement. It came on a Saturday morning when I'd reluctantly agreed to have breakfast with the ladies from the Booked 4 Murder book club at their favorite meeting spot, Bagels 'N More, across the road from Sun City West. I arrived a few minutes late, only to find the regular crew talking over each other, in between bites of bagels and sips of coffee.

"Who took the blueberry shmear? It was right in front of me."

"It still is. Move the juice glasses."

"I hate orange juice with the pulp still in it."

"If it didn't have pulp, it'd be Tang."

Cecilia Flanagan was dressed in her usual white blouse, black sweater, black skirt, and black shoes. Don't tell me she wasn't a nun in a former life. Shirley Johnson looked as impeccable as always, this time with a fancy teal top and matching earrings, not to mention teal nail polish that set off her ebony skin.

Judging from Lucinda Espinoza's outfit, I wasn't sure she realized they made wrinkle-free clothing. As for Myrna Mittleson and Louise Munson, they were both wearing floral tops and looked as if they had spent the last hour at the beauty parlor, unlike poor Lucinda, whose hair reminded me of an osprey's nest. Then there was my mother. The reddish blond and fuchsia streaks in her hair had been replaced with . . . well . . . I didn't even know how to describe it. The base color had been changed to a honey blond and the streaks were now brunette. Or a variation of brunette.

The only one missing was my Aunt Ina, and that was because she and her husband of four months were in Malta, presumably so my aunt could recuperate from the stress of moving into a new house.

"You look wonderful, Phee," Myrna announced as I took a seat. "I didn't think you'd ever agree to blond highlights."

My mother nodded in approval as she handed me a coffee cup. "None of us did. Then all of a sudden, Phee changed her mind."

It was true. It was a knee-jerk reaction to the fact my boss, Nate Williams, was adding a new investigator to his firm. An investigator that I'd had a secret crush on for years when I was working for the Mankato Minnesota Police Department in accounting.

"Um . . . gee, thanks. So, what's the big news? My mom said the club was making an announcement."

Cecilia leaned across the table, nearly knocking over the salt and pepper shakers.

"It's more than exciting. It's a dream come true for all of us."

Other than finding a discount bookstore, I couldn't imagine what she was talking about.

My mother jumped in. "What Cecilia is trying to say is we have a firsthand opportunity to participate in a murder, not just read about it."

"What? Participate? What are you saying? And keep your voices low."

"Not a real murder, Phee," Louise said. "A stage play. And not any stage play. It's Agatha Christie's *The Mousetrap*, and we've all decided to try out for the play or work backstage. Except for Shirley. She wants to be on the costume and makeup crews."

"Where? When?"

Louise let out a deep sigh. "The Sun City West Footlighters will be holding open auditions for the play this coming Monday and Tuesday. Since they've refurbished the Stardust Theater, they'll be able to use that stage instead of the old beat-up one in the Men's Club building. All of us are ecstatic. Especially since we're familiar with the play, being a murder and all, and we thought in lieu of reading a book for the month of October, we'd do the play."

I thought Louise was never going to come up for air, and I had to jump in quickly. "So . . . uh, just like that, you all decided to join the theater club?"

"Not the club, just the play," my mother explained. "The play is open to all of the residents in the Sun Cities. Imagine, Phee, in ten more years you could move to one of the Sun Cities, too. You'll be fifty-five."

I'd rather poke my eyes out with a fork.

"She could move sooner," Myrna said, "if she was to marry someone who is fifty-five or older."

"That's true," Lucinda chirped in. "There are lots of eligible men in our community."

I was certain Lucinda's definition meant the men were able to stand vertically and take food on their own. I tried not to shudder. Instead, I became defensive, and that was worse.

"Living in Vistancia is fine with me. It's a lovely multigenerational neighborhood. Lots of activities . . . friends . . . and it's close to my work."

Louise reached over and patted my hand. "Don't worry, dear. I'm sure the right man will come along. Don't make the mistake of getting a cat instead. First it's one cat, and then next thing you know, you've got eleven or more of them and no man wants to deal with that."

"Um . . . uh . . . I have no intention of getting a cat. Or anything with four legs. I don't even want a houseplant. I went through all of that when my daughter was growing up. Now she can have pets and plants in St. Cloud where she's teaching."

The women were still staring at me with their woeful faces. I had to change the subject and do it fast.

I jumped right back into the play. "So, do all of you seriously think you'll wind up getting cast for this production?"

My mother nodded first and waited while the rest of the ladies followed suit. "No one knows or understands murder the way we do. We've been reading murder mysteries and plays for ages. I'm sure the Footlighters will be thrilled to have us try out and join their crews."

Yeah, if they don't try to murder one of you first.

"Well, um . . . good luck, everyone. Too bad Aunt Ina won't be able to try out. Sounds like it's something right up her alley."

My mother all but dropped her bagel. "Hold your tongue. If we're lucky, she and your Uncle Louis will stay in Malta until the play is over. It's bad enough having her in the book club. Can you imagine what she'd be like on stage? Or worse yet, behind it? No, all of us are better off with my sister somewhere in the Mediterranean. That's where Malta is, isn't it? I always get it confused with the other one. Yalta. Anyway, leave well enough alone. Now then, where is that waitress? You need to order something, Phee."

The next forty-five minutes were spent discussing the play, the auditions, and the competition. It was ugly. Like all of the book club get-togethers, everyone spoke at once, with or without food in their mouth. I stopped trying to figure out who was saying what, and instead concentrated on my meal while they yammered away.

"Don't tell me that dreadful Miranda Lee from Bingo is going to insist on a lead role."

"Not if Eunice Berlmosler has any say about it."

"She's the publicity chair, not the director."

"Miranda?"

"No, she's the lady who brings in all those plastic trolls to Bingo."

"With the orange hair?"

"Miranda?"

"No, those trolls. Miranda's hair is more like a honey brunette. Perfectly styled. Like the shimmery dresses she wears. No Alfred Dunner for her. That's for sure."

"Hey, I wear Alfred Dunner."

"You're not Miranda."

"Oh."

"What about Eunice?"

"I don't know. What about her?"

"Do we know any of the men who will be trying out?"

"I'll bet anything Herb's going to show up with that pinochle crew of his. They seem to be in everything."

I leaned back, continuing to let the discussion waft over me until I got pulled in like some poor fly into a vacuum.

"You should attend the auditions, Phee. Go and keep your mother company." It was Cecilia. Out of nowhere. Insisting I show up for the Footlighters' tryouts.

"You can scope out the men, Phee. What a great opportunity."

Yep, it'll be right up there with cattle judging at the state fair.

In one motion, I slid the table an inch or so in front of me, stood up, and gave my best audition for the role of "getting the hell out of here." "Oh my gosh! Is it eleven-thirty already? I can't believe the time flew by so quickly. I've got to go. It was great seeing all of you. Good luck with the play. I'll be sure to buy a ticket. Call you later, Mom!"

As I raced to my car, I looked at the clear blue sky and wondered how long I'd have to wait until the next monsoon sponge made its return visit to the valley. Weather I could deal with. Book club ladies were another matter, and when they said they were going to participate in a murder, I didn't expect it to be a real one.

Meet the Author

J.C. Eaton is the wife and husband team of Ann I. Goldfarb and James E. Clapp. Ann has published eight YA time travel mysteries. Visit their website at www.jceatonauthor.com

CPSIA information can be obtained
at www.ICGtesting.com
Printed in the USA
LVHW091533150319
610803LV00001B/71/P